Right By You

Cara D. Smith

Dedication

For Isaac and Steven.
And for you, dear reader.

One more time, for the people in the back!
The following story contains mature themes, strong language, and sexual
situations. It was written for a mature audience.

Contents

CHAPTER 1 1
CHAPTER 2 12
CHAPTER 3 15
CHAPTER 4 21
CHAPTER 5 31
CHAPTER 6 37
CHAPTER 7 43
CHAPTER 8 49
CHAPTER 9 54
CHAPTER 10 56
CHAPTER 11 65
CHAPTER 12 72
CHAPTER 13 77
CHAPTER 14 80
CHAPTER 15 82
CHAPTER 16 87
CHAPTER 17 99
CHAPTER 18 106
CHAPTER 19 113
CHAPTER 20 118
CHAPTER 21 120
CHAPTER 22 129
CHAPTER 23 137
CHAPTER 24 139
CHAPTER 25 145
CHAPTER 26 150
CHAPTER 27 155
CHAPTER 28 163
CHAPTER 29 167
EPILOGUE 173

If you are struggling with substance abuse or depression, please seek help.
<u>You matter.</u>
1-800-662-4357

CHAPTER 1

Tara

The parking lot of Martin, Parker, and Warner Realty is packed. Gabe's lime green Dodge Charger is nestled in his favorite parking spot, far away from other cars to protect it from door dings and scratches. I detour to walk by it on my way in and lay my hand on the hood. It's cold. *At least he didn't blow me off to go somewhere else.*

A polite chime alerts the various receptionists when I yank the door open. I know most of them at least in passing from office parties and whatnot. They're all smiles when they see me, but those smiles fade quickly. I don't have it in me to smile right now, so I nod to each of them and walk around the corner to my husband's office door.

Stef, his receptionist, is talking into her Bluetooth earbud while she taps away on her keyboard. She holds up a finger, asking me to wait, without ever looking at me. Angry as I am, my blood pressure skyrockets. *Would it kill her to at least glance at me?* Stopping here is only a formality. She wouldn't keep me from barging on in, but Gabe would be annoyed with her for it later if he's in the middle of a meeting.

If he's here.

She finally hangs up the phone. Her smile is in place before her eyes travel the distance from her computer screen to my face. When she finally meets my eyes, her smile wilts. Her eyes widen as they zoom around, taking in the barely restrained fury I saw on my face when I fixed my lipstick in the visor mirror before I came in.

"C-can I help you, Mrs. Martin?" Stef has been our go-between for years now, passing messages for me when my husband is too busy to answer his phone or reply to an email. She's probably as tired of it as I am. This isn't her fault, though, so I make an effort to smile.

"I need to see him. Is he with a client?"

"No, ma'am. He's working through lunch."

And that's the problem! "Thank you, Stef."

I march past her desk to his door, not allowing her time to warn him. I don't want him to have a heads up. The door opens easily, and I silently slip inside. Gabe doesn't look up from his computer even when the door closes behind me with an audible *click*. "I'll be right with you," he murmurs, clearly distracted with whatever he's reading.

Some part of me is inclined to soften once I lay eyes on him. A minuscule part. It's what I've done for years. I see him and turn into a schoolgirl again. It's not working this time, though.

I take the opportunity to admire him, though I know him well enough I could draw him with my eyes closed. He's even more handsome than the day we met in high school. His focus and dedication drew me to him then—the same traits he's displaying now.

Studying his profile, I can picture the exact look on his face right now. I've seen it a million times. His gray eyes are slightly squinted while they scan whatever is so important on that screen. He'll have his brow furrowed, making his eyebrows look like mirrored slashes. I always tease him about that. Nothing has changed in the last eleven years, not even how he wears his dark blond hair.

"Sorry about that, I was—" His eyes finally turn my way. "*Tara?*" He says my name like it's a four-letter word. A bad one anyway. "What are you—" He stops. His face goes slack, marking the exact moment he understands what my presence here means.

He winces and rubs the back of his neck. "Lunch," he whispers. "I swear I told Stef to remind me! Time got away from me."

Of course, it did. "Again," I snap. I've lost track of how many times in the last six months he's missed and rescheduled the lunch date that was his idea. He's lost track of time, had emergency meetings, run late with a client. I'm over it!

He dips his chin. "Again. Why didn't you call?"

I plant my hands on my hips. He *would* try to find a way to make it my fault. Through clenched teeth, I tell him, "I did. Ten times."

Frowning, he checks both pockets for his phone, then starts opening desk drawers to find it. "Shit," he mutters. "It's still on silent from the meeting this morning," he says, citing the realty team's Monday morning "planning" session where his father spends the last half of the hour "encouraging" them to work harder and sell more properties. Those meetings are where it all started. He came home every Monday complaining about the pressure his dad was putting on him. Then the drinking started.

He offers me an apologetic smile. That used to work, but I've seen it so often I'm immune. "I'm sorry, Tara. You know how it is. Dad's pushing me to get my numbers up to impress Blake and Tim."

Ah, yes. Blake Warner and Tim Parker, his father's partners. Gabe has busted his ass to impress them since the day his dad got him this job, all so they can put his name on the door someday. I get it; he doesn't want anyone to say that he got the promotion because his father is one of the owners. But man cannot live on work alone.

I was happy to support his dream of becoming a partner here at first. But every year that passes, I lose a little more of him. At first, it was working through dinner once or twice a week. Then it escalated to every night. Then, he was up before the sun to have time to exercise and still make it to work early. And now, he comes home late, drinks his dinner, and keeps drinking until he passes out with his tablet in his hand, still working.

I can't do this anymore. Am I not important, too? I'm tired of being taken for granted. "I want a divorce," I say as calmly as if placing my order for lunch.

The words seem to come from nowhere. I can't believe I've said them. It's like my tongue took on a life of its own and forced the air to make the sounds necessary. It wasn't my plan coming in here today, but this has been a long time coming now. That focus and drive I admired so much before is the very thing driving us apart. We swore to love, honor, and cherish each other, but I'm the only one upholding my end of the deal.

Gabe stares at me, his mouth opening and closing like he keeps changing his mind about what he has to say. I silently plead with him to give me a reason to take the words back. *Just give me something, Gabe. A vacation, marriage counseling, anything.* "Who is he?"

Did he just . . . ? "I beg your pardon?" I ask, giving him a chance to think it through and retract that question. I would *never* cheat on him.

He curls his lip into an ugly sneer. "You accused me of cheating a few years ago when you *know* I don't have time for that. I wondered then if you were having an affair, but I *knew* you wouldn't do that to me. But now, I'm questioning that. So, *who is he?*"

His question comes out in an angry hiss, the prelude to one of his temper tantrums. For once, I don't care that he's about to make an ass of himself. He's only proving that I'm fresh out of fucks to give—that this might really be the end.

"You," I say, packing as much disgust as possible into one word. "When am *I* supposed to have time for another man, Gabe? I clean your house so you can come home and make another mess. I wash your clothes and take care of your dry cleaning. I make sure the bills are paid on time. I buy the groceries to cook the meals you never come home to eat. I keep myself in shape so all of your co-workers can tell you how lucky you are when we're at your stupid office parties!"

"Fine!" he cries when I run out of things to list. "But you won't get a penny. You know that, right?"

Because accusing me of cheating isn't bad enough, he has to make me out to be a money-grubbing bitch too. My high school sweetheart should know me better. I've never cared about money. If I did, I wouldn't have agreed to be a housewife until his career took off. I'd be making my own money and probably be happier for it. "I don't want your damn money! You can shove it up your ass! I want you!"

Tears of relief sting my eyes. I can't believe I just said that, either. It needed to be said, though. He needs to understand that I want nothing from him except for him to be my husband. The man by my side, holding my hand through life's ups and downs. Not the reason life has more downs than ups.

We stare each other down across his desk in the silence that follows my outburst. It's so out of character for me; maybe it'll shock him into pulling his head out of his ass and realizing I'm miserable. The silence reigns, though. Without a word, he waves to a chair across from him. I know what'll happen if I sit. He'll make me all sorts of pretty promises he won't keep because he'll be too busy working or too drunk to follow through.

This is it. I'm done being his afterthought. I'm done sitting on the sidelines and watching life pass me by while I try to keep our marriage afloat.

"No, thank you."

A muscle in his jaw jumps at my refusal, letting me know it was the right thing to do.

Is this what power feels like? No, power is the wrong word. Control. That's it. For the first time in years, I'm in control here instead of blindly going along with his wishes like a good little Stepford wife. I like it. It's too little, too late, though. *It's time to seize control of my own life.*

I cross my arms under my chest, not over it, which would hide the one thing about me I know he loves—or he used to—and stare him down. "Do you not see how ridiculous this is? This lunch date was your idea, but it never happens because you're always too busy for your wife! Well, guess what? I don't want to be the wife you're too busy for anymore!"

"I'm sorry," he says softly. *What happened to the tantrum?* I'd like to believe I got through to him, but I know better. He isn't looking at me. He's looking at his screen like I'm not even here. Like I don't exist. *I'm tired of not existing.*

His apology only serves as fuel for my anger because he doesn't mean it. If he did, he wouldn't be sitting there still. "No, you're not. If I took it all back right now, everything would be the same tomorrow. I can't even say you're going to be sorry because you'll be too busy with work to miss me. Don't come home, Gabe. You don't have a home anymore."

My sense of self snaps in half, and I struggle to draw a breath. Who am I without Gabe? I don't even know anymore, but I refuse to fall apart in front of him. There will be time later to overanalyze everything I've said since I walked into his office. And to put myself back together. I steel my spine, level my chin, and stare him down, waiting for him to insist that we'll talk about this when he gets home this evening.

Gabe only hangs his head. He doesn't try to argue, doesn't try to fight. He sits there and takes it. *Fight for me, you coward!*

But he won't. That's why this didn't happen sooner. I knew he wouldn't try, and I wasn't ready to face it because he means the world to me. Trying would be admitting that he's done something wrong, and Gabe never does *anything* wrong.

I've never felt as alone in my entire life as I do right now. He doesn't want me anymore. This is a confirmation of what I've suspected for a long time.

I'm an inconvenience.

I only get in his way.

Hold him back.

Without me, he can finally succeed.

Gabe wants a wife who is seen and not heard at all times. He doesn't want someone who wants something from him, even if that something is only his love. Being married to me doesn't serve a purpose for him aside from having a trophy to show off.

"I'm sorry," he says again like he's apologizing for something inconsequential, like not having a house to show in the neighborhood I specified.

No, you're not. "Is that all you have to say?" Do I not deserve even an ounce of that determination? I won't beg, but it would be nice to know I mean *something* to him after all this time.

His head moves up and down, but only just. It's barely even noticeable.

"You're not even going to try?" *Please? I don't want much . . .* It's not like him to be so passive. He really is giving up. He's abandoning me.

With one swift motion, he lurches to his feet and sweeps his arm across his desk, sending papers and office paraphernalia flying. He's not trying to intimidate me. It's just his flair for the dramatic showing. I hate myself for flinching when he shouts, "What do you want from me?"

His hands slam down on his desk and the resultant sound is loud enough to be felt. *They definitely heard that in the lobby.* "I work twelve hours a day to buy you a nice home, and a nice car, and all the other asinine little things you want while you sit on your ass and do nothing! But that isn't enough for you, is it? No, gotta come in here and make a scene when something doesn't go the way you think it should. *Nothing* makes you happy! What more do you want from me, Tara? Just tell me! You don't have to make idle threats!"

"Idle threats?" "Sit on my ass and do nothing?" I'll show you idle threats . . .

I don't have a desk to clear, or I might. Maybe there's something to the way he acts out when his emotions are too big for him to handle. I don't have things to throw or break. All I can do is stand here and stamp my foot, but I refuse to stoop to that level. *I'm done.* It's not worth it. He might not care that everyone in this building can hear him, but I do. I keep my voice down and tell him, "I don't care about the jewelry, or the car, or any of the things! I want the same thing I've always wanted! I. Want. You! The rest can burn! I'd trade it all for the damn date that you keep blowing off."

Gabe's chest heaves with his breath. I wouldn't be surprised to see steam coming out of his ears due to the effort his brain is undoubtedly putting into processing what I've just said. How can I not care about any of that? It's what other women would want, right? I'm not other women, though. I married Gabe, not a car, or a house, or a pretty new necklace. I want my husband to come home before dinner at night. I want him to give me a hug and a kiss and be happy to see me. When the day is done, and the lights are out, I want him beside me in our bed. I want him to reach for me.

But I have Gabe, who is never home before eight, walks through to door with his phone stuck to his ear, shuts himself in his office with a bottle of scotch, and never comes to bed before I'm already asleep—if he makes it there at all. The idea of him reaching for me to make love is laughable. I can't remember when the last time was. My knight in shining armor turned out to be an asshole in shoddily spray-painted cardboard. Not even tinfoil. Tinfoil would require more effort on his part.

I take a deep breath and swallow my tears. Gotta hold it together just a little longer. "You accused me of coming here and making a scene, but where else am I supposed to talk to you, Gabe? You practically *live* here. And if you are home, you're still working and too drunk to string two words together!"

Slowly, the lines in his face, born of anger, not laughter, fade away. After eleven years, I should know how every emotion alters his face, but I can't put a name to the softness that replaces the fury. This is a Gabe I've never encountered before, and that scares me. "Tara, I'm sorry. Can we start over? Let me get—"

I cut him off. It's too late now, no matter how badly I want to let him convince me that things will be better. I have to be resolute, or he'll walk all over me for the rest of my life. "No, we can't! I can't. I can't keep giving you second chances. I can't keep looking the other way while you put everything else before me. Don't worry, I won't bother you anymore. I'll have my people call your people. I'm sure we can settle out of court, so you don't lose any time from your precious schedule."

I turn on my heel, yank the door open, and march out of his office before he can make me promises he won't keep. I feel eyes on my back, tracking me on my way to the door. It takes every last ounce of determination I have to keep my chin up and walk out like I own this place. Behind me, Stef calls a soft goodbye, but I don't acknowledge it. I don't want to see the pity in her eyes. It'll destroy the fragile dam I'm hiding my hurt behind.

Gabe

I should have followed her. I've only told myself that ten million times since she slammed the door behind her. Each time I tell myself it'll be the last, that I won't let myself dwell on should've's. *What's one more, though?* The garage door opens automatically as I approach. The house is dark, but her burgundy BMW is right where it's supposed to be. She's probably in bed already, pouting while she watches one of those stupid old movies she and her father love so much.

Her car in the garage eases the tension that's tying my insides into knots. If she's still here, I still have a chance. I can talk her out of this if she hasn't already changed her mind. At the same time, it pisses me off. She didn't mean anything she said today. She came in and made a scene for no reason. *Idle threats.*

I couldn't chase her down. How would that have looked? It's bad enough we were yelling at each other in my office. *Everyone* heard. Well . . . I was yelling. She stood there looking at me with her sad eyes and hardly raised her voice—the eye of my storm. I'm glad I didn't follow her now. I still have my dignity.

Dad ripping my ass once she was gone was bad enough. *"How dare you cause a scene like that! There were clients here! Do you have any idea how that makes us all look? If we lose business because of it, it's coming out of your paycheck!"* The echo of his voice in my head makes me flinch. Facing him was almost harder than hearing Tara say she wants a divorce. I always swore I wouldn't take after him. *Look at me now . . .* I made it two years longer in my marriage than he did, though. I don't have any kids to put through *that* hell, either. *Winning!*

I pick up the second copy of the divorce papers from the seat beside me and fight the urge to destroy these too. I can't believe she wasted time with this sham—hers, mine, and her uncle Den's. He must've dropped everything in order to serve me today.

After I ripped the first copy to shreds in front of him, Den—the asshole—calmly handed me a second set, advised me to call my attorney, and left. It's probably a good thing he did. I would have said or done something I'd regret. It would've served him right, though. He's clearly in on whatever game she's playing to scare me into falling in line.

"Tara!" I call for her before the door is all the way open. Unsurprisingly, she doesn't answer.

I should be on the phone with a client in Cali right now. I have a reputation for punctuality and reliability. Rescheduling is neither, so I never reschedule. After Tara's outburst, I knew I was going to have to make an exception this time. *Why is she trying to ruin my hard work when I'm so close to my promotion?*

Out of habit, I glance at our Word of the Day calendar as I pass it on my way to the bar and smile to myself. Today's word is "narcissistic." *How fitting for her today.*

Her rant about my drinking rings in my ears again as I pour myself a healthy measure of scotch, but only half as much as I usually would, to appease her. If cutting back will smooth things over, I can do that. But a drink when I get home helps me relax after dealing with my father all day. She said all she wants is my time, and tonight that's what she's getting. But first, I need to mellow out. I'm too angry with her for putting me in that position and with my father for chastising me like a schoolkid to be good company.

I finish that drink quickly and stop myself in the act of reaching for the bottle to pour another. *Not yet.* I need to talk to Tara first. She needs to see me sober.

I get it; I'm busy. I'm busting my balls to make partner. To make Dad proud. She knows that. She should understand, but pleasing them both has proven to be impossible.

Once I'm a partner, life will be gravy. She knows this, too. We've talked about it. We just have to hang in there for a bit longer. Then, there will be time and money for her to do her thing. In the meantime, I buy her all the pretty things she wants. Her friends are all jealous as hell of her life. That should be enough, but she wants more.

"Tara?" I call again. Silence answers me. Sighing my irritation, I charge upstairs, ready to get this over with. I don't care if I have to wake her up. She can sleep in tomorrow. She doesn't do anything all day, anyway. No matter what she says about all that house stuff.

"Tara!" I throw open our bedroom door, and my eyes are immediately drawn to our king-sized bed. The headboard itself is a work of art, thick wires that look like vines woven together. She fell in love with it the second she saw it. I bought it, not caring that it cost almost as much as the rest of the bedroom furnishings combined. Anything to make her happy. There's no little Tara-sized lump in the bedding, though—no sound of her deep, even breaths beckoning me to join her. The bed is empty.

My heart slams against my ribs. I turn on my heel and dash down the hall to the next bedroom. She's never moved out of our room before, but maybe this is part of her plan to scare me? It's empty as well. As is the next. And the next. All the beds are empty.

Panicking in earnest now, I run down the stairs to check the den. It's empty as well. Panting, I run back upstairs and nearly rip my bedroom door from its hinges. Nothing looks out of place. *The bath!* That's it! She's taking a bubble bath, probably listening to a book. She didn't hear me yelling for her because she's got earbuds in.

The bathroom door slams into the wall when I throw it open, likely denting the drywall. My hope deflates. It's dark in here save for the moonlight streaming through the window. As I turn to go, my eyes sweep across the vanity, and I freeze.

Something is missing. The pretty little box that always sits next to her sink. The one with her makeup in it.

My mind tries to deny what my heart already knows. She's not just out with the girls, bitching about what an asshole I am. She's gone. *Gone*, gone. With concrete feet, I trudge to the closet and push the door open. A black garment bag is the only thing left on her side. She took everything, not just enough for a night or two. That means she's not planning to come home.

I sag against the doorframe. My stomach turns, the alcohol curdling like old milk. Squeezing my eyes closed, I imagine her standing in front of that bag, agonizing over whether or not to leave it. Curiosity gets the best of me and I unzip the bag. The white lace of her wedding dress glows in the gloom of the closet, mocking me. *I should have followed her.*

Her phone doesn't even humor me with a ring. She's either turned it off or blocked my calls. After the tone, I leave a message demanding she call me. This is ridiculous! We're adults, but she's acting like a spoiled brat who heard "*no*" for the first time.

Mad as I am, I'm still worried. She's never *left* before. I don't know what to do or think. Where is she? Is she alright? How did she get there if her car is here?

The only way to get answers to my questions is to talk to someone who knows where to find her. I call Noel, her best friend. It rings twice and stops, meaning she hit the fuck-off button. I can feel a vein jumping in my temple. *I never liked that bitch anyway* . . . She's probably with Tara, which means she's not alone at least. Next, I try her other best friend. I should have called this one first. She's too passive and eager to please to reject a call.

The call rolls to voicemail. I pull the phone away from my ear and stare at it. *Did that really just happen?*

I try her mother, then her father, and all four of her brothers. None of them answer. A chill sinks into my soul. I know she'll go to her parents' house, but should I go beat the door down and demand to see her, or respect her decision until she's ready to talk?

She'll call me. She just needs some time to think things through and see that she's overreacting. Then, she'll come home.

***

The doorbell rings, snapping me out of my daze. I have no idea how long I've been sitting on the closet floor, waiting for someone to call me back. Anger can only get me so far when there's no one in front of me to be angry at. After repeatedly rehashing the events of the day, I have to admit Tara might have a point. This could have been avoided if I'd taken a little bit of time off to smile and enjoy life with my wife. But Dad doesn't approve of taking time off. For anything. He barely made it to our wedding because he was showing a house that day.

I jump up and almost fall on my face when my knee refuses to cooperate because I've sat too long. Ignoring the ache, I run down the stairs again and yank the door open, only to find myself on the receiving end of a fist to the nose that knocks me on my ass and causes yellow spots to explode across my field of view like my own personal fireworks display.

My attacker grunts with the effort he put into his swing. Distantly, I hear him cursing under his breath about the damage my face did to his fist. *Trade ya* . . . "Just wanted to let you know Tara is safe. I'm not sure why you deserve to know. I'm not even sure if you care. I know if I had a wife and I came home to find she had packed her shit and left, I'd be pretty fucking worried. You're not me, though."

Sitting up, I spit a mouthful of blood onto the tile. His fist is roughly the size of a soccer ball, so he split my lip, too. Wiping my mouth on the back of my hand, I glare up at him. Tara's brother, Colton, is built like their father, short and stocky, lacking only the barrel chest to round out the likeness. I haven't seen him in a while, but it would appear his biceps are finally bigger than my face. His attitude is even bigger. The bastard hits like a truck, too.

Odds are, he'll just knock me down again if I get back up, so I stay where I am rather than risk him giving me a black eye. Or worse. If I hurt him, Tara'll hold that against me, too. "Where is she?" I ask though I'm sure I know. I want to hear that she's somewhere safe.

"None of your concern. She's safe. That's all you need to know."

"She's my *wife!*" I spit the words at him, then spit more blood on the floor. "It is my concern."

He snorts and scuffs the sole of his boot on the concrete. "Maybe if you treated her more like a wife and less like a pet that stopped being cute when it grew up, we wouldn't be having this conversation." He shakes his head, sneering at me in disgust, and turns to leave.

Pissed enough to forget the risk, I surge to my feet and shout, "I gave her everything she wanted!"

"She didn't marry your fucking bank account, dumbass," he calls over his shoulder loudly enough for the neighbors to hear.

That's the second time I've heard something similar today. It's bullshit. My hands clench into fists at my sides. "Will someone please tell me how missing a lunch date is bad enough to justify this shit?"

Colton stops and spins around to double-time it back to my front door. He shoves his finger in my face, and the snarl on his own could curdle milk. "Let me ask you something, dipshit. What was Tara's dream?"

His question brings me up short, stopping me before I can do something stupid like pushing his finger aside. Instead, I take a step back, diffusing the situation even though I'd rather punch him. Colton is a champion MMA fighter. If I give him a reason, he'll tie the long hairs on my head to the short hairs on my ass and roll me down the driveway without breaking a sweat.

Tara's dream? I know I know this. "Her dream was to be a designer and have like a dozen kids."

His eyebrows climb halfway up his forehead. "Close." He sounds a little surprised. I should be proud, but somehow his surprise hurts. "She did want to design wedding dresses. And she wanted four kids, not a dozen. What was your dream, Gabe?"

I don't have to think. Half of my dream is still in the works, at least the half I can achieve since I'll never play soccer again. "To join my Dad's agency and make partner before thirty."

"Uh-huh," he says, nodding. "Now, tell me, of the two of you, which one is living the dream here?"

I am. Saying that feels like admitting guilt, though. I didn't do anything wrong. "I told her she didn't have to work until I was making enough to fund her business!" We're almost there. As soon as I'm promoted to partner, she can do her dress thing. I'm taking care of her, though, damnit. He should respect that.

He smirks at me. "No, you told her you didn't want her to work because it would be too risky for you to both start new careers and a family at the same time. You wanted her to focus on raising babies until you were making enough money to support your family *and* fund her business." He throws his arms out wide and makes a show of looking around. "Where are the babies, Gabe?"

The asshole pauses to give me time to answer. I don't have one, though, or even a decent excuse. We tried for a while. Each subsequent failure hurt her worse than the next. When Dad started throwing more responsibilities my way, I had to work later. A lot of times, she was already asleep when I went up to our room. Taking care of it myself was easier than waking her up and getting her interested.

Saying she was sleeping sounds like a cop-out. *What kind of man uses that as an excuse night after night?* Damn, now that I think of it, I can't remember the last time. I was celebrating something. A big commission, I think. I remember hearing her crying in the shower a few weeks later and seeing a pregnancy test in the trash. I thought she was silly to cry because we could try again. We didn't, though. She was never awake.

"You're not hurting for money, either. So, where's her business? She put her dreams on a shelf for you, and now they've collected so much dust they can't be salvaged. She has nothing to show for the last seven years of her life. Nothing to be proud of. All because she put way too damn much faith in you. It's not that you missed lunch, Gabe. You missed *everything.*

"Leave my sister alone. If you want to do something for her, let her make a life for herself without you there to ruin it. Enjoy that partnership. I hope it'll keep you warm at night."

I watch him storm away, glaring at his retreating back, and wipe away more blood. *Why is everyone blaming me?*

CHAPTER 2

Tara

Six months later . . .

*T*he door of Uncle Den's office stares at me, waiting for me to get out of the car. The sooner I walk in there, the sooner I can put this all behind me. But I don't know how to make myself. Is this what it feels like to get an amputation? To walk into a hospital knowing that you're going to walk out missing a piece of yourself? Because when I walk out of there, the part of me that has belonged to Gabe since the day we met will be gone.

I can do this. I haven't put up with that asshat he hired all these months to flake now.

Asshat is an excellent way to describe Gabe's lawyer. Dylan Walsh is the reason we meet at Uncle Den's office instead of the much more conveniently located office suite he operates out of, and why Dad comes with me to every meeting. I look around and find his beat-up Chevy two cars down. The sight of that hunk of junk eases my anxiety, reminding me I don't have to face him alone. One of my brothers usually tags along too, because Walsh isn't happy until someone is crying and they want it to be him.

Gabe actually threatened to fire him on the spot if he drove me to tears again. It shocked me. Isn't it in his best interest for his lawyer to beat me down? After that, Walsh backed off just enough to ensure my eyes well up at least once, but the tears don't actually fall.

There's no reason for him to be so mean. If I wanted all the fancy things and no Gabe, I wouldn't've left. I didn't want to ask for alimony, but Den insisted. It's a pittance compared to what he brings in, but it will help a lot until I get something figured out. Finding a job isn't proving as easy as I thought it would be. Den also insisted I get my car and half of the resell value of the house. I protested. Gabe agreed. It's up to him to decide if he wants to sell it or cut me a check.

"I work twelve hours a day to buy you a nice home, and a nice car, and all the other asinine little things you want while you sit on your ass and do nothing! But that isn't enough for you, is it? No, gotta come in here and make a scene when something doesn't go the way you think it should. Nothing makes you happy! What more do you want from me, Tara? Just tell me! You don't have to make idle threats!"

Gabe's words to me the day everything blew up echo in my mind, putting some steel in my spine. *Let's do this.* I step from the car a different woman than the one who forced herself to get behind the wheel.

The incessant clicking of a pen greets me when I open the door. It grates on my nerves, leading me to grind my teeth together to vent my frustration before I snap. It's probably Walsh's new idea, psychological harassment. *Wonder if he's opposed to having that pen inserted like a suppository . . .*

But he isn't the one holding the pen. Gabe looks like hell. *I wonder if he's drunk.* His hair is standing up all over the place instead of his usual meticulously arranged style, and his stubble can't be called stubble anymore. He hasn't shaved in a week or longer. It's been just as long since he slept if the dark circles under his eyes are any indication. The bags there are big enough I could've packed in them. *I hate seeing him like this.* He rises when he sees me, and the clicking gives way to blissful silence.

Walsh stands too, which is surprising. I didn't know the bastard had any manners to speak of. He sweeps an errant lock of his soul-black hair into place and offers me what other women would probably consider a panty-dropping smile. It makes him look like even more of a pretentious asshole than I previously believed him to be since I know what he's really like. Or at least what he's like on the job. He could be a nice guy outside of work. He might save kittens, feed the homeless, rescue drowning children. For his sake, I hope he does. Otherwise, Karma is going to have a field day with him when she comes around. *On second thought, I hope Karma makes him her bitch.* Great, now I have to do something to balance that thought out later. Maybe enduring years of neglect with a smile entitles me to a free pass or two.

Uncle Den was already on his feet when I walked through the door. He's not the kind to sit around and wait. He bustles forward to hug me the instant he sees me. "Hey, Tiger."

"Hi," I rasp back, trying to smile but failing miserably. Seeing Gabe like this, it hurts because I know he hurts. That's not what I wanted. I knew I'd suffer, but I didn't think he would even notice my absence.

Before he lets me go, he whispers in my ear, "Gabe has requested a few minutes alone with you. You don't have to agree, Tara."

Nodding to let him know I understand, I consider it while I hug Dad. I'm not afraid of my husband—soon to be ex-husband. He's never done anything to hurt me. Not physically, anyway. Refusing feels cowardly. It says I'm not resolved enough to hear him out.

"You wanted a word?" I ask Gabe, infusing the question with counterfeit confidence. *Fake it 'til you make it.*

From the corner of my eye, I watch Dad and Walsh file out. I'm not sure where they're going. Den's office isn't huge by any means. Not my problem, though. They can loaf around in the parking lot and talk about football or something for all I care. Or my family can gang up on Walsh and teach him some manners.

Gabe watches me across the table, his gray eyes dull. Emotionless. There's nothing of the old spark I know so well. I *knew* so well.

Bracing myself for the heartbreak, I try a smile on for size. It's a bit too small. It feels too tight. "Hi," I say awkwardly and cringe. I don't know what to say to him, but anything would be better than *that*. I'm supposed to be confident and poised. This is what I want, after all.

His head bobs slowly, reminding me of the dog my grandmother used to have on the dashboard of her car. The stench of his favorite scotch wafts across the room when he opens his mouth, "Tara Bear." *Ah, there it is, the knife to the heart.* He hasn't called me that in years. I didn't know he remembered his old pet name for me. "You've proven your point, alright? I get it. You think I've been a shitty husband. Let's put all this on hold and try again. Give me six months. If you're still not happy, we'll sign. We can go home right now, watch some of your corny old movies, and talk about this."

My heart stutters to a stop. He has a point. Six months isn't much in the grand scheme of things. It's nice to hear him admit he was in the wrong for a change. Maybe I . . . *Wait a minute!* He didn't admit to anything! He put it all on me! And he showed up drunk, or well on his way there!

Trying again is not an option. No more doormats here. In six months, nothing will be different and he'll beg me for more time—just like he is now. That knife in my heart twists a little. Tears sting my eyes. "I can't do that, Gabe. I'm truly sorry this is so hard for you. I'll always love you, and I never wanted to hurt you, but I have to do what's best for me."

I grab a pen off the table and sign on the appropriate line.

His eyes screw closed and the pen in his hand clicks once more. "I love you," he says, twisting that damned knife one more time for good measure. I wait, watching as he scrawls his name on the line to make sure it's actually done. The clatter of his pen hitting the table echoes in my ears as I walk out the door.

CHAPTER 3

Tara

Two months later . . .

"This looks wonderful! Tara, I can't thank you enough for coming in on such short notice!" My boss gushes on and on while her eyes drink in every detail of the Halloween themed window display I spent the morning assembling. It might be early in the month, but we want customers to think ahead to buying costumes, and Madison *loves* to make Halloween costumes. I've heard about it since she hired me. "And on your day off, to boot."

"Teagan can't help that she's sick." Well, she probably could help it, in this instance. The brew flu isn't serious, though.

Madison gives me the side-eye, and we both dissolve into giggles.

She pats me on the shoulder and shakes her head. "You're too damn sweet. We both know she did it to herself. She likes to party a little too much."

Very true. I don't begrudge Teagan that. She's young and carefree. Let her live it up before life ties her down.

"That may be, but she's suffering enough. Praying to the porcelain goddess is never fun, even less when you know you're the one to blame." Flashbacks from my own personal D-Day—Divorce Day—assault me. Bless Colton's heart, he carried me home and held my hair back after I drank half my weight in liquor. *I still owe him for that.*

"True that. I hope you didn't have big plans for your day?" Madison always tries not to pry. Instead, she throws out leading questions and hopes I take the bait.

I don't mind indulging her. Trista and Noel are the best friends I could ever hope to have, but I'm slowly discovering this thing called a life. I'm branching out.

Madison didn't have to hire me. Having no previous experience in sales, I was a risk, and we both knew it. Selling dresses in her little boutique is probably the closest I'll ever get to living my dream. If she wants to be friendly, I'm all for it.

I smile to reassure her. "Nothing I can't do tomorrow instead. I was going to curl up by the window with my sketch pad and see what inspiration I could find." Since I have a parking lot view on one side and the other overlooks the road, there's not much to see that inspires me. But I have a good imagination.

The view might suck, but there's a roof over my head, and I'm paying to keep it there. I'm alright with that tradeoff.

My sketch pad and pencils were the first things I purchased once I had a steady income. I didn't quit designing when Gabe and I decided that I would wait to launch my career. *I never imagined how long I'd have to wait.* I drew every day, even going as far as to submit some of my designs in contests. It took a few years and a few negative pregnancy tests for me to get discouraged enough to give up on all of my dreams. It took a few more years for me to recognize my depression for what it was. I told myself to hang in there, and things would get better. And they did. After I left.

"Do I ever get to see these sketches?"

My face burns with embarrassment. The idea is laughable. Almost everything in this shop is Madison's own design, and it's all *gorgeous*. Every sketch I ever submitted to a competition was deemed unworthy. And she doesn't know *what* I sketch. When she finds out I'm a fashion designer too, she might not want me here anymore. She might worry that I'll copy her designs or something.

"C'mon, Tara!" She bats her eyes at me when I fail to reply. "You're always talking about drawing. You see my drawings come to life; the least you can do is let me look at yours!"

"I'll try to remember my book on Monday." It's not much of a promise at all. I'll probably 'forget' to bring it with me, or she'll forget she even asked. I'm not sure my fragile confidence can handle her laughing at them. And if she suspects I'm only here to copy her designs, she might fire me. Then I'm back to searching for a job and relying on alimony to pay the rent.

"How about you go grab it and meet me at that new bistro down the block for lunch on me?"

My breath stalls in my lungs. Madison regularly invites one or two of her veteran employees out for lunch, but she's close with all of them. This is the first time she's extended that invitation to me. It's more than friendly chatter to pass the time. This is straying into actual friend territory.

"S-sure." My cheeks heat up in excitement this time. It's been a long time since I've made a new friend. There's a flutter in my chest and a wiggle in my body that I can barely contain. Surely I can convince her that I'm really not here to steal her work. And if she laughs . . . Well, I'm a big girl. I'll deal. A new friend is worth the risk.

"Great! I'll lock up and go snag us a table!"

***

Madison took the liberty of ordering us both chicken salad on giant croissants. Best. Thing. Ever. I'm dying of sandwich bliss, and what a way to go! Compulsively eating is better than biting my nails down to the quick, waiting on her to pass judgment. Madison has the restraint to wait, preferring to flip through my sketches in silence, which might kill me before the deliciousness in my hands.

She reaches the end of the book at the same time my stomach reaches its limit. At least I have the other half to look forward to tomorrow. I might be extra grateful for that if she does fire me. My sketchbook closes with a snap, and her eyes meet mine. "You've been working for me for *how long?* And you're just now showing me this? Woman, why didn't you tell me you're a *designer?*"

I can't decide if that's a good reaction or not. Anxiety turns the food in my stomach into a hard, uncomfortable lump. *She says that like I've worked there for years instead of weeks.* My last bite goes down hard. "It was on my resume," I point out, knowing full well nothing I wrote down indicated what sort of designing I do.

"Tara!"

"What?" I cry, holding up my hands in surrender. Embarrassed by her outburst, I glance around the dining room. Several other diners shoot me dirty looks for interrupting their lunch but are mollified by a smile. I bite my lip and debate the wisdom of revealing my fears. What if that hasn't occurred to her yet and I give her ideas? *Better to get it all out in the open now.* "I was afraid you wouldn't hire me because I was competition or something. I needed a job!"

Her lips twitch to one side, then the other. "Yeah, you might have a point there. I don't know if my ego would have allowed me to hire another designer. But, these are good, Tara! Really good. I've wanted to expand to weddings, but wedding dresses aren't my thing. I don't do floof."

"You don't do *white* floof." Her ballgown line is to die for, but she loves color. If she ever marries, she'll probably wear neon pink or electric blue—anything but white.

Her shoulders slump. "White is just so boring. But you make it look appealing!"

"Aww, thank you!" There's no greater compliment from her regarding wedding gowns. I'm touched. I don't relax, though. I'm not safe yet.

She opens the book again and flips until she finds a specific design. I barely breathe while her eyes dart around the page she stops on. I wait literally on the edge of my seat for her to decide how she's going to handle this. After studying it for a few minutes with her bottom lip between her teeth, she finds my eyes again. "Alright, don't get your hopes up, but how would you feel about spending some of your days off in the back with me? We can maybe put one or two of these together and put them out on the floor?"

The hopes she told me not to get up are somewhere in the stratosphere. The tension that had me close to snapping in half melts away. I have to stop myself from slumping back into my chair. "That sounds like a dream come true."

She grins at me. "Come to the back door tomorrow at ten."
"It's a date."

Gabe

"Is this seat taken?"

Squinting, I look over at the man I'm here to see and shake my head, playing my part. "All yours."

It's much too bright in here. But that's what I get for picking some high-end watering hole that caters to pricks with their heads so far up their own asses every breath is a fart. Without light, people might not recognize them. *What a shame.* No one bothers me here, though. I'm a small fish in a small pond teeming with other small fish who think they're bigger than they are. And—what can I say?—they're my people.

The man settles onto the stool. When the bartender approaches, he jerks his chin in my direction. "I'll have what he's having."

I relax back into the high-backed barstool. "Make it two, my tab. I'm feeling generous," I say, still following the script.

"Thanks." He leans forward, resting his elbows on the bartop.

The bartender delivers our drinks. "Anything else?"

"I'd like to tab out," I tell him.

"Yes, sir." He leaves to get my receipt. I get out my wallet to put my card away and 'accidentally' drop some folded-up cash.

The man next to me picks it up and holds it out with a smile greasier than his hair. "You dropped this."

"Thank you," I tell him, reaching to take it back. He winks at me and palms it.

The bartender returns, so I sign my receipt. That done, I finish my drink in two long pulls. "Got places to be. Have a good one," I tell the 'stranger.'

He extends his hand. "Thanks for the drink, man."

I grasp his hand, transferring the baggy he's holding from his palm to mine. "You're welcome."

I casually slip my hands into my jacket pockets and make my way to the door doing my best to ignore the sensation of eyes on my back. It's all in my head. It happens every time I do this, which is ridiculous. The pills are prescription. Nothing illegal about them. *Except for how I get them.*

I force myself to maintain a slow, steady pace, but I'm dying to run. I *need* my fix. Alcohol doesn't touch the pain anymore. Pot only numbs it. My dealer promised the stuff in my pocket will take the pain away. I'm steps away from the elevator and privacy when someone grabs my arm.

I stop and turn on my heel to glare at the offending prick, immediately on the defensive. The offending prick isn't a prick at all. She's not a welcome sight, though. I hate for anyone to see me like this, let alone someone I work with. She offers me a small smile while her eyes roam over my face, the corners crinkling in disapproval.

Her brown hair cascades freely around her shoulders instead of being bound back in the tight bun she favors in the office. It's a good look on her. It softens the severity of her features, which makes her look younger, more girlish than the strict taskmaster I know her to be. She's gorgeous, which surprises me. She's worked for me for years, and I've never noticed precisely how stunning she is before. I don't recall ever encountering her outside the office, though.

Swallowing a groan, I try for a smile and fail. She's used to that by now. Smiles have been in short supply since Tara left. "Hey, Stef."

She doesn't pull her punches here, either. "Hate to say it, but you look like shit, boss."

"Duly noted." I grind my teeth, but it can't stop the heat of embarrassment creeping up my neck. Something outside the wall of windows draws my eye to the skyline, all lit up for the night. "What brings you here?" I ask her, tracking the distant blinking lights of a plane coming in for a landing. I shouldn't be asking her questions, encouraging her to stick around.

"I was here for a date. Got stood up," she says wryly.

"I'm sorry." I do mean that. It's nothing on the pain eating me alive, but I'm sure it hurts all the same.

"I'm not." Her teeth close over her bottom lip for a moment, and something changes in her eyes. "Not anymore. You wanna get out of here?"

I thumb the baggy in my pocket. Maybe that fix can wait a bit . . .

CHAPTER 4

Tara

The bell over the door chimes a warning, dragging my wandering thoughts away from how much my life has changed in the three weeks since my lunch with Madison. I glance up from the mannequin I'm dressing in time to watch a blast from my past strut in. It's funny to consider her part of my past when it hasn't been a year since I asked for the divorce. She's part of Gabe's circle, though. Not mine. We're friendly enough for the guys' sake, but I've never cared for her. I've always felt Felicity is using her boyfriend, Mason. He's much too sweet for someone like her. She'll ruin him.

"Tara!" she squeals, as extra as always. "I didn't know you worked here!"

I don't owe her an explanation, so I don't offer one. I know how she is. This kind of work, and everyone who does it, is beneath her. "Yep, I love it." I'm not ashamed of what I do, but I'm not going to give her ammunition, either. "What can I help you with?"

"Well . . ." She makes a show of ducking her head bashfully. "I saw Madison's post on Instagram about the wedding dresses from a new designer. I want to try the ballgown!"

I bite my tongue to hold back my excitement. *She's here for* my *design!* My brain sputters to a stop. That means . . . *Please, God, no.* "Mason proposed?" I squeak out, managing to pass it off as enthusiasm. Would it be out of line if I invited him out for lunch to tell him he's making a huge mistake? I have nothing against marriage—I wouldn't design wedding dresses if I did—but he needs to keep looking for a bride, or he'll end up like Gabe and me.

Her face falls. I barely hold in a sigh of relief. "Not yet. But soon! I just know it! We're meant to be. We've been together so long, I can't imagine what he's waiting for!"

For you to grow up? "I'm sure you're right." I plaster on my customer service smile and wave my hand toward the dressing rooms. "I'll bring it right in!"

Once I see her to the fitting room, I race to the back where Madison is working. It's only been a day since Madison posted pictures and we already have interest? I'm beside myself. But why does it have to be Felicity? And is there some law against trying on wedding dresses when you only have delusions of being engaged?

I bolt through the workroom door and struggle to keep my voice down. "Madi! We have an issue!"

She takes one look at me and drops the bolts of chiffon she's holding onto her work table. "What is it?"

"Someone is here to try on a wedding dress!" I think I need her to pinch me. I can't believe this is happening. *But what if she hates it? Oh, my gosh. What if it isn't good enough? What if I messed something up?*

Her eyes go comically round, then she breaks into a huge grin, which snaps me out of my panic. "That's amazing!" She bounces on the balls of her feet. "Why is this an issue?"

"It's someone I know, and she's not engaged . . ." *She might never be engaged.*

Madison's smile becomes a frown. "Not your problem. Your job is to sell the customer what she wants. If she wants to blow a few thousand dollars on a dress she may never wear, that's her business." She strides to the rack where my dresses hang, shielded from dust and debris in clear plastic garment bags. "Which one?"

"The Princess," I reply, rattling off the nickname we gave my ballgown design. We only finished it two days ago. It took me three weeks, often burning the midnight oil, to complete them both. I've never been prouder of anything in my life, except for growing a set of lady balls and demanding a divorce.

She grabs the bag of floof as she affectionately dubs anything with a full skirt and grins. "Well then, what are we waiting for? Let's go sell a dress!"

My feet follow obediently, leaving my mind to wonder if this is really happening while my stomach churns and threatens to reject the apple I finished an hour ago. I *need* this to go well. I hate that this is happening to Mason, but Madison is right. It's between the two of them. I need to worry about myself right now, as callous as that makes me feel.

Madi's customer service switch flips and her enthusiasm for her work—and mine—shines. "Felicity! So good to see you again!"

I step through the doors and watch them air kiss each other on each cheek. It's no surprise that Felicity knows about the boutique—she's a fashion influencer, after all—but I had no idea she and Madi were on a first-name basis.

Felicity somehow manages to look amazing in the satin robes we keep in the changing rooms so customers can wander around to look at the merchandise between bouts of trying things on without having to redress. It's hard to fit between racks in a ballgown.

"Madi! I can't believe you're breaking into weddings! You said you'd never do it!"

"I know, but I can't deny talent when I see it. And she has talent." Something flutters in my chest at her praise. I never get tired of hearing her say that.

"Do I get a hint about this mystery designer?" Felicity asks, probably fishing for a lead for her blog.

A feature from her could be huge. One little post could send tons of business my way. But using her to further my own career feels a little icky. *What do you think she's trying to do to you?* Is it worth it, though? Felicity is absolutely the type to hold that over my head. That can only get her so far. Madison knows what she's doing. I just have to trust her to handle this situation. She won't let Felicity take advantage of me.

"Well," Madison begins, drawing the single syllable out. "You know her."

I nearly choke on air. *Oh, Madison, no! Wait until we know if she likes the dress!*

Felicity perks up at that, and the wheels begin to turn. "I do?"

"She's local."

"That was a given," Felicity says dismissively. "Who is it?"

"Let's get you in it first. Then we'll talk. Tara?" Madison passes me the bag with a wink.

My stomach is rebelling against the apple again, but I follow Felicity dutifully and close the door to the dressing room behind us. The size I chose to make the dress should fit her hips, and the corset back will adjust to accommodate her waist and bust. Without an ounce of shame, she drops the robe and grabs my shoulder for support while she steps into the layers of fabric.

"What made you decide to come to a local boutique for a dress instead of a big fashion house?" I ask, both to be polite and because the curiosity is going to kill me. Felicity is the biggest snob I know when it comes to clothing, and I'm no Vera Wang. I've always felt that the name on the tag means more to her than the design.

"Well, I was going to until I saw Madi's post. It got me thinking. I want something one-of-a-kind, and Mason likes to support local businesses. It's a win-win! He'll be so proud!"

"Well, it's definitely one-of-a-kind! It was just finished two days ago." As for Mason, he would flip if he knew she was trying on a wedding dress. Madison is right, though; that's between them. And maybe things have changed since I saw them last . . . *Doubt it.* It's not fair for me to assume, though. I've known him since high school, but I've never pretended to understand what he sees in her.

"Can you tell me who the designer is?" She whispers her question, glancing toward the door like Madi might come barging in and bust her.

"I've been sworn to secrecy!" It's the truth too. I promised I would let Madison handle the announcement since it's her boutique. She *tsks* her disappointment while I finish tying the laces and cinch the waist in with a clamp. "There."

This is the first time I get to see someone else wearing one of my creations. I've made my own clothes for years—even my wedding dress—but this is different. My hands tremble on her shoulders when I guide her to face the mirror. Fortunately, Felicity seems to mistake my reaction as a response to her beauty because I can't hold back my gasp. And she *is* stunning. Her body is perfect for a dress like this.

But my *dress!* I made that! It's gorgeous!

"How's it coming?" Madison asks from right outside the door.

"Oh. Em. Gee!" Felicity bounces on the balls of her feet. "I swear, this dress was made for me!"

Madison opens the door and squeals while she does a little happy dance.

"Right? How much is it going to set me back to ensure this dress is never made again?"

"Twenty-five for the rights, ten for the dress," Madison replies without hesitation. My head spins. I need to sit. Madison and I haven't discussed prices yet. She's aiming higher than I would've dreamed of. "And that's a steal. We could make a lot more than that off this dress."

Felicity nods sagely. "Without a doubt. Consider it sold! Now, who *is* this designer?"

Madison's grin turns mischievous. "Turn around."

Felicity's eyes find mine in the mirror. *"You?"*

"Me," I say because it's all I can manage to get out. My brain is still struggling to comprehend the amount of money they're discussing like it's pocket change. There was a time it wouldn't have phased me at all, but now . . .

The skirt swirls prettily when she turns to hug me. "You're a genius! I can't believe I've known you all this time and never knew this about you!"

"Th-thank you."

Madison winks at me behind her back. "Do you want to see it in the big mirror?"

Felicity's head snaps up. "Definitely! And I need pictures for my blog!"

She skips the full treatment—the veil, a quick updo, and jewelry—since the pictures will be on the Internet. For whatever reason, she's delusional enough to think her boyfriend checks her blog religiously and will see her all dolled up before the big event. I don't have the heart to tell her the man isn't the least bit interested in her fashion blog. She'd have to write about things like sports or raising children to catch his interest. Neither of which is her forte.

A million and one pictures and a swipe of a credit card later, she's out the door, and I sit down on the floor before my knees give out. "Is this real?" I ask, terrified I'm about to wake up from a very bizarre dream.

"Congratulations, Tara!" Madison says on the verge of laughter. She leans against the counter and watches me. "Do you realize what just happened?"

"I just sold a dress to a woman who will probably never wear it?"

She laughs at that. "You made thirty-five *thousand* dollars, less the cost of materials. Do you know what that means?"

That I don't need Gabe's help anymore! I can hardly breathe for my excitement. I can tell him to stop sending me alimony. I can make it on my own! If he ignores me, I'll tear up the check. But I'm not telling Madison that; she'll think I'm crazy. "Unless Mason had a change of heart, which I *doubt,* he's going to kill me for letting her spend that much of his money on a dress she might never wear."

She giggles. "Well, maybe that too. But, Tara, it's official! You're a designer. We need to talk about where you go from here."

I pop to my feet and leap to hug her. "Thank you! This was—is—a dream come true!"

The door opens again, and Felicity comes back in, empty-handed. The bottom drops out of my stomach. *She's changed her mind.*

She comes straight to me. Her bottom lip is going to bleed at the rate she's gnawing on it. "Tara, I wasn't gonna say anything, but . . . I just can't keep it to myself."

So it's not about the dress? What could she possibly have to say to me that has her so upset if she doesn't want to return her purchase? "What's wrong?" I ask, extending a hand toward the waiting area where we can sit.

Madison's eyes dart between the two of us, and her lips stretch into a flat line. "I've got a dress to make," she mutters, excusing herself.

Felicity waits until the swinging door to the backroom is motionless again, letting the suspense build to the point I'm chewing on my own lip.

"I was at Alchemy a few weeks ago," she begins, naming what I think is a bar. I've seen the name on billboards. "I hate to be the one to tell you this, but . . . Gabe was there . . . and he left with another woman."

Blood pounds in my ears. She holds up her phone to show me a picture of Gabe and . . . *Stef!* The shameless bitch has her hand in a very inappropriate-for-public location, virtually leading him by the dick. I knew this day would come, but I didn't think it would happen so soon. Or that it would be his *secretary.* It stings that he can make time to go out to drink with another woman, but he couldn't manage to be home by dinner time for me. *Really puts things in perspective.*

"Thank you for telling me," I say on autopilot like one of those annoying automated operators. "But we're divorced now. He can do as he pleases." I need to get her out of here before my control crumbles. I'd go home, but I don't know if I can make it that long.

"Divorced?" she says, her voice ripping through the octaves at the end to make it a question.

"Yes, months ago . . . Did he not tell you?" I ask, not trying to hide how surprised I am. It's not like he can hide it. His friends are bound to notice.

Felicity pokes her bottom lip out and slumps her shoulders. "I'm sorry, Tara! Mason must've forgotten to mention it. I hated to be the one to tell you, but I would want to know if it were me. I feel bad for bringing it up now, though!"

"I appreciate it." And I do. Now I know. He's moving on. The divorce didn't hurt nearly as bad as he thought it would. Maybe I'll shred those alimony checks after all. I don't want to talk to Gabe right now.

"Are you alright?"

I blink a few times to clear the past from my eyes and force a smile. "I'm fine, Felicity."

She smiles back. "That's one of my favorite things about you. You're so strong. You manage to roll with everything without falling apart. I've gotta go. See you around!"

She shoots to her feet as if we just wrapped up a chat about something mundane. Like she didn't just drop a bomb on my head. But she's right; I never show my pain.

"See ya," I call before the door closes behind her.

Madison was obviously eavesdropping because she rushes past me and pops the *'Closed for lunch'* sign in the window. After all the hours we've spent locked up sewing in the back room, she knows the essential details of my divorce. She doesn't bother to ask if I'm okay, just hugs me tight. I rest my chin on her shoulder and watch the world move on outside, but I don't break down like I thought I would. I'm too numb.

"It was his secretary," I mutter.

I didn't know it was possible to have both the best and the worst day of your life on the same day.

Gabe

The crack of the cue against the ball and the resultant cracks of the break makes me flinch. My head is pounding like a motherfucker. Last night's bender wasn't worth it, but *fuck*. I've fought with Stef more in three weeks than I did with Tara in eleven years. Nothing makes that woman happy. And since she controls my schedule, she *always* knows when I'm free. I thought that moving on would fix things, but it's making things worse. I miss Tara more.

Sex would probably shut Stef up. Correction, sex *would* shut her up, but since that first night, when she caught me by surprise, I can't. I can't get Tara out of my head. Stef is just a stand-in, and what we're doing—whatever it is— isn't fair to either of us. Firing her doesn't seem fair either, but it's the only way I can see to get out of this mess. If I do, I'll have to hire a new secretary because mine had to go and get clingy.

"I thought you had a showing today?" Ryan asks. The question snaps me out of my angry musings. Mason's game room falls silent. All eyes are on me. Ryan raises his pierced eyebrow in query when my gaze lands on him.

I grunt, unhappy with the topic that was the subject of the most recent fight. "Rescheduled. Stef's doing so I can go to a wine tasting with her tonight." It's like she took a lesson from Tara but took it to the extreme.

Tara . . . Fuck, I miss her.

"You going to be sober enough to go?" he asks. His eyes bore into mine as he takes a swig from his longneck.

I clear my throat and slip one hand into my pocket to thumb the little baggy containing the pills that will counteract the blast of bitter anger flowing freely through my veins. "I hope not."

Maybe if I'm not, she'll get mad enough to end things herself.

The others freeze. Both of Ryan's annoyingly mobile brows climb his forehead.

"Gabe, if you're going to be in a relationship with her, would it kill you to try?" Mason asks, disapproval heavy in his tone. The man is a fucking paragon of morality, if you overlook the whole premarital sex thing. Disappointing him is almost worse than disappointing my ol' man. Dad at least yells and lets you know exactly where you fucked up. Mason just shakes his head and asks confusing questions in a calm, rational manner until you come to the conclusion he reached twenty minutes prior—the one he wanted you to figure it out on your own. *Asshole.*

"Y'know, I think it might." I sigh. Stef is a rebound. I know it. They know it. Deep down, she knows it. None of this would be happening right now if I hadn't failed at the im-fucking-possible task of keeping my wife happy.

Predictably, Mason shakes his head. His little brother, Austin, frowns and drops his gaze to the rug under the pool table. He's the black sheep of the family, but he was still raised by fucking saints and had the same sense of right and wrong instilled in him that Mason had.

Chris props himself up with his pool cue. "Alright, man, we've respected your wishes this long. We haven't bothered you—or Tara—about the divorce because you didn't want to talk about it, and you didn't want us to influence her decision. I think it's time you tell us what the hell is going on. Because I don't like the rumors I'm hearing."

"Rumors?" Visions of the check-out line tabloids flash through my head. I don't know why anyone cares anymore—I blew my shot at fame—but let them get wind that I've put a toe out of line and it's all over the front pages of the bottom-feeding local news rags.

"Word is you cheated on her," he says matter-of-factly.

Wait, what? "I—" I have no fucking clue what to say. They think I *cheated?* How could I have time to cheat? That's the root of the fucking problem, according to Tara. I didn't make time for a woman. A damn good woman, at that. This is one of those cases where truth is stranger than fiction. And their version of the truth is a lot less painful than the actual fact. At least in their minds, I actively did something to fuck up.

"I don't want to talk about it." There. I will neither confirm nor deny. They can make of it what they will. What can it hurt? The end results are the same: Tara and I aren't together anymore.

Ryan growls, undoubtedly pissed at me. Tara is like a sister to him. "Dude, how the hell could you cheat on T?"

I stare him down. It hurts he thinks I would cheat on her. I channel that into anger and try t back him down. "I said I don't want to talk about it." They sigh collectively, followed by mutterings I can't quite decipher.

"What's up with you and Felicity?" I ask Mason to get the heat off me. Sure enough, the discontented whisperings die down. Tara is—was—a general favorite. Felicity, on the other hand . . . thinking about that two-faced bitch makes my lip curl.

Mason won't hear a word against her, though. He's blind to her shortcomings, insisting the problem is that we don't know her better. I knew all I needed to know about her when she cheated on him all those years ago. *Poor bastard . . .* She'll show her true colors sooner or later. It's amazing she hasn't already. I only hope she does it *before* he proposes. I don't want him to end up like me in a few years.

He tries to hide a grimace behind the act of taking a sip of his bourbon. *So maybe the truth is starting to come out.* "Well, I had to approve a thirty-five thousand dollar purchase on her card yesterday, and she won't tell me what she bought. Only that it's necessary, and I'm going to love it . . ."

We all recoil as if the blow landed in our own wallets. It's chump change to that asshole now, but how does a woman casually spend *that* much money without coming home in a new ride?

Chris smirks at Mason across the pool table. "Maybe she booked a vacation? Or bought out a lingerie store?"

Something shifts in Mason's eyes and his usual, easygoing demeanor vanishes. *Uh oh, definitely trouble in paradise.* A soft knock on the door saves him.

He sighs and rolls his eyes skyward. We all know who it is. Only one person would knock, especially since the door is open. "Come in, Fern," he calls, moving around the table to intercept the gorgeous little slip of a thing who keeps his household running smoothly.

Fern is a perk of holding our monthly meeting of the minds at Mason's, and not just because she's hotter than sin—a fact that seems lost on Mason, like the look she gives him through her eyelashes when she sweeps into the room. Barely north of five feet and curved in all the right places, she also comes equipped with a smile that packs a punch and eyes that can stop traffic. But his eyes are fixed on the tray in her hands instead of on her chest like any normal male's would be. Something is going on there. *Maybe that's the reason he didn't give me the third degree over Stef?*

Her looks are just the cherry on top, though. The woman can fucking cook. After months of take-out and burnt dinners, because I can't cook for shit, my mouth is already watering at the thought of what she might be bringing us.

"Wings?" Austin asks at a near shout, the volume piercing my skull and shooting through my pounding head like an arrow.

Fern's entire body shakes with her delicious little giggle. "Wings. And the sauce you all liked so much last time."

Mason reaches to take the tray, but she brushes by him because her eyes are studiously fixed anywhere but on him, as they almost always are after that initial look. The way they dance around each other fascinates me. This thing between them could set the house on fire with a glance, and they have to know it. She effortlessly, but obviously, avoids him while he plays it cool. Oblivious. Which is fitting because he's too fucking straight-laced to be getting any on the side. He probably doesn't even think about it.

"Thank you, Fern," he murmurs. There's more gravel in his voice than his driveway, but that happens when she's around. The others follow her like Pavlov's dogs, conditioned to her presence meaning food, and crowd around the tray she slides onto the table.

Over their appreciative moans, she says, "No problem! Gabe, need another beer?" She pins me in place with a smile and a blink of her large green eyes. Eyes that are much too open and expressive to hide secrets of that magnitude. There might be a possibility between them, but that's all it is, and has ever been. *Fools.* I don't condone cheating, but Mason's relationship is a joke. The sooner it's over, the better off he'll be.

"Sure, sugar." I watch Mason from the corner of my eye to catch his reaction to the endearment. He doesn't even twitch. *Damn.* Guess that answers that question.

"You got it! Anyone else for a refill?" There's no reason for her to offer. There's a beer fridge in the corner and a stocked bar next to it. We're capable of getting our own drinks. It's something she does. She gets us all another round and drifts out the door, somehow managing to leave the room a little tidier than it was before, though I never noticed her picking anything up.

I owe her, though. Her timely arrival was a much-needed distraction. If I have my way, these guys will never know my wife left me because she thought my job was more important. The pills in my pocket whispers their promises like a siren's song. Caught in their spell, I excuse myself to the bathroom so I can take them without anyone asking questions.

CHAPTER 5

Gabe

Two weeks later . . .

I frown at my cell phone. I *know* I had another appointment this afternoon. It's not on my schedule, though. *Maybe they had to reschedule?* Stef will know. I cradle the handset for my desk phone between my ear and my shoulder and jab the button to call her.

"Yes?" she purrs in my ear. She needs to knock that shit off at work. We're supposed to be professional. Dad will have my ass if she keeps it up.

I'll talk to her about it later. "Hey, did the McEntires reschedule?"

"Yes," she says. There's an edge to her voice I don't like. I've done something to piss her off. Again. "I *told* you not to take any appointments after four today. We have plans."

Are you shitting *me?* My hands clench into fists, and the dull thud of my pulse thrums in my ears. I swallow hard to keep my anger in check. Dad will kill me if I blow up in the office. Again. "I'm sorry, what?"

The unhappiness in her voice is gone now. "I rescheduled them so you can go to my cousin's wedding with me. It's no big deal. They're coming Tuesday instead. Actually, they said that works better for them, so I did you a favor!"

Breathing heavily, I count to ten. Then to twenty. It's the principle of the thing, really. I've told her repeatedly that she can't rearrange my schedule to suit her. I don't need someone trying to micromanage my fucking life that way. "I told you I wasn't going."

"But—"

"No buts. I took off work to go to your stupid art exhibit last week. The week before, it was the wine tasting, and let's not forget the appointments you've rescheduled so I could take you to lunch!"

She huffs out an impatient sigh. "You know this is why you're divorced, right?"

I grit my teeth to keep from yelling at her. *One . . . Two . . .* I make it all the way to ten before asking, "What?"

"You're treating me like you treated *her!*" Her loud whisper is more of an angry hiss than anything. "You're not *trying* to give me a chance! If you don't go tonight, I'm leaving."

I almost laugh. Is she threatening me? Really? She's got another think coming if she thinks I'm going to fall for that. I'm not going to let her manipulate me. "You do what you gotta do, but I'm not going. I won't repeat myself again. Why don't you take the rest of the day off?" *Please? Because I don't want to see you right now.*

I need some time to cool off before we have to deal with each other, or I'm going to be called into Dad's office for another ass chewing. He doesn't give a damn that she and I are dating so long as we keep it professional at work. This is *not* professional, and what comes next if she walks through that door won't be, either.

"Are you kidding me?" she shouts loudly enough to guarantee me a few stern words from Dad later. *Better than an all-out lecture.*

I don't answer.

"I quit." She slams the phone down hard enough I hear it through the door.

That went well. Relieved that it didn't get any worse than that, I throw myself back into my chair and scrub my face with my hands. Without any conscious decision to do so, I reach for the little baggy in my pocket. *No!* I'm in control here. Not it. I'm not *that* bad. I don't need a high. I need a night out.

I grab my cell and tap the icon to call Ryan. He's always ready to party.

"Gabriel," Dad's disapproving voice comes through the intercom on my desk.

I cringe automatically, conditioned to the tone of his voice and what it means for me. I'm in for it. "Yeah?"

"My office. Now!"

I thumb the baggy again while I walk down the hall. *I need more.*

***

"Wherethe fuckami?" I shift around to get away from the light stabbing me in the eyeballs. There are cartoon characters on the walls, and I don't recognize any of them. *Why the fuck isn't* Scooby-Doo *a thing anymore?* If a kid is going to idolize a cartoon dog, it should be that one.

"Mornin', Sunshine," Chris's overly chipper voice answers. *Keaton's room . . .* That's a relief, but I still have questions.

How did I get here? Why does my head hurt? Why does my lip hurt when I talk? The drugs don't do this to me. Did I overdo it? *What the hell is going on?*

"Wha' th' fuck didja do ta me?" I ask, managing to enunciate more of the words this time. It's not perfect, but at least I'm not speaking in cursive.

He smirks. "Ah, that was not me. I take it your memory is a little spotty?"

A flash of Mason's angry blue eyes and the sharp pain of a fist connecting with my bottom lip rolls through my mind. Wincing at the memory, I lightly touch the sore spot on my lip, then the knot on my forehead I have no recollection of. "It's coming back."

"Good." In one swift movement, he draws his arm back and snaps it forward fast enough that it's blurry to my alcohol-addled brain.

Air evacuates my lungs forcibly. I curl into the fetal position to protect my assets. Pain shoots from my balls to my stomach, up to my chest, and on to my already tender brain. Bile climbs my throat, seeking escape from the roiling in my stomach while the absurdly dressed cartoon dogs on the walls spin around me.

"Fuck," I gasp on what little air remains to me. My lungs haven't remembered their purpose in life yet. If I'm lucky, maybe I'll pass out from inadequate oxygen and be spared this pain. Tears stream from my eyes, lessening the effect of the glare I turn on Chris. *How could you, man?*

Calmly, he holds up a baggy—what remains of the new stuff my dealer convinced me to try last night. Blood drains from my head fast enough to make the world spin again. Puking is a possibility once more, though there's nothing but acid to come up. *He knows.*

"What. The. Fuck?" Each word drips with disappointment and disdain for my life choices.

Hundreds of excuses spring to mind. *It's not mine. Someone is trying to frame me. It's not what it looks like.* I discard them all. He knows what it is, or we wouldn't be here right now. I'm not an addict. Defending myself is what an addict would do.

"How'd you know?" I ask instead, hoping to distract him. The new stuff was good. *For a while.* Instead of sinking into a numb oblivion on my couch I was happy again. I went out with my friends and lived it up like I'm supposed to. I want that feeling again. I need him to put the baggy down.

"Fern." Another flash of memory, this time of a bright ass light in my eyes while my friends held me down and soft, gentle fingers on my face. And worried green eyes behind that blinding light. "Even after you assaulted and insulted her, she cared enough to connect the dots."

I cringe again as the hateful, high-induced words I spewed last night echo in my head. *"Are you going to let him dictate what you can and can't do like some whipped little bitch? . . . Fucking stuck up bitch!"* I'm lucky Mason didn't do more damage. I would've in his shoes, friend or not.

"Austin and Ryan spent the morning tossing your apartment, looking for more," he says, swinging the baggy so I know what he means. My eyes track its sway. I don't give in to my cravings until the pain becomes too much. Right now, it's bad. Bits and pieces of what the new stuff made me say and do compound the pain from Tara leaving.

"There isn't any. That's all I've got." That's how I keep in control. I only keep one on me for those bad days and contact my dealer when I run out. I met him last night to restock before I picked up the others because the temptation was too strong after Stef pulled her shit and Dad jumped my ass again. Thanks to her meddling, I had an unexpected opening to find some relief and arrange a meeting before anyone expected me anywhere.

"How long?"

The breath in my lungs forces its ways out nearly as hard as when he hit me in the nuts. I don't want to tell him, but there's no way out of it. Lying will only make things worse at this point. It's what an addict would do. I'm not an addict—I can quit whenever I want. "Since the divorce . . . Two months ago. Wait, closer to three now." *Three months without my Tara Bear. Nine, technically.*

Chris blows out a breath and plants his ass on the foot of the irritatingly small bed. "It's time, Gabe. Tell me what happened . . ."

I close my eyes, too humiliated to face him. What will he think of me when he learns the truth? This is worse than him finding the drugs. "There's nothing to say."

"I know what you said the last time we talked, but I don't buy it. You'd never cheat."

"No. Never." I was alright with letting them think that before, but now . . . It hurts more than I thought it would.

"Then what happened? You two were perfect together."

I knew this moment would come eventually. I hoped to avoid it longer, but there's no putting it off now. Chris won't let it go now. Neither will the others. But what do I say? *The truth, dumbass. You've dug yourself in deep enough.* "She said my job was my only love, and she was the other woman."

He sucks air between his teeth. "Ouch," he says sympathetically. "Why'd you let us believe you cheated then?"

One eye cracks open. He's watching me, probably waiting for me to redeem myself. But I can't. "Would you believe me if I said letting you believe I was that kind of asshole hurts less than the truth?"

The sound of a key in the lock filters back to us. The door opens, and closes. "Honey! We're home," Austin calls. Heavy footsteps warn us of their approach before they crowd into Keaton's room. It's not a small room, but between the toys and four full-grown men, it feels tiny.

"Hey, fuckface." Ryan's greeting is cold, but I expected that. Drugs cost him something once. None of us know what because he doesn't talk about it. My using, even casually, is the ultimate betrayal in his eyes. Worse than not telling them the truth about Tara. Worse than their fabricated version of events. But he should understand better than anyone.

"He says this is it," Chris says, tossing the baggy toward Ryan. He deftly plucks it out of the air, noting the way my eyes follow it. Without a word, he turns on his heel and stomps from the room.

"Hey!" I cry, attempting to rise for the first time since I opened my eyes. "Wait!"

"Fuck off," he calls over his shoulder.

"I *need* that!" My shout is deranged, even to my own ears. Some part of my brain registers this and what it means for me, but I can't stop myself. I lunge out of bed to stop him before he can flush it, because I'm sure that's where he's going.

Austin intercepts me at the same time Chris lunges to tackle, so all three of us go down in a flailing pile of limbs, giving Ryan all the time he needs. A toilet flushes and my body trembles in response. *Fuck.* All the fight drains out of me, leaving me nothing but dead weight on Austin. Chris gains his feet first, then shoves my uncooperative ass off our buddy so he can get up. I don't even try to help.

Thundering footsteps announce that Ryan has rejoined the party. "He's telling the truth about his stash, or he wouldn't've tried so hard to stop me. The first step is admitting you have a problem." His voice is coarse at the best of times, but just now, the pain of my betrayal has him sounding like a five-pack-a-day smoker.

He glares at me, likely waiting for me to say what he wants to hear. It's not enough that Tara couldn't understand I was working to secure our future. The fucking drugs are jeopardizing my relationship with the only brothers I've ever known. *Is this what rock bottom feels like?*

"Gabe, we want to help you," Chris says, adopting his dad voice since Mason isn't here to do so.

Where is that asshole when I need him? As much as I hate to see his disappointment, talking to him about it would be easier. Like a good father, you know he's always going to have your back, no matter what. Even when he's not your own damn father. *My* dad would've disowned me already, and that's if I'm lucky.

"Where's Mason?" The question comes out a whine. I hate whining. I'm a grown-ass man. Just now, I'm more like an overgrown child.

"He isn't answering his phone," Chris says

"He better be getting laid," Austin grumbles.

Right, the thing with Felicity and Fern . . . After what the drugs made me do last night, Mason might *not* have my back no matter what.

Ryan sinks to his knees, putting himself on my level. "Why would you do this?" he growls at me.

My head rolls toward Chris. "It's not my fault. Chris, tell him." I'm whining again, begging him to explain and spare me the pain of repeating the words.

Chris sighs and glances between our other two friends. "He wasn't cheating; Tara left his workaholic ass. He said he started using after the divorce."

Austin cusses. "Why didn't you tell us you were struggling, dumbass? We would have been there for you."

You have no idea what it's like to be me, Austin. I fight the urge to roll my eyes. Austin doesn't know what it is to be beaten down by his own family. His family always has his back. He doesn't know what it's like to fuck up to this degree. "Because I failed, alright? Tara left because she didn't understand the importance of what I'm working for! At least I didn't fucking knock her up at any point, so we don't have kids to drag through the hell of every other fucking weekend!"

"You wanted to be numb," Ryan interjects softly, understanding lightening the disappointment in his eyes into something even harder to look at: pity.

"Yeah," I snap, wishing I could black his eye for looking at me like that. "Guy promised it would make the pain go away."

He growls at me. "It'll make *everything* go away. Get up, dickweed." He surges to his feet and lightly kicks me in the ribs when I make no move to follow. "Get up. You're not doing this to yourself. You're not doing it to me, or to them, or your family."

I scoff at him. *What family?* Parents aside, Tara was the only family I had, and I don't even have her. *What would she think if she found out?*

"Your ass is going to rehab if I have to carry you there, so you might as well show a little fucking dignity and walk!"

I flinch at his tone more than his threat. He couldn't carry me if he wanted to. "I don't need rehab."

He snorts. "Yes, you fucking do. We're not taking any chances. You're going, even if they send you out the door in two weeks. The question is, are we doing this the easy way or the hard way?"

The easy way or the hard way? I can pick my ass up off the floor and accept the olive branch he's offering, or I can lay here like the sad sack I've become and be a whiny little bitch. Option two would be so much easier, but what's it gonna cost me? Respect? Definitely. Friendships? Possibly.

Mom's words to me the night before I signed the papers to terminate my marriage ring in my ears. *"The right thing to do is rarely the easiest option, Gabe. Sometimes, you have to straighten your spine and do it anyway."* She was talking about getting Tara back at the time, though going through with the divorce seemed counterintuitive. She advised me to give Tara what she wanted, then prove to her that I can do better and win her back. That it took years for my marriage to fall apart. Fixing it isn't something I can do overnight. The drugs haven't done permanent damage to my friendships yet, but I can fix this before it does. I just have to do the hard thing.

All three of my friends sigh in relief when I climb to my feet. Ryan's hand lands on my shoulder, knocking me off balance. I'm not sure if I'm still drunk or massively hungover. Between the split lip, the headache, and the lingering pain in my groin, if you looked up the word miserable in the dictionary, you'd probably find a picture of me.

Ryan steadies me and nods his approval. "There's the Gabe we know. Now, let's get your ass cleaned up. You reek."

CHAPTER 6

Tara

Four days later . . .

"You can't go back there!" Teagan's shout alerts me to a problem up front. Madi and exchange glances. I drop my shears to go help her, but Madi stops me with a wave of her hand.

"Let her handle it. She'll let us know if she needs us," she murmurs.

A masculine voice answers Teagan, but he's not yelling, so I can't quite make out what he says. The voice is familiar, though, which is enough to give me shivers. *Did he find me?* I haven't seen Gabe since the day we signed the divorce papers. I haven't gone out of my way to avoid him, but I don't want to see him. Especially not after the picture Felicity showed me.

One door opens just enough for Teagan's head to pop through, her purple hair blending with the other bright colors in the room. "T, you have a visitor. He says it's urgent."

"Who is it?" I ask. There's no point in hiding. Whoever it is, he obviously knows I'm here. If he didn't before, Teagan gave it away.

"It's Mason," he calls, obviously standing close enough behind her to hear. "It took me three days to find you. You changed your number, and your family wouldn't tell me anything. Can I buy you lunch?"

I sigh my relief and smile at Teagan. "It's okay," I tell her. "He's a friend. Madi?"

"Is he a cute friend?" she whispers, a teasing gleam in her eye.

"Yes," I whisper back. "But he's also the cute friend who is dating Felicity Green, so . . ."

Her eyes go round. "Didn't you hear?" She stops and shakes her head, rolling her eyes. "Of course, you didn't hear. You live under a rock. The short version is, she got caught cheating, he threw her out."

Oh shit! I freeze and tamp down my panic. Is Mason here to return the dress? Is he mad at me? I'll gladly give his money back—hopefully, he'll take payments— if it means he's away from her. No matter what, he's a friend, and he'll be civil about it.

"I can hear you, you know," Mason calls dryly.

Madi dissolves into a fit of giggles while my cheeks attain a temperature to rival the sun. She waves me off, still laughing too hard to speak. Our dynamic has changed since Felicity bought that dress. I don't work on the floor anymore, but I'm still her employee. Now, I make dresses. My dresses. And business is booming after Felicity's feature. The phone is ringing off the hook with the who's who calling to book appointments for daughters and granddaughters.

Up front, I find Mason and another familiar face. Wide-set green eyes smile up at me from his side, where he's holding her close. "Fern!" I cry, genuinely happy to see her. She's an absolute darling and one of my favorite parts about visiting Mason's with Gabe, at least when Felicity isn't around to insist upon 'decorum.'

He could never make time for me *but always had time for his friends.* I never resented them for that, but it was hard sometimes. I couldn't begrudge anything that got him away from work for any amount of time. The hope that he would make time for me when we got home always lingered in the back of my mind.

The possessiveness in Mason's hand on her hip is a surprise but a pleasant one. On more than one occasion, Gabe and I discussed how the two of them were one spark away from exploding. It was cute how neither of them ever saw it, though. Gabe insisted they did, but I knew better. Mason was too wrapped up in Felicity, and Fern was too dedicated to her job.

She steps away from him for a hug when I open my arms to her. She's a good hugger, and I didn't realize how badly I needed one. "It's so good to see you!" she sighs into my shoulder.

"You, too! So, what's so important that you're kidnapping me for lunch?" I'd rather hear what happened to bring them together, but chances are, Mason is on a schedule, and whatever brought them here must be big.

They exchange nervous glances. Mason checks his watch. "Let's get going," he says, changing the subject. "I have a meeting this afternoon."

He leads the way to the door and opens it for us, admitting a rush of crisp Autumn air. I follow Fern out onto the sidewalk. Mason steps around me and gathers her to his side again before he offers me his other arm like the gentleman his mother and grandparents raised him to be. Hesitantly, I take it. It's not fear of Fern's wrath that gives me pause. Any fool could see they're so gone for each other there's no need for jealousy. It's fear of what he has to say.

Before we merge with the steady flow of lunchtime shoppers clogging the side- walk, he lets out a sigh that originates from the tips of his toes. "It's Gabe," he says softly enough it's nearly lost in the general susurration of humanity.

"He's alright," Fern adds hurriedly, some sixth sense alerting her to my impending panic attack.

Instead of leading me to the car at the curb, where Len, Mason's driver, is waiting, we walk down the block to the same bistro Madi and I went to. The bistro where missing pieces of the puzzle that is my life started to fall into place. Each step we take adds to the sense of doom building within me, like some of those recently placed pieces are about to vanish.

"Gabe . . . didn't tell us the reason for the divorce until Sunday," Mason finally says. "He let us believe you left because he was cheating."

"Why would he do that?" I ask, but I don't recognize my voice. I don't even remember deciding to ask the question. It's a crazy thing for him to do. His friends are insanely loyal men and wouldn't condone his behavior.

"He said he'd rather have us believe he was that kind of asshole than admit the truth."

Mason holds the door for us, sneaking a kiss from Fern on her way by. In the back corner, I spy another familiar face. Austin stands and waves, beckoning us over to where he waits with two other familiar heads of hair, Chris and Ryan.

"Sorry," Mason murmurs to me. "This was supposed to be Ryan and me, but he suggested bringing Fern for female solidarity. Then the other two found out, and we couldn't keep them away."

"It's okay," I tell him, my voice thick with tears. I swallow the lump in my throat and smile away the tears. I miss them all. They were a huge part of my life for years, but I've avoided them for fear they would resent me for leaving. They were his friends first. I'm still not sure why I'm here, but having them with me means more than they'll ever know.

"Hey, T!" Austin greets, immediately folding me into a hug. "I've missed picking on you!"

"I'm sure you have." He's the youngest in their group—the de facto baby brother to all of us. Since I'm the youngest in my family, he's the only baby brother I've ever had.

Chris shoots to his feet to sweep me up as soon as Austin releases me. His red hair is a little on the shaggy side now, but he still smells like I remember, the expensive cologne he's used since high school, a hint of sweat from the gym, and the chocolate chip muffins he and Keaton have for breakfast every morning.

It's Ryan who gets to me the most. Seeing him brings tears to my eyes. Gabe is the only member of this group I know better than Ryan because they've been best friends since before I moved here. The pierced eyebrow quirks up in a way that always annoys Gabe.

"Hey, T-Bird. Missed you." He bends to rest his chin on my shoulder when he hugs me, and his scruffy stubble scratches my cheek. The lump I forced down before comes back for revenge. A few tears come out of nowhere, rolling down my cheek to drip onto Ryan's shoulder.

"You need to shave," I tease him, because that's what I do. "But I missed you, too."

"How you holding up?" he asks.

"Oh, as well as can be expected, I guess." Chris vacates the seat next to Ryan for me, joining Austin on the other side of the table. Mason helps Fern into the chair next to me, then grabs the last empty one and drags it around to the end to sit beside her.

"I got a job," I say pointlessly, because if Mason found me, I'm sure they all know. "I'm selling my designs now." I wince and shoot Mason a guilty look. "Sorry about that . . ."

His brows sink low over his ocean blue eyes. "What are you talking about?"

I groan, burying my face in my hands. I just let the cat out of the bag. "Felicity was in a couple of weeks ago and bought a wedding dress," I tell him, peeking between my fingers.

Comprehension blooms in his eyes. "You're charging thirty-five grand for a dress?"

My eyes squeeze shut. *Now I've really done it.* I might as well tell him everything and get it over with. After all, he's not likely to take it out on me. "Um, no . . . I *wish.* She also bought the rights to the design, so to speak. She wanted to ensure no one in the world would ever have a wedding dress like hers."

His eyes squeeze shut and he clenches his jaw. Hesitantly, Fern reaches out and lays her hand on his cheek. At her touch, his eyes fly open and the anger melts away. Pure love looks back at her, and it's the most beautiful thing I've seen in years. *I miss that.* "She's gone," Fern whispers to him.

It's been ages since I saw that look in Gabe's eyes. I hope Fern realizes how lucky she is. And I hope she never loses that like I did.

Mason captures her wrist and brings her palm to his lips for a kiss. "And that's not why we're here."

"Why *are* we here?" I ask, unhappy to be getting back on track. It's inevitable, but I'd prefer to delay it a little longer. Watching the two of them restores my faith in true love. *Maybe I'll find that again someday.*

The guys all look at each other and cringe. It's Fern who rolls her eyes and takes one for the team. Her hand finds mine under the table and she gives it a squeeze. "Tara, Gabe is in rehab. We wanted you to hear it from friends rather than headlines."

'Gabe is in rehab.' Her words flutter around in my brain like a balloon that got away before it was tied off. I can't quite catch them to fully comprehend what she's saying. Finally, they lose momentum and drag me down with them. "Rehab?" I ask, my voice flying through octaves. *Is he finally trying?* The hubbub of our fellow diners cuts off, interrupted by my outburst. "For what?" I whisper, conscious of eavesdroppers now.

Gabe was on his way to fortune and fame in college, before he ripped up his knee. That one moment ruined his chance at ever playing at a professional level two days before he was supposed to sit down and sign with the local MLS team. Between that, his mother's own fame as a soccer star, and his father's relentless ad campaigns for his realty business, Gabe's name is recognizable. He's not as well known in town as the other men at the table—who are already garnering a fair bit of attention from fellow diners—but tabloids would still have a field day with this bit of information.

"Drugs and alcohol," Ryan says, his tone hinting at the depth of his own depression. "I checked him in Sunday afternoon."

"What happened?" I ask, fearing the worst. Did they find him passed out from an overdose? Did he nearly die? Is this because of me?

"Fern realized something was wrong Friday night and put the pieces together. He's going to be fine, Tara," Ryan says. He slings an arm around me and pulls me sideways into a hug. "I'm sorry to upset you, but we thought you'd want to know."

"No, you're right. I-I'm glad you told me. I just . . . I didn't realize it was this bad for him. When Felicity showed me that picture," my throat clogs with the tears I'm trying to hold back, "I thought he was doing alright. I thought he was moving on." Some part of me will always love Gabe. That part of me is suffering along with him, suffocating herself with 'maybes' and 'what ifs.'

As one, all four men scoff, saving me from the whirlpool of useless guilt. "Not exactly," Austin says. "It took some coaxing, but we finally got the story out of him. He was at the bar to meet his dealer but ran into Stef. She came on to him, and they left together. That led to a brief . . . let's call it a fling, shall we? He says they fought like cats and dogs because she tried to control him and change his schedule to suit her. She left him on Friday because he refused to take a day off to go to some wedding with her or something."

"Right," I say to let him know I'm following. No matter how badly it hurts, Gabe is a free agent. He can date whomever he pleases. "So, now what?" I ask, praying the subject shifts to something other than his love life.

Chris blows out a breath, puffing out his cheeks. "Now, we wait," he says. "The place has visiting hours if you'd like to—"

Fear stops my heart. I can't see Gabe right now. I can't. I'm finally achieving my dream. Seeing Gabe again might jeopardize all I've worked for because I might forgive him. Especially after this. And that wouldn't be healthy for either of us. "I don't think that's a good idea," I cut in, trying to keep my voice gentle. "I think Gabe needs a clean break."

I need a clean break. Leaving Gabe is the hardest thing I've ever done. I still miss him—the old him anyway. *Can I really say I've moved on if I can't handle seeing him?*

I glance over at Ryan. His black coffee eyes freeze me in place. "T, none of us really knows what went on. We didn't even know you were unhappy." He grabs my shoulder and squeezes it. "I wish you would've said something. I don't know, maybe we—"

Anticipating his next words, I shake my head. "There's nothing you could've done, Ryan," I tell him softly. "We just . . . drifted apart." It's sweet of him to care, but no one outside my relationship had the power to fix it. I didn't *want* anyone to know things weren't going well. I felt like a failure in more ways than one. I had *one job,* and I couldn't do it.

He nods. "Be that as it may, I hate that I didn't know. I know he'd love to see you, but I think I speak for all of us when I say I won't blame you if you don't want to go. But don't be a stranger to the rest of us, alright? You left him, not us."

A tear slips down my cheek, but he's tactful enough not to mention it. I squeeze my eyes shut to stop any others from following and smile. I'm so glad to know they feel that way.

"Yeah!" Austin says, a goofy grin splashed across his face. He winks at me. "We like you better, anyway."

I shrug and choke back more tears. "You were his friends first. I was afraid—"

"That's not how friendship works, T," Mason says. "We didn't stop caring because you two split up."

I don't know why I thought these four would let me tiptoe out of their lives without having a thing or two to say about it. I don't know why I worried they'd hate me for leaving Gabe, either. It was silly of me, but it doesn't matter anymore. I just hate that it took Gabe going to rehab for this to happen.

"I'll try. I saved your numbers when I changed mine. I'll text you all later." That's the best I can do, at least until I know I can see Gabe without crushing my heart all over again. It must be good enough for them because they all nod and grab their menus.

While they compare notes on what looks good for lunch, I fish my phone from my purse and fire off a quick SOS text to my sister-friends. They were with me through it all, and I need them to shake some sense into me because I'm thinking about doing something stupid.

CHAPTER 7

Tara

Trista sips at her appletini. She'll nurse it all night and still manage to catch a buzz. Noel quickly downs her lemon drop martini and happily licks her finger to get the sugar off the rim of her glass. The jukebox in the corner cranks out an old country tune I haven't listened to in years. Throw some sawdust on the floor and voila, this place would be the stereotypical honky-tonk from any movie, ever. I love it. It reminds me of the bar and grill in the little town where I grew up.

Noel casts another dubious look around the joint and sighs. "Alright, we're here, we're as loaded as can be expected since we just got here," she eyes Trista's nearly full glass and rolls her eyes, then crinkles her nose at my untouched margarita, "why are we here?"

The sour of my drink suits my mood, but I need something with a little more burn tonight. I know I can count on Tris to be sweet and supportive and on Noel to give me a healthy dose of reality, but I don't know how I'll handle telling them. I do know that I don't want to get trashed, though. That is Gabe's schtick. It's appealing after being the sober one for years, but the memory of my post-divorce hangover is still too fresh. I don't want to play that game again. I'm only drinking to loosen up.

Still, I pick up my glass and down half in one go. Noel's eyes get huge, and she signals the bartender for another round for the pair of us. I shake my head when he looks to me for confirmation. "Water, please," I tell him.

Noel is going to need a drink for this, so I wait while the bartender does his thing. I close my eyes and let the song that's little more than background noise permeate my brain and carry me away. This isn't Noel's typical scene, but there's something good to be said about a dive bar from time to time. And I was curious to see this one after learning Felicity was caught with her skirt up right outside the back door. It's *definitely* not her scene. She was slumming it.

"Here y'are darlin'," the bartender says, his twangy accent more pronounced than I'm used to hearing. He's definitely a transplant from elsewhere in the state. Probably a college student. Brown hair curls around his ears, but every time I look at him, his gray eyes turn my thoughts toward Gabe. Each time that happens, I have to remind myself why I shouldn't chug my drink and two more because those thoughts are downright depressing.

"Thank you," I reply, answering his smile with one of my own. He winks at Noel. In the mirror behind the bar, I watch her smile become edgy. Predatory. The girl knows what she wants, and she goes for it. If you don't like that, you can kiss her scrawny ass.

"I saw the guys today," I tell her between one sip and the next so she doesn't spew alcohol everywhere. There will be no party fouls tonight. Aside from the one I'm about to commit.

"The guys? Gabe's guys?"

"Uh, oh," Trista mumbles, grabbing my arm, ready to prop me up or hold me back, as always.

"It was good to see them, actually." I can't help but smile. They were like honorary brothers-in-law to me, and I felt like I lost them in the divorce. Until today.

"What, did you bump into them somewhere? Was Gabe with them?" Noel asks, shifting into business mode.

I cringe and ready myself for the hard part. "Not exactly, and no . . . They tracked me down to talk to me. Gabe . . . Lied to them about the divorce. I guess he wouldn't talk about it for a long time, then let them believe he cheated on me."

"He did *what?*" they ask in tandem. Loudly.

"Shhh!" I came here over our usual haunts because I wanted the anonymity, and they're making a scene. The nice thing about dive bars is that no one really cares unless or until things get out of hand. "The guys took me out to lunch. Gabe told them letting them believe he was cheating was easier than admitting to his failure. But that's not the worst of it."

Noel blows a raspberry. "And they bought that? If he were going to cheat, I'd think he'd at least trade up—something that wouldn't be easy to do since he already had a queen. They should've known she was nothing more than a rebound."

I raise my glass in thanks for the confidence boost. We've done this once already, but it's still nice to hear.

"What's wrong?" Trista asks, the corners of her pretty brown eyes tightening.

I down the rest of my margarita. The alcohol hasn't kicked in yet, so there's no pleasant buzz to numb the pain and make this any easier to say. I thought I was going to die when Fern told me. Gabe, my Gabe, the love of my life, turned to illegal substances to numb the pain of the divorce. At least, that's why Ryan says he did it.

"Gabe is in rehab," I blurt out.

"Oh, for his knee? Isn't it a little late now? I thought he made a full recovery?" Trista asks, ever the optimist. *Bless her.*

Noel leans around me to stare at our tiny friend in disbelief. My two best friends are polar opposites. Trista is every inch a pixie—all four-foot-eleven of her—from her short-cropped dark hair to her sparkly pink toes. Her features dominate her pale face, giving her a childlike look that is only amplified by her optimism and innocence.

Noel, on the other hand, is a foot taller and blond as blond can be without the help of chemicals. Her eyes are such a pale blue they almost appear white, and they glow next to her perma-tan. To round out the juxtaposition, she oozes the confidence of a model strutting the catwalk, which she very well could be if she wasn't so damn vain. One would think vanity and modeling go hand in hand, but Noel is too hung up on what she perceives as imperfections to embrace her beauty.

And then, there's me—average on every level. I'm comfortable in my own skin, though, and that's all that matters. At least I am now that I'm not constantly trying to fix something about me that isn't broken in a doomed effort to repair my marriage along with it.

"What?" Trista asks.

"Not that kind of rehab, you ditz!" Noel says, flinging her hair over her shoulder. "Spill it, woman. Drugs or booze?"

"Both," I whisper, thankful she's taking charge here. It's easier to answer questions than to volunteer information.

Trista presses her hands to her mouth to stifle her gasp while Noel whistles long and low.

"Did *not* see that coming," Noel says. She wraps a stick-thin arm around me and pulls me sideways until my head is on her shoulder. "I'm sorry, babe. That's rough. Is he alright?"

Her concern warms my heart, but I know it's more for me than for him. She probably wants to know exactly what kind of basket case I'm going to be when this booze kicks in. "Yeah. He hasn't overdosed or anything. I guess he was out with the guys and Mason's new girlfriend on Saturday, and she recognized the signs when he started to crash."

"M-Mason's new girlfriend?"

I curse, kicking myself for my careless tongue. Trista has crushed on him since the moment she laid eyes on him. I've tried to tell her they never would've worked, but she's hopeless.

She's too timid to fit into his life. I've met tiny women who absolutely dominate. Hell, Fern isn't much bigger than Trista, and her personality can knock you on your ass—as long as Felicity isn't around. But fate saw fit to gift Trista with all the spunk of a wet noodle. Or maybe her overbearing mother robbed her of her fire. Either way, she's not up for a life with him.

"Sorry, Tris." I offer her a hug, and she takes it. "Yeah, he's finally kicked that bitch to the curb. If it's any consolation, he seems happy now!" It's not a consolation at all, but if you really care about someone, you should want them to be happy, no matter what. *Easier said than done.* I wish Gabe and I had figured that out before it came to divorce.

"That's good, at least," she says, but her eyes are dewy. She snatches up her glass and takes a healthy drink this time instead of the little sips that are more her style.

Noel and I shrug at each other. We both knew this day was coming sooner or later. At least we are all together to get her through it. I'm sure it'll be all over the news any day now, because there's nothing better to report about than the personal life of the man who will soon own one of the biggest businesses in town. *Unless they hear about Gabe first.*

"Anyway," Noel says, drawing the word out and motioning for me to get on with it. She's smart enough to know I'm not done dropping bombs.

"I want to go see him."

"Record scratch! Stop the music. Hold the phone. Not fucking happening!" Noel manages to grab the attention of every last patron of this surprisingly busy hole in the wall.

I smile weakly and wave a hand to let the onlookers know everything is alright with us. "I feel like I need to," I say, toying with the salt on the rim of my glass.

"Why?" Trista asks.

"Because . . ."

Noel rolls her eyes. "Oh, well, *that* clears it up."

I sigh and take my time putting the feelings and thoughts that have tumbled around my brains since lunch with the guys in words that make sense. "I thought I said all of the things I needed to the day I asked for the divorce, but maybe I was wrong. I blame him for a lot of things, and I can't move on until I'm not carrying that anymore. I don't want to throw it all on him and hurt him more, but I need to say it all so I can let it go. And I think maybe he needs that too."

That's the only reason I don't feel selfish for even thinking it. He's clearly struggling. Maybe we can talk it out and resolve our separate problems. Then, life will be better for both of us. He won't need help, and I can move on.

Noel rolls her eyes at me. "You mean, you want to give him a chance to defend himself and change your mind."

"It's too late to change my mind. The divorce is final. I'm happier than I've been in years. I have a job I love. By some miracle, I found a boss who is helping me make my dream come true—"

"Not all of your dreams," she mutters.

I sigh. I knew the harsh reality check was coming sooner or later. Expecting it doesn't spare me the pain. "Maybe that just wasn't in the cards for me. I've made my peace with it now that my life doesn't revolve around starting a family and being a good little housewife. I thought I needed children to be happy, but I've learned that's not true."

The fulfillment I get from making my dresses isn't the same as I imagine raising children to be, but it's close enough. Maybe I'm not being entirely honest when I say I've made my peace, but I am working on it. I'll get there. More time is all I need.

"It's not too late," Trista says. "Women have children in their thirties all the time."

I offer her a smile for her unfailing support, even when she has to feel like her own heart is in a blender. "Can't do it alone, Tris. And I'm in no rush to dive into another relationship."

"Pfft," she scoffs, waving a hand around. "Pick one, any one. Men are all the same."

I bite my tongue to stop a smile. She doesn't mean that. She wouldn't say it if she weren't so upset. Though, her offhanded bitterness reminds me of an option I consider and repeatedly discard: sperm donors. The official channels, though. Not random hookups or approaching a guy and begging him to get me pregnant. But I want what I grew up with—a big family. Without the father in our lives, a chunk of that dream is missing.

"Trista! I do believe you're toasted!" Noel says, a wicked glee sparking to life in her eyes.

Trista hiccups. "Seems like the thing to do." Determination hardens her eyes as she stares at what remains of her appletini. With a sharp nod, she snatches it up and throws it back. *Oh, shit.* She doesn't *have* a tolerance for alcohol. In roughly ten minutes, she'll be dancing-on-the-bar drunk and love everyone. It doesn't happen often, but when it does, it's an experience to remember.

Frantic, I reach for her back pockets, searching for her phone. To an onlooker, it probably appears as if I'm groping her, but I don't care. I do care that I don't find what I'm looking for.

"Give me your phone!" Like everyone else in the world, alcohol overrides her common sense and blesses her with false confidence. Most people grunt and bear the aftermath with passing grace. Trista isn't most people. She'll be crushed in the morning.

Trusting as she is, she hands it over without question, only thinking to protest when I pocket it. "For your own good!" I say over her promises. "Do you remember last time? I didn't take your phone and you drunk dialed your ex?"

Her arguments die a swift death. "Thanks."

"That's what I'm here for."

"No." She shakes a finger at me, "you're here because of Gabe. Because you want us to talk you out of doing the right thing."

Whoa! She's got me there, but I didn't expect either of them to call me on it. I expected the exact opposite from them. I was ready to explain that I'm not taking two steps back if I do this, that I'm trying to move forward.

Noel's chin tilts to a dangerous degree. She holds up a hand in the universal sign for stop. "Hold up! How is going to visit him the right thing? He couldn't be bothered to take time for her when they were married; she doesn't owe him a single second!"

Trista crosses her arms over her chest. "If she still has things to say, she owes it to herself!"

Noel's eyes go round. "Well, shit. She's got me there." She shrugs at me and grimaces. "If you think he's still dragging you down, then by all means, go let him have it. He deserves it. Do you need us to go with you?"

I have the best friends in the world. My eyes well up with tears because I'm so lucky to have them. I hug them both. "I love you two so much. But no, if I'm going to do it, I need to be strong enough to do it by myself. But afterward . . ."

"Ice cream, cookies, and bad movies?" Trista asks.

"Yes. I might need all of that."

CHAPTER 8

Gabe

"You resent your father," the doctor says, nodding confidently, once I've run out of things to tell him about growing up with a famous mother and a father who let his love drown in his feelings of inadequacy.

Fuck, what's his name again? I shake my head in response while I rack my brain for his name. I don't want to be here. I don't want to be doing this. I know my childhood wasn't perfect, but big deal. Show me someone whose was. I'm not going to sit here and listen to this shit.

"Now, hear me out," he says. I don't like this guy. Dr. Johnson. That's it. *He is a johnson.* "That doesn't make your father a bad person. It doesn't make you a bad person. It only means your father made decisions you can't reconcile. For instance, why marry your mother and start a family if he was only going to ignore you both later?"

Fuck. Maybe he's onto something. Uncomfortable, I scratch at the stubble that's almost too long to be considered stubble anymore. I need to shave, but I don't want to. There's no one to impress. And it's exhausting. Everything is exhausting.

It's been two weeks since Ryan dumped me out here. He visits every day and the others take turns. Between the four of them, I have two visitors a day. Three when Mom comes, because one of those assholes told her.

Dad hasn't been in yet, not that I'm surprised. He won't tarnish his reputation. My chances at making partner are toast. *It was all a waste.* My knee begins to bounce to relieve the agitation and the restlessness. I'm too tired to move, but I can't sit still.

"Because of that, you want to prove you're better than him. And you want to make him proud," Dr. Dick says, bringing my brain back to the subject at hand.

No shit, Sherlock. I swear he knows I can't concentrate. Come to think of it, they warned me that would happen . . .

"But you let that desire to prove yourself eclipse everything else in your life."

Tell me something I don't know.

"You neglected your hobbies and your marriage."

Thanks for pointing that out, asswipe.

"You blame your father, indirectly, of course. The fact of the matter is you deflect the blame. It's not your fault you had to work so hard to be better than him. Your ex-wife should have understood. If she loved you, she would have supported you."

My hands ball into fists where they rest on my knees. My body shakes with the need to leap to my feet and beat the guy to a bloody pulp. I'm here to get help, not to have him make me out to be an asshole. I *am* an asshole, but he's got it all wrong. It's *not* my fault!

"You blame your father for your ruined marriage, and you blame Tara for your substance abuse. I say they're both your fault. How does that make you feel?"

"Like you're a fucking idiot." I sneer at him. "It's not like I *wanted* my wife to leave me. And I didn't *want* to get hooked on Oxy." I don't list the cocaine and fentanyl cocktail I let that greasy prick talk me into trying. I only know what it was because they tested me when I got here. And they told me I'm lucky to be alive.

The insult rolls off him. He smiles blandly and crosses his legs. "But you made the decisions that brought you to both outcomes, Mr. Martin. No one made those decisions for you. Your father didn't force you to work as you did. No one forced you to buy the drugs. I think that's enough for today. We'll talk more next week. In the meantime, I'd like for you to consider actions and consequences."

I squint at him. He's crazy if he thinks I'm going to put up with his bullshit for another week. As soon as I'm over the withdrawals, I'm out of here. "Who says I'll be here next week?"

"I do," he says, a smile coloring his voice. "Our purpose here is not only to get you over your addiction, but also to address the problems that pushed you to drugs in the first place, Mr. Martin. Until you can accept that you are in control of your own life, and therefore are to blame for your own actions, we won't release you."

My jaw clenches. What did Ryan get me into? They can't force me to stay, though. I'm not here on court orders. I can leave whenever I want. "I don't need you to release me! I checked myself in!"

"True," he says, nodding like a bobblehead. "But how long do you think you'll make it before you're turning to drugs to hide from the truth again? Better to accept it now and stay clean, don't you think?"

"Fuck off!" My chair falls over backward when I stand up. I don't take the time to right it before I storm out the door. He can kiss my ass.

"Mr. Martin?" a nurse calls after me. I'm halfway back to my ten-by-ten cell of a room. The temptation to keep walking is strong, but the nurses have been so kind. It's not her fault Johnson is a johnson. I compromise and turn around to walk backward.

"You have a visitor," she says, tilting her head toward the so-called family room.

Her words lift my spirits. That's just what I need after my visit with Dr. Dick. My friends will cheer me up. I can tell them what that dipshit said, and we can have a good laugh.

I nod my thanks and change direction. This place isn't all bad. It sucks that I have nothing to numb the pain anymore—and I feel like shit—but they're teaching me to distract myself. All the same, I'm ready to go home. These visits are the best part of every day. I've seen my friends more since I got here than I have in years. Life got in the way. Jobs got in the way.

Who's it gonna be? Ryan has already been in today. Mason brought Fern and Ronni in yesterday. *That girl is a clown.* Their happiness is a slap in the face considering what I lost, but I'm happy for them. *Chris.* It's been nearly a week since he was in last. It's gotta be him.

I round the corner into the public space full of furniture arranged to give some semblance of privacy and freeze. The room is empty, save for the nearest sofa. Over the back, a head of curly blond hair I'm intimately familiar with is visible. *I can't believe she's here.* "Tara?"

She looks over her shoulder and tries to smile. It doesn't reach her eyes. "Hey, Gabe." She stands and turns to face me, looking me up and down. Her gaze lingers on my shaggy hair and the ragged beard. Blood rushes to my face and neck. Ducking my head, I reach to rub at the scruff on my cheeks self-consciously. If I'd known she was coming, I might've cared enough to put forth the effort to visit the barbershop here.

She looks good, but she always did. She lost weight while finalizing the divorce, too much to be healthy, but she's filling out now. Her outfit reminds me of the day we met, a pair of faded jeans and a concert tee for some obscure country band. And her boots. Mustn't forget her boots. Her eyes are missing their spark, though. *Good. She misses me.*

The satisfaction that knowledge gives me probably makes me a bad person, but I don't care. It's only fair. I miss her, too.

I miss everything about her. I'll never tell her that. I've missed her for years, but it took coming here to realize that. It took *Stef* to realize that.

I miss her head on my shoulder when I hug her and the way she giggles when I kiss her sometimes. The way she'd cuddle up to me in her sleep, mumbling incoherently. Her skin under my lips. The taste of her on my tongue. Her smile when I walk through the door, and the way she'd run into my arms. *She took all that from me.*

"What are you doing here?" She had her chance to reconcile. I gave her plenty of them and she threw them all back in my face.

"Well," she looks around to stall for time. Classic Tara maneuver. She knows what she wants to say; she likes to waste my time. "The guys told me you were here."

I say nothing because I'm smart enough to figure that out on my own. I don't know why they thought they needed to drag her into this. It's embarrassing enough without her seeing how far I've fallen. They could've warned me at least instead of letting her blindside me like this. *I'll deal with them later.*

"And . . . I thought maybe we should get some things off our chests. See if we can . . ." Frowning, she stops for a second. The crease between her brows smooths out, and she nods to herself. "Maybe we can resolve our separate problems since they both stem from the same issue."

My mind skips back to the conversation with Dr. Dick. She's right. I do have some things to get off of my chest. I shove my hands in my pockets and smile, but it feels more like a sneer. "Oh, you mean like how I'm mad at you for ripping my heart out and walking all over it?"

Her eyebrows shoot up toward her hairline, and her entire body shifts with the verbal blow. I watch her reaction, patting myself on the back for getting to her before she can hurt me. And then she smiles. *Oh fuck.* Nothing good happens when she smiles after something like that.

"I was thinking more along the lines of how you took my heart and left it to shrivel up and die in some forgotten corner, but okay, we can go with your version."

Angry at her assumption that I would abuse my greatest treasure, I glare at her and raise my voice. "I never did anything—"

She rolls her eyes and cuts me off, her voice rising to match mine. "You're right! You didn't! You never did a damn thing! It's always all about you, Gabe. What you want. What about me?"

"What about *you*? I gave you *everything!*"

Not to be outdone, she shouts back with all she's got. "You gave me *things*! I didn't want things; I wanted *you!* I wanted a family! I wanted my dream! You expected me to sit at home and be the good little wife while you went out and chased yours. You said there would be time for me to work later. You wanted me to focus on our family first, but you never gave me that family!"

Crossing my arms, I glare her down. She always has to throw that in my face— the one thing she wanted I couldn't easily give her. "I was busy!"

"And whose fault was that?" She screams the words hard enough that her face turns a brilliant shade of red.

There's that word again, directed at me when it's quite clear I didn't do anything wrong. I thought she achieved maximum volume before, but I was wrong. If she's not careful, she's going to strain a vocal cord. She'll be lucky if she has a voice after this, and I'm not even trying. Hell, I'm just getting warmed up. "I had a job to do!" I yell, giving it all I've got.

Tara snorts out a derisive laugh. "Oh, yeah, you had a job to do. That's a lame excuse and we both know it. You did what you did because you wanted to hear your father say you did good and show him what a self-centered jackass he is! Well, guess what, Gabe? Now, you're the self-centered jackass. At least he admitted he was in the wrong when your mother filed for divorce because he turned into a bitter, money-hungry bastard who worked all the time!"

Whoa, wait a minute. I'm nothing like my father! "What are you saying? I didn't do anything wrong!"

"If you didn't do anything wrong, why did I leave?"

"Because you didn't understand that I was trying to secure our future, and you didn't support that goal!"

That smile makes a comeback before she tosses her hair and laughs. Warning bells chime in my head. Shit is about to get real. Her voice is so soft I have to strain my ears to hear. "What future, Gabe? The future where I sat home by myself every night, wondering if you'd be home before dinner was cold? The one where I went to bed and woke up alone every damn day because your job and alcohol were more important to you than making sure your wife knew you loved her? *You* drove me away, Gabe. Your job, your drinking, your need for your father's approval, and your need to prove some stupid point ended our marriage, and that's on you.

"I tried to stick it out. I tried to make it work. In the end, you didn't until it was too late. And that's on you too. Grow the fuck up and take responsibility for your damn actions! I came here in hopes we could forgive each other and work toward being friends again, but now I see I can't forgive you because, in your mind, you've done nothing wrong."

She flips around and marches straight for the emergency exit, ignoring me when I call after her. An ear-splitting siren cuts through the relative peace of the building, but she doesn't falter. She's apparently so desperate to get away from me, she'd rather run around the building than come near me, which was her only other way out. *What the fuck have I done?*

A throat clears behind me. My eyes snap shut. I offer up a quick prayer that I'm wrong. But I'm not. Dr. Dick is standing there, fighting a smirk. "Consequences and actions," he says before continuing on his merry way.

CHAPTER 9

Tara

The number on the screen of my ringing phone is unfamiliar, but I answer it on a gut feeling. "Hello?"

"Tara Martin?" a man asks.

"This is she . . ." *I swear if this is another damned call about my car's extended warranty . . .* But it might be a wedding dress emergency or something. My cell number *is* on our business cards now.

"Hello, Ms. Martin. This is doctor Evan Johnson. I'm the psychologist working with your ex-husband. I got your number from Ryan LeDoux."

Damnit, Ryan. ". . . Okay?"

"Gabe is doing remarkably well in our program now. He has you to thank for that, by the way. Your visit two weeks ago made a huge impact on him."

"Okay?" *I'd like to make a huge impact on Gabe's stupid face with a chair.* I am happy to hear that the doctor feels he's doing well, but I'm not sure what has to do with me.

"He's being discharged this weekend, and I was hoping you'd consider joining us for a little . . . meeting of sorts, that evening. Gabe has some things he'd like to say to everyone."

I recoil as if hit. My phone slips from my fingers. I manage to catch it before it hits the ground and press it tightly to my ear. Dr. Johnson waits in silence while I try to remember how to speak again. "I don't think that's a good idea, Dr. Johnson." I'm still too angry with Gabe to talk to him rationally. Someday . . . Maybe.

"I understand, but if you change your mind, the meeting is at six o'clock on Saturday."

"Thank you." I lower the phone and look down to tap the button to disconnect the call. I don't know what I'll be doing Saturday at six o'clock, but I know what I *won't* be doing.

CHAPTER 10

Gabe

There's a soft knock on the door before it opens. "Hi, honey," Mom murmurs. "How are you feeling?"

I toss the last of my belongings into the bag on my bed without bothering with neatness. I'll get home to my shithole apartment soon and unpack them anyway. Maybe. Or I might leave them in the bag for a few days as a reminder. I'm still learning the finer points of doing laundry. Any excuse to put it off is a good one. "I'm good, Mom. Thanks for coming."

"Of course," she says, beaming at me. "I'm so proud of you."

"Mom, I was an alcoholic and a drug addict."

"For three months, and you turned your life around!" she says, always ready to defend her only child to the death. A smile tugs at the corners of my mouth. Mom is always in my corner, no matter what. Even when I don't deserve her support or her optimism.

She's right, though, in more ways than one. Tonight is about proving that. Or at least showing that I'm making an attempt. My hands shake, betraying my nerves, as I zip my bag. I reach for the handle but change my mind and leave it on the bed. I'll get it after the meeting. I need to quit stalling.

"Is everyone here?" I ask, turning to face her.

She smiles her approval of my clean-shaven cheeks and my freshly trimmed hair. "You don't look like a bum anymore!"

"What have you got against beards?" I ask, teasing her because I know full well the new man in her life sports one.

"Nothing, when they're well kept," she says, nudging me in the ribs with her elbow. "To answer your question, yes, everyone is here. I just wanted to check on you. You take your time, alright?"

"Thanks, Mom."

She latches onto my ear with her thumb and forefinger and tugs me down to her level to kiss my cheek. Something else that will never change. But sometimes, change is good.

"I'm ready. Let's do this." It'll only be worse if I wait. I'll work myself into a mood wondering if Tara is here because Mom didn't specify. She didn't answer when I called, not that I blame her. She hit the fuck off button and rolled me to voicemail. I have no way of knowing if she got my message or if she even cares anymore if she did. Hell, I'm not even sure if it's her number anymore. She never took the time to change her voicemail message, leaving it as the default automated message everyone starts with, so there's no way to tell. Mason said something about having a hard time tracking her down. It's not that hard when she's only a phone call away.

Mom holds my hand like I'm still her little boy as we walk through the halls to Dr. Dick's office. My heart beats a little faster with every step, forcing adrenaline through my veins. This is harder than the day I fucked up my knee. Harder than graduation. Scarier than waiting for Tara to walk down the aisle so I could promise to love her forever. But I survived all of those things *and* signing the dotted line that put an end to my marriage. I can survive this, too.

You could hear a mouse fart when we open the door. My eyes sweep the room, searching for a head of curly blond hair. Mason still looks a little worse for the wear, but he smiles brightly, as does Fern, who is tucked under his arm. I'm glad she came. I owe her my life. Ryan, Chris, and Austin are arranged around them. Dad is sitting as far away from Mom's boyfriend as he can get. But there's no Tara. A sense of dread settles into my bones.

I take a step back and check the hallway. Tara has to be here. I need her to be here. I told myself she might not come, but I never really believed it. She came here to make amends once. Yeah, that kind of . . . blew up. But surely she wouldn't give up that easily? It took her *years* to give up on our marriage.

Dr. Dick pushes to his feet. "Excellent! We're all here!"

"But—"

"She's not coming, Gabe," Ryan says softly. "I called and offered to pick her up. She's at work."

At work. The significance isn't lost on me. Mom squeezes my hand and abandons me for her seat next to Russell, the boyfriend.

Numb, I take my seat next to the good doctor because I know it's what I'm supposed to do, and he gets the ball rolling. "Thank you all for coming tonight. I'm doctor Evan Johnson for those of you I didn't get to speak with before. Working with Gabe hasn't been easy, but I'm sure I don't need to tell anyone here that."

Everyone chuckles, and again when I call them assholes for it. My heart isn't in the teasing, but I'm trying. For them. I can't believe she didn't come. Her absence tonight birthed a black hole in my chest that grows a little each time she crosses my mind.

"So, tonight is all about Gabe. He's done a lot of soul searching in the last couple of weeks, and I believe he's ready to rejoin the world. He's going to need a strong support system in place to hold him accountable and help him through the bad days, which is why you are all here. Gabe, you ready?"

"As I'll ever be, Dick." I underestimated how much I was relying on her to come. How much I was counting on this chance to make amends. Her absence speaks volumes, and it says I really fucked up this time. Whatever brought her here that day we fought; it was my last chance. *I'll just have to go to her.*

But first, I have to do this.

He grins and pantomimes beating me over the head with his notebook. What started in bitterness became a joke between us. Luckily, he gets my sense of humor.

I stand up, because this isn't the sort of thing you do sitting down, and take a deep breath. If any of these clowns calls Tara afterward, I want them to tell her I did it right. "Doc told me to speak from the heart instead of writing things down, so I'm going to stick to the last few months, or we might be here all night." Laughter. Good. My eyes travel the circle, trying to decide where to begin. I thought I had a plan, but I've lost it. Fern shifts under Mason's arm, and a sparkle catches my eye. Nodding to myself, I make my decision.

"Fern, thank you for coming."

"Of course," she says, offering me an encouraging smile. Her words surprise me. She wasn't exactly a friend before; she was my friend's nanny and housekeeper. Human furniture that is pleasing to the eye and can cook better than anyone I've ever met. The last time we spoke outside the walls of the rehab center I treated her like a second-rate whore. She doesn't owe me shit, especially not kindness. What I said and did is inexcusable. But that's Fern, determined to do the right thing no matter the cost to her.

With the memory of that night fresh in my mind, I'm almost too ashamed to make eye contact, but I'm too proud not to. "Part of my road to recovery has been revisiting the decisions that brought me here. And learning to accept that I am responsible for those decisions. I wouldn't be where I am today without you, Fern. I would like to apologize for being a complete dick that night. I was out of line. There are no excuses, and it won't happen again. I'd also like to thank you for being you and caring enough to alert everyone to my drug usage."

That wasn't so bad. Embarrassing, yes, but also . . . empowering. I can do this.

She touches Mason lightly on the thigh and pops to her feet. It's cute how they can communicate without words. They probably don't even realize they're doing it. I'm almost jealous of it—which is ridiculous. That sort of understanding is not something Tara and I ever had, but I'd kill for it now. *Or maybe we did once, but I took it for granted.* But then again, when Fern taps my shoulder I lean down without even knowing I'm supposed to and accept her hug, returning it with interest. Maybe it's just something about her.

"Hey, now!" Mason says, teasing us both when she kisses my cheek.

"Gabe, I'm just glad you're better. And I'm always willing to apply a boot to your butt when you need it nudged back in line." After one more squeeze for encouragement, I let her go and wait until she's tucked safely against his side before moving on.

"Mason—"

"There's nothing more you need to say, Gabe," he says softly. Apologizing to her is apparently enough for him. I need to say this, though. I have to hold myself accountable.

"Yeah, there is," I say, grinning at a memory from our high school days. He caused a scene in the hall by forcing a senior to apologize for shoulder checking a freshman into a locker. Having Mason around always ensured that none of us were ever bullies.

"Thank you for not killing me that night. I know that an apology is only so much air, but it's all I've got right now, along with a promise to do better. You have my word."

He lays a hand on Fern's shoulder before standing to hug me as she did. "Your word has always been good enough for me."

I don't deserve to call these people my friends. Their easy acceptance and unwavering support chokes me up. Mason lets me lean on him until I pull myself together, then he pounds me on the back a couple times and returns to his seat. His eyes are a little red when he faces forward again.

One by one, I go around the circle, thanking my friends and family for their support and apologizing for all the ways I now know I've wronged them.

Dad is the hardest. I'd rather swallow my tongue than apologize for holding things against him, but it feels so good to say the words and let it go. Predictably, he doesn't react as the others do. He fixes me with an indignant stare and thanks me for my honesty as if he's thanking me for passing the milk at breakfast. My time here taught me that deflecting blame is something I learned from him. *He could use a few weeks with Dr. Dick.*

It hurts to know that he can't even attempt to meet me in the middle. Since he never has a problem pointing out exactly where he went wrong with Mom, it hurts even more. *He can acknowledge it, but he blames her.* Instead of dwelling on that, I focus on the dissipating tightness in my chest. I will not allow his bitterness to poison me again.

***

I follow Ryan to his restored '67 Camaro, feeling like a free man. Almost.

Tara's absence is a dark cloud hovering over my head. I *need* to see her. I carefully close the door, because Ryan gets snippy if you slam them, and buckle my seat belt.

Ryan does the same and puts the key in the ignition. He doesn't turn it over, though. "Ask."

"What do you mean?" I ask so I don't seem so . . . pathetic. I have so many questions; they're burning my tongue. I was going to look for openings to casually drop one here and there on the drive home.

He looks over and rolls his eyes. "I know you've waited this whole time to ask about Tara. Ask."

Well, shit. Guess I wasn't as calm and collected as I thought. There's no use in arguing with him, not when he's giving me a free pass to answers. "Where does she work?"

Snorting, he leans back in his seat. "You know she'll probably kill me for telling you that, right?"

I roll my eyes at him. "Yeah, because you can't stop her or anything. Please, I need to know. I need to see her."

There's a chance she won't hear me out, but there's also a chance she will. As long as that possibility remains, I have to try. Because I'm going to make all this up to her if she lets me, and I'm going to become a person she can at least tolerate. But, if nothing else, I have to talk to her one more time. The weight of the things I need to say to her will suffocate me if I don't. She was right when she came to see me. I'm glad it didn't work out at that time, though. The things I thought I needed to get off my chest then . . . They're not the same things sitting there now.

He looks me square in the eye but takes his time making up his mind. I see something shift in his eyes when he decides to give me what I want. "She works in a little boutique downtown. I'm not sure where she's living. I'm not sure I'd tell you if I did."

That's better than nothing. It's not quite the answer I was hoping for, though. I pick at a hangnail while I consider my options. The last thing I want is to show up where she works and upset her, but it might be my only chance. At least there, I'm not completely invading her privacy, and she probably won't be alone. "But you know where she works, and you said she's working, so take me there?"

Frowning, he scratches at his stubble, a subconscious tell that he's uncomfortable about something. He's done it since we were kids—before he even had facial hair. "Maybe you should start with a phone call, man?"

"She won't answer."

"Can you blame her?"

". . . No. But how am I supposed to talk to her if she won't answer calls or texts?"

He sighs, and I ride the rush of victory. "Fine, but I'm going too, and if she asks you to leave, you're leaving. I don't care if I have to drag you out."

"Deal," I say before he can change his mind. I'm so excited the only thing keeping me on the ground is the seatbelt. I don't want to cause a scene or upset her. I need to see her and ask for a chance to say my piece.

"Are you sure she'll be there?" I ask, looking out into the darkness. It's late enough that most little shops will be locked up by now.

"Yeah, she'll be there. They stay open late on Saturdays. And she told me she'll be there all night." With a turn of his wrist, the car roars to life. He navigates the turns from memory and pulls into a tiny parking lot behind an unfamiliar building.

"Remember what I said," he growls, killing the engine. "I don't care if you're my best friend, I *will* dot your eye if she asks you to leave and your answer isn't 'yes, ma'am.'"

Fucker will laugh while I pick myself up too. I grumble my agreement and climb out of the car. He leads the way around the building to a door flanked by displays of dresses, brightly colored on one side and white on the other. Ryan opens the door and strolls on in. I grab the door before it closes in my face and follow him in.

There is color everywhere, so much that it almost hurts to look at. Here and there, a spot of white breaks up the rainbow. A girl with purple hair appears between two racks of dresses. She stops in front of us, and her eyes quickly drop to the floor and work their way up Ryan's body. She takes a small step back and does it again, caught up in the Ryan conundrum—the war between his pretty face and his fuck-off vibe.

Anyone else might miss the amusement lacing in his voice, but I know him well enough to catch it. "Can I speak to Tara, please?" he asks her.

"Uh . . ." The girl—for she can't be much older than jail bait unless that purple hair makes her look younger—looks to me and back to him. "She asked not to be disturbed."

I bite my tongue to stop myself from insisting. Ryan can handle this. My best chance is to let him.

"Tell her it's Ryan." He shoots me a glare, letting me know that he's putting his ass on the line for me. I nod my thanks while holding my breath, crossing my fingers in my pockets, my toes in my shoes, and praying it works.

"O-okay," she says. She turns around and hurries off, shouting for Tara as she goes. Over the racks, I watch her open a swinging door enough to stick her head in. Murmurs filter back to us, then the girl looks over her shoulder right at me. *Damnit.*

The girl looks away, then backs up. The doors part and Tara slips through. *Thank God!* Her hair is twisted up in a knot on top of her head and fixed in place with a pencil. She hasn't done that in years. One of the overhead lights reflects off glitter clinging to . . . all of her. She glows like an avenging angel sent to punish me for my transgressions. The scowl on her face completes the likeness—beautiful and terrifying.

Somehow, after everything we've said and done to each other this year, I love her more than ever. I stuff my hands in my pockets to keep from reaching for her. It's easy to forget that I can't do that anymore. Especially when I want to hug her tightly and beg her to forgive me.

She stops in front of us and crosses her arms over her chest. I cringe at the glare she aims at Ryan. "Really?" she asks him.

He mimics her stance right down to the glare, though he ruins it with a smirk. "Really. He's not here to cause problems. I'm here to ensure that. I've already promised him a black eye if he can't behave. Otherwise, feel free to pretend I'm not here."

The stiffness in her posture softens a little. She reaches out and squeezes his forearm. Causing problems suddenly sounds like a good idea because I'm jealous as hell of that touch. "Alright. I can handle that," she says.

I brace myself for that glare, but she just looks tired when she turns to me. "I'm glad you're doing better," she says. I have no doubt that she means it, even if she doesn't love me anymore. "What did you want?"

"Why didn't you come tonight?" I ask. I squeeze my eyes shut and bite my tongue to keep myself from begging Ryan for a fat lip instead of a black eye. I finally get a chance to talk to her, and *that's* what I say?

"Because the last time I went to visit you didn't end well. And because I'm pushing the limits on my deadline." She sounds as tired as she looks, which probably means that she's working too hard.

I know how that goes . . . Ironic that I can recognize that in her when I couldn't in myself. "When's that?"

"Monday."

A crazy idea pops into my head. A lunch date was our coffin nail, so to speak. Maybe a lunch date can be a new beginning as well. "Can I take you to lunch on Tuesday?"

"I—" She stops and blinks at me a couple times. "What?"

I smile. There's no way she missed the significance there. "It's a dress, right? If you have to have it done Monday, you should have a little breathing room Tuesday, right?"

She purses her lips. "Yes," she finally says. I take it as the answer to both questions.

"Then can I take you to lunch? You name the place."

"Why?" she asks, watching me through narrowed eyes like she's searching for the catch.

"Because I have things I'd like to tell you—part of my recovery process. I stood up tonight and apologized to my friends and family. I had something to say to you as well, and I'd like a chance to say it." We lock eyes and stare each other down. I don't know what she's looking for, but I hope she can see that I'm determined to make this happen. *For both of us.*

"Won't your father be mad?"

I shrug. Yes. He definitely will be. The real question is, do I care? I'm not so sure that I do anymore. Caring about what he thinks cost me too much.

She rests her fists on her hips. "Fine. There's a little bistro just down the street."

I punch the air, celebrating like I'm back on the soccer pitch and just won a championship game. I'd bet everything I have that she only chose that place because she doesn't expect me to show. At least if she's nearby, she's not losing a lot of time if I don't. I don't care, though. She agreed. That's all that matters. I still have a chance. "Noon?"

"I'll be there."

"Thank you, Tara." I scratch my jaw and look around, trying to find something to talk about to draw this out. My eyes land on one of the white dresses. *Did she design that?* Inspiration strikes. "Can I see what you're working on?"

She looks at Ryan, who shrugs his indifference. "Sure," she says, waving her hand for us to follow her.

We follow her through the swinging doors. I stop short, amazed at the chaos around me. There are bolts of material, beads, and sequins in every shade of the rainbow on shelves, tables, and chairs. Mannequins stand about, showcasing gowns in various stages of progress. Most of them are decked out in jewel tones, but Tara bypasses them all for one of two wearing white. It's so sparkly it almost hurts to look at it. *Guess that explains the glitter.*

"This is the one I have to finish by Monday," she says. She stoops to lovingly straighten a bow. "They're paying a rush fee for it."

My heart swells with pride. She wanted this so much, and she's making it happen. *Without me.* I brush that thought aside and smile at her, but she's too focused on her creation to notice.

"It's beautiful," I tell her, but I'd tell her that if she showed me an old potato sack and said she designed it. It's nothing compared to her wedding dress, but I'm probably biased or something. It's white and puffy, and I'm sure the groom will feel the same way about it as I do about Tara's. After all the years she supported me, it's my turn to do the same for her. I look around at the brightly colored ones. "Any others?"

"Thank you," she says, shifting her weight from foot to foot uncomfortably. "Just this one right now." She moves to the second mannequin in white. "Madi does the formals. I do wedding dresses."

"So the all of the white ones up front?" I ask. There were nowhere near as many wedding dresses as formals, but I doubt they're something she can make in a day. Looking around at the various examples of progress, it's astounding that she has so many completed. And that's not even all of them!

She smiles, pride sparking to life in her eyes. "Yes. Those are mine."

"They're beautiful. I'm proud of you." *Have I ever told her that? Surely I have . . .* No instances come to mind, but I'm sure there were plenty of opportunities . . . *But did I take them?*

Tara stops fussing with the dress to look at me. She swallows hard. Twice. Her eyes search my face for a long moment. "Thank you," she says as if the words are foreign to her.

Or maybe it's what she's thanking me for.

Happy to catch her off guard in a good way, I smile at her. "I'll . . . let you get back to work. Tuesday at noon."

"Um . . . I'll walk you out," she says.

Yes, please. "No, that's okay. I don't want to pull you away from work again. I'd hate for you to miss your deadline and have to reschedule."

The role reversal here sucks. This was her reality for years, though. She dealt, and so will I.

Tara smirks at me. "Sucks, huh?" she asks as if reading my mind.

I swallow hard and nod once. "Very much so."

Lowering her eyes, she bites her bottom lip. "You know I'm not just doing this to get even with you, right? This is just how it worked out . . ."

I shake my head. "The thought never crossed my mind. You wouldn't do that. Good night, Tara. I'll see you Tuesday."

"'Night," she says softly.

I turn and walk away before I try to hug her. I might never let go if I do. And then I'd kiss her. And I don't get to do that anymore.

Behind me, Ryan bids her a good night, and I have no doubt he hugs her like I wish I could. I hate him for it, just a bit, but at least she's getting a hug.

CHAPTER 11

Tara

I check the clock for the twentieth time in ten minutes. *I can't believe I agreed to this.* I can't believe I'm so *nervous!* It's just lunch. With Gabe. There's nothing to be nervous about.

He probably won't even show.

I'll walk out of there feeling like a fool for believing him.

But what if he does?

"Just go," Madi says without looking up from the fabric she's cutting.

"Hmm?" I ask, trying to play it cool so she doesn't mistake my anxiety for excitement to see him again. That's not it at all. If I'm excited, it's because I'm ready to put all of this behind me finally.

"Woman, all your clock-watching is making me antsy! Just go already!" She reaches the end of her cut and pauses to flap her hand toward the door, shooing me away.

"I don't want to be too early . . ." I don't want Gabe to misconstrue it as an eagerness to see him, either. Yes, I want to do this. I want us to be able to meet as . . . indifferent acquaintances when our friends invite us to things. But I don't want to give him false hope of anything more. He has too much of that already if the way he looked at me Saturday is any indication.

Madi looks up. "I guess I get that. You don't want to have to wait even longer if he doesn't show."

"Well, that, too," I agree grimly. It's the more likely outcome. That's half the reason I chose somewhere nearby. I'm not losing a lot of time out of my day driving across town to be stood up, and, if he upsets me, I have a quick escape.

"Too?" she asks, arching her eyebrows.

"What if he thinks I'm early because I forgive him or something and I'm happy to see him?" I'm walking a minefield while blindfolded! I *am* excited to see him, but admitting that—even to myself—is terrifying. I don't know how to be his friend. And what if we can't be friends? What if we fight again? *What was I thinking?*

"Oh, honey . . . You're thinking way too much about this. It's only ten 'til. You've got a five-minute walk ahead of you. It's not like you're showing up thirty minutes early. And we both know you'd rather be a few minutes early to show him how it's done. Stop overthinking it. Pretend he's Ryan or Mason. Speaking of Ryan, for the love of God, keep him out of here when Teagan is working." I burst out laughing, but she carries on, "Poor girl can't decide if she should climb him or run from him."

"He's a teddy bear," I say, wiping tears of laughter from my eyes. Teagan was so intimidated by Ryan, she hid in one of the dressing rooms until they left, but she hasn't stopped talking about him since. "A big, admittedly gruff, teddy bear."

"I've only seen pictures, and I'd like to snuggle with him," she mutters under her breath.

I ball up a piece of notepaper I don't need anymore and throw it at her. "Bad girl. One, you have a boyfriend. Two, Ryan . . . isn't housebroken." Maybe not the best way to word it, but it's nicer than saying he's a bit of an asshole where women he doesn't consider family are concerned. To my knowledge, there aren't many women he considers family, and none of them are his kin.

"What, does he pee in the corners?" she asks, barely restraining a giggle to get the words out.

"No," I say, laughing again. "He doesn't know how to sit and stay."

"I don't care about 'sit' and 'stay.' It's 'roll over and play dead' that concerns me. I'm tired of that trick."

"Things still a little . . . dull?" I ask, delicately navigating the turbulent waters of her dating life.

She heaves a sigh. "I've seen old pennies with more shine than my relationship. I think it played dead so long it actually died."

"I'm probably not the best person to talk to about fixing broken relationships," I admit.

She looks down, hiding her face behind a curtain of long, strawberry blond hair. "I think we're past the point of fixing. I think we have been for a long time now, but we're comfortable, so neither of us wants to be the one to end it."

"Maybe you should try a weekend away? Just the two of you. Go somewhere with no distractions. Leave the electronics at home so you have to focus on each other."

She blows a raspberry. "So we can be completely bored while we ignore each other on opposite ends of the couch?"

I know she's being sarcastic, but I hate to see her long-term relationship fall apart without either of them making one last attempt to fix it. *Not like it would've helped Gabe and me.* I can't prove that, though. And they're not us. "Well . . . I would suggest not being on opposite ends. More like . . . naked and taking up the whole thing."

Her phone chimes with an incoming text. She automatically glances at it where it rests on her work table. "Hey! You're stalling now! Get out of here!"

"Alright, I'm going!" I shrug on my jacket, grab my purse off the break table, and hustle out the door before she herds me out with a seam ripper and a pair of shears.

The walk is short but every bit as difficult as walking into Uncle Den's office to sign the divorce papers. The small chance that he might show has my stomach in knots because I don't know what happens next if he does. I don't get caught at a crosswalk by some magic and manage to make it with a couple minutes to spare. Gabe stands and waves when I walk in. Seeing him is such a shock, I nearly trip over my own feet. I didn't realize how much I doubted him until now.

He looks so much better than the day I went to see him at rehab. Not so gaunt and haunted. There's a shine to his eyes again, made even more obvious by the suit he's wearing, which is a couple shades darker than they are. His smile is brighter than I've seen it in years. *He looks good.* The drunken mess he used to be made it hard to remember how I ever fell for him. That's not the case now.

The heat that used to be so familiar courses through my veins. Memories of ragged breath, exploring hands, and hungry kisses flood my mind as I cross the little dining room.

I stop at the table and we both sort of smile at each other. *I wonder if he feels as awkward as I do?* What do we do now?

My body has a few suggestions, but those are better left unexplored.

"You're here," we say together. The ice breaks, and we laugh.

Gabe steps around me and pulls out my chair like we're somewhere fancy, or he has someone to impress. "I wouldn't miss this for the world," he says as I sit. Once my chair is pushed in, he reclaims his own and rests his forearms on the table. "But I don't blame you for doubting me. I know I've given you plenty of reasons to, which is why we're here."

The waitress bustles over and takes our drink orders. We both order water, and she returns with them swiftly. I wait until she's out of earshot, happy for a few more moments to get my thoughts under control, to pick up where we left off. The apprehension over what he might say helps. "Alright. You said you have something you want to say?"

A restaurant isn't the best place in the world for a private conversation, but it'll have to do. I'm not going to his place, and he's not coming to mine.

He frowns a bit. "I do, but, if you don't mind, I have a question for you first."

I fold my hands in my lap to remove the temptation to fidget. "Okay."

"Why did you come to see me at rehab?" He cocks his head to the side and watches me closely.

My mouth goes dry. Every muscle in my body tenses up. I know the answer, but I don't know what to say.

"It's alright, Tara. I can take it," he says softly.

Can you, though? I don't want to have another shouting match here. My throat works, but there's nothing to swallow. "I wanted to talk to you—to get some things off my chest so I could move on," I tell him in a voice as rough as sandpaper. "I wanted to prove to myself that I can see you in public and not . . ." Fear stops me. I don't know how to say it without revealing too much of myself.

"Not what?" he asks when I don't finish the thought.

I take a deep breath. This is what we're here for. Or what I'm here for, anyway. To be honest with myself and with him, and to put our past to rest. "Not hurt. Not be plagued by what-ifs and should-haves."

Silence falls between us, relieved only by the clatter of cutlery on plates and the dull murmur of our fellow diners. Gabe leans back in his seat and scrubs his face with both hands. "And?"

"I don't know." I refuse to lie to him. It might be easier, but I'm not going to hide behind a house of cards, counting on it to protect me when one wrong move will send it tumbling down and leave me exposed. Better to confront it all head-on. Seeing him doesn't *hurt.* It's more like a persistent dull ache in my chest. But I can live with it. I've dealt with worse. "It doesn't bother me as much as I thought it would."

And that feels good. I'm stronger than I gave myself credit for being.

Gabe winces and nods slowly. One side of his mouth curves up into a bitter half-smile. "Is it selfish of me to admit to hoping you wouldn't move on so easily?"

I shrug. I didn't come here to judge him. It's not my place. But yeah, kinda. I want him to be happy. Shouldn't he want the same for me? "Probably, but what did you expect? You made it easy, Gabe."

He blows out a long breath. "I did."

Did he just . . . ? I could swear I just heard him accept responsibility for something. "I'm sorry, could you please repeat that?"

He breathes out a little laugh. "I did. I put you last in every possible way, and for that and so much more, I am sorry. If you'd like me to start listing all the times I messed up, I'll do my best, but—"

"No," I say quickly. I'd rather not relive them all—if he can even remember half of them. This is hard enough—seeing him the way he used to be but knowing it's over. Having him drag up everything in our past . . . it would almost be as painful as the day we signed divorce papers. At least then, when he apologized and asked for another chance, I knew nothing had changed. I'm not so sure I can say the same now. Gabe just admitted that he did something wrong and *apologized like he means it.* Is the sky falling? Is hell freezing over? I don't know what to do with this.

He doesn't give me time to figure it out, either. "I spent a lot of time thinking about the past in rehab. By the way, thank you for your visit. It was very . . . enlightening. You were absolutely right. I needed to grow up and accept the consequences of my actions. I'm working on it."

"Um, you're welcome?" *Who are you, and what have you done with Gabe?* I can't believe he just said that. When he said he wanted to apologize, I expected a general 'sorry I was such an asshole.' I didn't expect him to be thoughtful and detailed. It's nice. He sounds like an adult instead of a coddled child.

He gives me a tentative smile. "I'm serious, Tara. The way you left paired with the conversation I'd *just* had with Dr. Dick . . . It was a turning point for me, I guess. It really drove home what he was telling me. Up until that point, I really didn't take anything he said to heart. Somehow, you showed up when I needed you most."

"Glad I could help." A what-if worms its way into the back of my mind, but I refuse to acknowledge it. I can't change the past, and it wouldn't've helped anyway.

The waitress reappears at our table as if she knows I need a savior right now. "Are we ready to order?" she asks while she refills our waters.

I glance at the daily special—a Monte Cristo and coleslaw—and order it because I haven't touched my menu. Gabe orders the same, which surprises me because he hates eating fried foods, and the waitress disappears as quickly as she came.

"So, how's work going?" I ask to change the subject. I don't think Gabe has said everything he has to say, but I can't take anymore right now. The weight of the words spoken is crushing me already. Work is a safe subject. And I'm very interested to know how his father handled his absence—if not the scandal of it.

A frown flits across his face. He waits for a beat to answer, like he really can't believe I asked that. "It's going. I didn't lose my job, but Dad is . . . Dad. He's made it known in no uncertain terms that I will never be promoted to partner. However, the other partners went around him and decided to feature me exclusively in our promotional materials for the next year. Their theory is that it'll put an end to any rumors if people see that I'm perfectly healthy. And that any publicity is good publicity."

I instinctively reach for his hand and panic halfway there. *What the hell am I doing?* Snatching my hand back feels callous at this point, so I follow through. I can still comfort him, right? It's a normal thing to do. His hand is warm under mine, and familiar—like home. He sighs as soon as I touch him, and the tension bleeds out of his shoulders. "I'm sorry about the partnership. And your Dad."

His eyes drop to my hand on his. "You should've seen him at the meeting, Tara. He barely looked at me. He didn't even accept my apology, just thanked me for my honesty."

"Maybe he can't forgive you because he can't forgive himself?"

"That's what Mom says," he whispers.

"You don't need his forgiveness, Gabe. Don't let him drag you down again. He's a grown man. He made his bed. You make yours and let him lie in his."

"Thanks, Tara." He turns his hand palm up and cradles my hand in both of his. I force myself to relax when panic sets in. This is what I feared—sending mixed signals. He looks up at me, his gray eyes burning with desperation, before I can take my hand away and that look stops me. "I never wanted to hurt you. You know that, right?"

"I know," I whisper, too breathless from the intensity of his gaze to speak louder.

He goes on as if I never said a word. As if he can't possibly hold the words back one second longer. "I got caught up in being the best, in making Dad proud, and it cost me the only thing that ever mattered." That knife he left buried to the hilt in my heart twists again. Maybe seeing him will hurt more than I thought. "When we spoke last, you said you hoped we could work toward forgiving each other and learn to be friends. If that offer still stands, I'd like to take you up on it. I can never make all this up to you, but I can try to be better and be worthy of your friendship going forward."

"Gabe . . ." I don't know what to say. I don't know if he *can* make it all up to me. I can forgive easily enough, but forgetting is another story. I don't know if I can trust him. And if I can't trust him, I don't want him in my life. *But life is better with Gabe in it . . .* Or it used to be. Could it be again? Is it worth the risk?

"Just think about it, alright? Tell me about your dresses. How'd your deadline dress go?" he asks, blatantly changing the subject.

I appreciate that, though. Come to think of it, I appreciate that he recognizes that I've reached my limit on this conversation too. *Maybe we can be friends after all.* "It went great, thank you for asking. She absolutely loved it, and it fit like a glove."

All that hard work was worth it for the smile on the bride's face. *I love my job.* Helping brides make their dream dresses a reality is the best.

"That's great, Tara! I'm happy for you."

***

Our waitress whisks away the last of the dishes and lays the ticket on the table. Gabe and I reach for it at the same time, but his hand lands first, like a game of Slap Jack. I open my mouth to argue—I don't need him to pay my share—but he doesn't give me a chance.

"I invited you!" he says. He slides it from under my hand and winks at me. "You can get it next time."

Once we moved away from the topic of our turbulent past and our uncertain future, lunch was actually fun. Old Gabe really is back. He's not just a stranger who looks like him. I could see myself doing this again. He's going to be okay. I can move on. We can get along. "Well, thank you for lunch. I . . . had a good time." I hate to confess that, but he's come so far I feel he deserves to know.

He stops in the act of separating a couple bills from the others in his wallet to look at me. "I did, too. Thank you for agreeing to come. It means a lot to me." He folds two twenties and leaves them under the ticket. I gather my purse, and he's right there to help me with my jacket when I stand up. "Can I walk you back?"

The question catches me off guard. We've exhausted his lunch hour. Between taking our time to eat and catching up on each other's goings-on since the divorce, the hour flew by. He's going to be late already.

"Sure." I'm not sure why I agree, because he is offering the time he deprived me of before, or if I only want to thumb my nose at his father. Both are appealing.

I resent Sam as much as Gabe does, maybe more, for his indirect contribution to the failure of our marriage. And I'm not sure I'm magnanimous enough to forgive him. A father shouldn't treat his child the way he treats Gabe.

The walk back is quiet. It's a comfortable quiet, though. The awkwardness has passed now. At the door, I turn to face him and smile. "This was nice."

"Yeah," he says. He looks down and lightly scuffs the sole of his shoe on the pavement. "So, there's a party at Mason's this weekend to celebrate my newfound sobriety. I'd love for you to come."

A refusal dies on the tip of my tongue. It's too much too soon. But is it? He didn't ask me to come with *him*, so he's not inviting me to be his date or anything like that. And I did promise the guys I wouldn't be a stranger. "I'll think about it," I promise.

He looks at me through his lashes and grins like a little kid. "Great. And . . . Do you think we could maybe do this again sometime? Not a date, just . . . lunch?"

That grin is infectious. I return it without meaning to. "We'll see."

He nods. "You've got my number."

"I do."

He opens the door for me. "Have a good afternoon, Tara."

I walk in and look back over my shoulder. "Thanks. You too."

Madi comes bursting through the swinging doors at the sound of the chimes. She watches me from across the room, waiting for some signal. I'm almost afraid to move. "So?" she finally asks.

"It wasn't all that bad," I tell her. "Little awkward at first, but that was to be expected, I guess."

"And?" She motions for me to get on with it.

"And he invited me to a party at Mason's this weekend to celebrate his discharge. And told me to text him if I want to get lunch again sometime."

Madi whistles long and low. "If you don't wanna go to the party solo, I'll go with!"

"That's actually not a bad idea." I'll have friends there anyway, but it'll feel less like I'm going *with* Gabe if I have a friend with me. "Maybe I'll clear it with Mason to invite Trista and Noel, too." Taking my tribe will keep things impersonal.

CHAPTER 12

Gabe

"How you doing?" Ryan asks, touching his glass of scotch to my water. I'm not ready to try drinking again yet. I don't trust myself to stay in control. Someday, when I'm more confident, but too much rides on my control right now.

"Great." Standing in front of my closest friends and family and owning up to my own bullshit was exhausting. It was worth it, though. At least, now that I've had a chance to talk to Tara. There's a weight missing from my shoulders. I feel like a whole new person. As much as it sucked, this is a good feeling. *The truth really does set you free.*

I hope she comes.

Ryan nods. "You're doing good, man. I'm proud of you."

"We all are," Mason adds. The guys' encouragement takes root in my chest and doubles in size. I've accomplished many things to be proud of in my life, but this one might take the cake if it weren't for the shame of ending up in this situation to begin with.

I hope Tara is proud of me too. I sneak a glance at the door, hoping to see her there.

Fern's voice drifts through the sound system like a seductive cloud of incense, wrapping around my eardrums and hugging them tight. I don't know what Mason dropped on that Karaoke machine and the sound setup for his back yard, but it was money well spent if it means we get to hear Fern sing more often. I'm sure the others will take a turn too. Once they're lubricated enough.

Maybe Tara will sing a duet with me.

They really went all out to make this special for me. There are lights strung about the perimeter of the patio, anchored to posts that were recently sunk in preparation for a pergola. Someone rented, borrowed, or bought patio heaters to ward off the chill of the December evening. There's also a fire pit, and Fern gleefully carried out the stuff for s'mores shortly after I arrived. There's even a humongous L-shaped picnic table that wasn't here last time I was, but I'm sure it wasn't purchased just for this.

Movement by the door catches my eye. *Please be her!* I hold my breath glance over as Tara steps out into the night. *Yes!* My growing smile turns sour quickly, though. Noel, Trista, and a strawberry blonde I don't recognize quickly follow Tara. I understand why Tara wanted them here—she probably wanted backup—but I wish she didn't feel that way.

The new girl gawks around, taking it all in. The other two are all smiles until they glance my way. I get glares. As hard as it is to admit, I deserve it. They'll never approve of me again, not that they have for years. I let them down by letting Tara down, and they gave up on me sooner. And they weren't quiet about it.

It doesn't matter what I say, what I do. They'll never trust me to take care of Tara. They'll be my biggest obstacle in earning her heart again. It doesn't take a lot of brainpower on my part to reach the conclusion that Trista will be the easiest of the two to sway. But that's not what tonight is about. Tonight is about celebrating second chances and new beginnings. Tomorrow, it's game on.

"Hey, y'all," Tara says brightly, throwing in a little wave. She gestures to the new girl. "This is Madi—Madison. My boss." She then names us off one-by-one, pointing around the patio as she goes.

"Nice to meet you," Madi says when Tara's done. She smiles at Mason and Fern. "Thanks for letting me tag along."

"Anytime!" Fern calls from the grill where she's turning steaks. "Make yourself at home."

"Don't tell me that. I might end up in that hot tub," Madi jokes.

"Well, if you're into skinny dippin', go right ahead," Fern says.

"I'm in!" Austin shouts to no one's surprise.

"When did *that* happen?" I ask, following Madi's gaze to the hot tub.

"Couple days ago," Mason answers. "I've wanted one for years, but I wanted to wait until Ronni was old enough I didn't have to worry so much. We'll probably add a pool this spring."

"Sweet," Ryan grunts. "Pool parties!"

"Can I teach Keaton to swim?" Chris asks.

I can't agree with Ryan on the pool parties right now. Not if Tara will be invited. Having her prancing around in her little bikinis for hours when I can't take her home after and show her what she does to me would be a new kind of torture.

Fern comes over and ushers the ladies to the bar, which is also new. Everyone was on board with this party being dry, but if I'm ever going to trust my control, I want to test it here where there are people who care enough to stop me from making a mistake. So I encouraged them to carry on as they usually would.

I'm beginning to wonder if the changes around here have more to do with Mason finding his happy again than anything else. I can't count the number of projects I planned to do that didn't get done because I was too unhappy to mess with it. And I didn't realize that was the underlying cause. Even the smallest tasks feel like climbing Mt. Everest when you're not happy.

If only I could go back and do things over. Divorce really alters your plans for the future.

I kick back in my chair, absentmindedly listening to the guys' chatter while I sneak peeks at Tara and ignore scowls from her friends when they catch me. I'm so happy she's here, but I can't help but wish she was here *with* me instead of *for* me. I'd hoped to spend more time with her this evening. *It's not over yet.*

The girls seem cozy enough at the bar for now, but I get up to refill my water purely so I can sit somewhere else when I come back. Somewhere with an open space beside me so I can hope and pray Tara will sit next to me.

A cloud of smoke rolls across the patio between me and the drink dispenser, bringing with the mouthwatering aroma of charred meat. "Dinner's done!" Fern calls from the grill. "Unless you like your steak well done. If that's the case, you're gonna have to take over. I don't burn food."

Laughter erupts behind me, cut short by Mason barking orders for everyone to go grab something from the fridge or oven. From the bar, I hear Trista ask someone if Fern is serious about the steaks. I glance over to see if Trista is joking, but her anxiety is written all over her face. "I got you, Tris," I call to her.

Relief washes across her features until she follows my voice. Her eyes get huge when they land on me. "Uh, thanks, Gabe!" she says quickly.

I'm probably ruining my chances of snagging a seat next to Tara, but that's okay. I refill my glass and turn my feet towards the grill to find Ryan standing over it, checking his watch.

I stop next to him. "What's up?"

"You go eat, man. It's your party. I'll take care of her. This won't take long anyway."

"You're only doing this to scare the shit out of her, aren't you?" I swear she's terrified of him. For no reason! He's never done anything to scare her. His very existence does the trick. And he gets a kick out of it.

He smirks at the steak. "Maybe."

"You're deranged."

"Damn straight."

Shaking my head, I walk back to the table to see if there's any food left for me or if the other fuckers ate it all already.

"I made you a plate," Fern says as I approach the table. "Ryan, too. I've seen all of you eat." *What did I do to get so lucky?*

"Thank you," I tell her with the general outcry dies down. "I appreciate it."

"It's here," Tara says, pointing to the plate in front of the empty space next to her. *Fuck yes!* I walk the last few feet with a spring in my step. My patience is paying off. This is exactly what I needed.

"Fern wouldn't let us touch anything until she was done," Austin whines. The man is like Brad Pitt's character from Fight Club. He never. Stops. Eating.

"I swear you have a tapeworm," Fern tells him.

Noel slaps her hands over her ears. "La la la la la! Not while we're eating, please!"

Fern grins at her. "Sorry."

"Tris!" Ryan calls. "Bring your plate!"

She gulps and awkwardly clambers off the bench to obey. Once her steak is plated, he follows her back to the table, eyes trained on the back of her head, smirking at the way she shrinks a little more with every step she takes. *Predator and prey.*

"This mine?" Ryan asks with a delighted grin when he sees the other unclaimed plate right next to Trista. He sits down a little closer than strictly necessary and smiles at her. "How's that steak?"

"Um . . ." She hurriedly picks up her knife and cuts into the middle. "Perfect! Thank you so much." She looks at him and beams, seeming to forget her irrational fear for the moment.

"Anytime."

"So Tara . . ." Fern calls down the table. "Know any good wedding dress designers?"

"You know, I think I might!" Tara calls back, running with the joke. "Can I have her call you Monday?"

"Oh, that would be fantastic. I'm starting classes in January, so the sooner, the better."

"And when should I tell her you'll need it by?"

"May," Mason says.

Silence falls. Everyone stops eating to look at Mason, but he doesn't seem to notice. If he does, he doesn't care. May seems a little soon to me. They haven't been together—really together—for a month yet. I wish them nothing but the best, though. Just because my marriage fell apart doesn't mean theirs will. They're kind of a special case.

"What's the rush?" Austin asks.

Mason snorts. "That's rich coming from you."

"Seriously though, I don't think she's going anywhere. What's the rush?"

"I've wasted enough time," Mason says with a shrug. He finally looks up and notices the rest of us watching him. "What? It's not like I'm dragging her to the altar by her hair! She agreed to it."

"So, about five months?" Tara asks. If she's worried about the timeframe, she doesn't show it. In fact, I'd say she's excited.

"Yep." Fern bites her lip. "Is that enough time?"

"Oh yes," Tara says, waving away her concern. "You're giving me a lot longer than the one I just finished."

"Good!"

"Hey, Tara?" Mason asks.

"Yeah?"

Grinning, he says, "This one doesn't have a budget, okay?"

Jaws drop. "Oh, damn!" Ryan says on a laugh.

Chris leans across the table to explain. "Felicity bought a dress from Tara a few days before she got caught behind that bar."

"Oh, shit," I whisper.

Tara wads up her napkin and tosses it at Mason. "Ass!"

"Hey!" He points at Fern. "My fiancée is *right there!* Don't talk about my ass!"

"Oh, so I can't talk about you at all then, huh? You're all ass."

A beat of complete silence follows, then everyone explodes into laughter as if given some cue to follow. *This is how it's supposed to be.* Tara beside me, our friends all around us laughing and having fun.

I hope she knows how happy I am that she's here. Maybe I should tell her that. It's the sort of thing I didn't take the time to do before.

"Good one," Austin shouts over the din. "I wish I'd thought of that!"

While everyone is distracted, I lean over to whisper in Tara's ear. "I'm glad you came."

She looks at me and smiles. Her lips form the words, "Me too," but the sound is lost in the laughter and good-natured banter.

***

"Are you sure you're okay to drive?" I ask Tara as I walk her to her car.

"Yeah, I didn't drink," she tells me. "It's Tris I'm worried about."

"Why's that?" I ask. I must've missed something. I didn't notice her drinking anything but water.

"Ryan tricked her into agreeing to drive him home."

"For fuck's sake," I mutter. "That's an accident waiting to happen." There won't be anyone to interfere when he decides to torment Trista. She'll get tense, he won't let up, and she'll end up causing an accident because she's so nervous.

"Tell me about it," she mutters.

"Don't take off yet. I'll take him home."

"Alright." Tara leans a hip against her car. "Hey, I thought maybe we could grab lunch again this week?"

My heart does loop-the-loops in my chest, but I do my best to contain my excitement. I don't want to seem over-eager and freak her out. "Yeah? When were you thinking?"

She draws her lips to one side. "How about Wednesday?"

"Eleven-thirty?"

"Sure. Same place?"

"I'll meet you there."

"Great."

A smile is my answer because I'm afraid to try and speak. I wouldn't be surprised to find my hands shaking with the effort it's taking to not grab her and kiss her. She came. And we have lunch plans. Definitely steps in the right direction.

CHAPTER 13

Tara

Four weeks later . . .

"Ah! I'm going to fall!" I shriek as my skates slip. Gabe grabs my waist in vain and goes down with me. We land hard on the ice in a groaning heap. "Sorry. It's been a long time."

He sits up and helps me do the same. "No worries. It was bound to happen."

"How's your knee?" I ask, anxiety strangling the words. I know he healed fine from his surgery, but I always worry that he'll tear those tendons again. He was so angry the first time, which made his recovery a struggle. And watching him suffer through the pain of the injury and the loss of his career . . . It was brutal for both of us.

His recent problems give me more reason to worry. A setback like that could cause a relapse. And what if the doctors can't fix him again?

He gives me an odd little smile. "My knee is fine. Ready to try again?"

"Yep!" I gingerly climb to my feet, watching him from the corner of my eye to make sure he's not downplaying any pain. He did that a lot at first because he was too proud to let anyone see him struggle. He kept pushing well beyond his body's need for rest and payed for it later.

"Let's go," he says, grabbing my hand.

My heart jolts. He takes off. I don't. *We're holding hands?* He sort of drags me along in a stupor until I almost knock us down again, then he stops. He grabs me by the waist again, but this time we both stay on our skates.

"Everything okay?" he asks, brushing a stray curl behind my ear with his gloved hand.

"Y-yeah." Gabe grabbed my hand like he did when we were kids. And I liked it. Despite the layers of clothes I donned to keep from freezing my tush off, I get goosebumps. *I miss this.*

His eyes burn with excitement. He loves this sort of thing—lives for it, really. "Sorry, I'm slowing you down," I whisper.

"You're not," he whispers back.

My eyes dip to his lips for a second. He's so close. The last month has been so fun, just like old times. I look back up, but his eyes aren't on mine anymore. He's staring at *my* mouth. What if I just . . . move a little closer? And maybe . . .

"Tag!" a little girl cries as she skates by and touches my back.

The moment shatters. *Thank you, kiddo!* I can't believe I was thinking about kissing Gabe. It doesn't matter that I still think he's the sexiest man on the planet—when he's not being an ass—he's not my husband anymore. He's my friend. I can't ruin that. No matter how much I want to.

"Tag! You're it!" I say, booping Gabe on the nose. I skate away, giggling, as fast as I can. He'll catch me, but I'm not going to make it easy on him.

Gabe

Fuck yeah! Tara nearly kissed me! If that kid hadn't tagged her, we could be—best not to think about could and might right now. There are too many kids here to be skating around with a raging boner.

Tara probably expects me to chase her. I turn and skate the other way around the ring, earning more than one disapproving look and a lecture from people I pass. I'm not going to hit anyone. And I'm not going to let anyone hit me except for Tara. She's watching her feet more than where she's going when I catch up to her and wrap her in a bear hug on collision. "Tag! You're it!"

"Oh!" she shrieks, pummeling my chest with her gloved fists. "You cheat!"

Her cheeks and nose are red from the cold, but her eyes shine in a way I haven't seen in a while—pure happiness. My chest swells with pride. I must be doing *something* right. She's so beautiful, and I want to kiss her so badly, but I'm waiting for her. At least I know she wants to now, but I'll wait for her to make that move. It's her turn. I just have to continue providing opportunities.

CHAPTER 14

Gabe

Three weeks later . . .

The parking lot at Tara's apartment is quiet after Easy Speak's noise and the music in the car on our way here. *Another successful outing in the books.* It's just a night out with our friends. I didn't even invite her. Fern did. But I offered her a ride, and she accepted without hesitation. I'm slowly gaining ground in my campaign to earn her trust.

I'm so nervous I can hardly breathe. These lunch dates and gatherings with our friends are great, but I want more. It's time to see if she feels the same. I hold onto the rail on the stairs to hide the way my hand shakes. The other goes to the small of her back to steady her as she navigates the risers in heels. She leans into me a little, just a slight increase of pressure against my shoulder. It's all the encouragement I need.

My patience frays while I wait for her to unlock her door. I want her to have a quick escape if she's not receptive to the idea. The last thing I want is for her to feel as if I've backed her into a corner. She'll never agree that way. But the few seconds it takes her is an eternity.

She opens her door and turns to smile at me. Her eyes shine in the glow of the streetlight like they did in the candlelight at our wedding reception. *I wish I could kiss her like I did then.* "Thanks for the ride, Gabe. I had a great time."

I clear the knot of emotions from my throat. "No problem. I did too. I'm glad you came."

Her smile droops. She squints at me in the dim light. "Are you okay? You look . . . scared."

I try to nod, but my head doesn't want to cooperate. "I'm fine. It's just . . ." I take a deep breath and try again. I will *not* stammer my way through this. "I was wondering if you'd like to get dinner sometime."

Better.

"Oh . . ." she says carefully. "Do you mean . . .?"

This isn't going well. Her hesitance pushes me to the edge of panic. Maybe I read too much into things and am rushing. Too late to quit now, though. *Confidence.* The worst she can do is shoot me down. "A date, yes. You don't have to decide right now. I just thought—"

She presses a finger to my lips, cutting me off. "I'll think about it."

My fingers close around her wrist. My eyes drift shut, and I allow myself a moment to enjoy the touch before I move her hand and let her go. "Just let me know," I tell her with a smile.

"I will." There's no hesitation this time. She smiles at me again like a replay of our early days, when our relationship was still new and tentative, and looking at each other was all it took to make us grin like fools.

If only things were that easy again. I could get away with kissing her good night then. It's a risk I'm not willing to take now, no matter how badly I want to.

Tara steps closer, her eyes fixed on my lips. My body missed the memo that sex is not an option tonight. Blood rushes south in response to her nearness and the possibility that her lips might land on mine.

She loops her arms around my waist and lays her head on my shoulder. "Good night, Gabe," she whispers.

Her breath tickles my neck. Rational thought flees, replaced by memories of her lips trailing kisses and that thing she used to do with—

Stop right there. I can explore that line of thinking later. It won't do me any good right now.

"Good night, Tara," I manage to say while returning her hug and maneuvering my hips away from her to avoid making this awkward for both of us.

Raising her head, she smiles one more time before slipping out of my arms and into her apartment. The door closes, and I wait until I hear the locks engage to leave.

CHAPTER 15

Tara

Madison sweeps into the back room like the tornado she is, startling a jump out of me from where I'm bent over, halfway in the fridge, searching for the container of soup I *know* I brought two days ago. When I jump, I bonk my head on the shelf, which leads to a flurry of curses my mother would be embarrassed to hear pouring from my mouth. *She'd probably attack me with the wooden spoon.* Never mind that I learned them from her when she didn't know I was listening.

"Alright, woman," Madi begins through her laughter. "He stole you for lunch every day I've been free for the last month. I call dibs today!"

"Works for me." I sigh, rubbing the sore spot on the back of my head. "I can't find my soup anyway."

She smirks at me. "I ate it yesterday. I didn't bring anything because I planned to go out with you. Then *he* dropped by, and you just vanished. *Poof!* Gone without a trace!"

"Are you done now?" I'm struggling to hold back my laughter. Gabe can be dramatic, but Madi can take it to a whole 'nother level when she's of a mind. Today, she seems to be of a mind. "You do remember me telling you yesterday morning that we had plans, right? And I didn't just vanish! I told you I was leaving."

She schools her pretty features into some semblance of sternness and points at me. "I'm done if you *promise* you're mine today."

My hands go up in surrender. "All yours! Let's go. I'm starving."

She does an impromptu happy dance. "Yay! The bistro?"

I nod, content with her choice though I've already been there twice this week. "You know, one of these days, you should actually learn the name of the place."

"I *know* the name of the place. I like the word '*bistro*.'"

"Fair enough." I chuckle as I follow her through the front door. Teagan will hold down the fort while we're gone. We don't have any fittings scheduled until two o'clock, so she'll be fine.

"Alright, I ask this every week, but has he fallen off the wagon?" she asks once we're seated, and the waitress has taken our order. We've grown close enough that she no longer tries to lead me into answering questions she doesn't ask. She just asks.

"Nope. Not even a sip yet." I'm so proud of him. He's had plenty of opportunities but has stayed strong.

"Do you think he'll drink again?"

"I'm not sure. He says he might try wine with dinner sometime, but he's not in a hurry for it."

"Good for him!" Her smile fades away as her eyes study my face. She cocks an eyebrow at me. "And you? How are you really? I know the answer you give me every day, but I don't want the party line."

"I'm good!" I say, and I am. But I'm not. Doubt is eating me from the inside out, but fear has kept me from voicing it.

The other eyebrow joins the first. "Tara, we might not have been friends since diapers, but I know you well enough to know something is bothering you. I've tried to give you time to bring whatever it is up on your own, but now I think you're too stubborn."

My smile fades. I don't want to talk about this, but I need to. I need an outside opinion before I make choices I might regret. And Madi might be the best person for this chat because she doesn't *know* Gabe, so she can be objective. "The day we signed the divorce papers, he asked me to give him six months to fix things. Obviously, I didn't. I regret it now. He's changed so much in the last five months."

She shakes her head. "You did the right thing! Nothing says he would've changed if you had stayed."

Bless her. That's exactly what I needed to hear. "I know, but now I feel like I threw away years of my life—all that time we were together—for nothing."

"No, you didn't. Look what you've done, Tara! Would we be here now if you had stayed?"

I drop my chin into my hand, depressed by her reminder of my old life. "No," I say, not liking the answer or the bitter taste it leaves on my tongue. "My life would have been an endless cycle of cleaning, cooking, daily runs with a bunch of judgy, hypocritical bitches, trips to a gym I didn't even like, and waiting for Gabe to come home, only to be disappointed when he did." That might work for some people. In fact, the women in my old running club thrived in very similar situations, and good for them. It didn't work for me, though.

"And now, you have all of that, minus the disappointment, *plus* a job!" she says with false enthusiasm that makes me laugh.

"Hey, I like my new gym! And I found a new running club, too. And I *love* my job. My boss can be a bitch sometimes, though," I say just to watch her reaction. She doesn't let me down.

Her eyes get huge. She leans across the table to shove my shoulder. "I resemble that!" But she laughs while she says it.

"I know you do, but I love you anyway. But, Madi," I hesitate, rummaging around my brain for the words I *need* to speak. She cocks an eyebrow and waits me out. "What if . . . What if letting him back in my life is a mistake?"

Madi's face softens. "Oh, honey." Her hand finds mine on the tabletop and gives it a reassuring squeeze. "There's only one way to find out. You have to follow your heart on this one, T."

"That's the problem." I trusted my heart before and look what happened. What if I end up right back where I started if I trust it again?

She smiles apologetically. "I'm not telling you to elope with him or anything. Do what makes you happy. And you *are* happy, Tara. Happier than I've known you to be since we met."

"He asked me out." The words have been tap dancing on the tip of my tongue all morning, just waiting for me to blurt them out.

Her brow furrows. "You've been going out for months."

"*Out*, out. A dinner date," I clarify, giddy with excitement. It's like high school all over again, only this time we don't have to ask our parents for permission. *That* would not go over well right now. My family will need time to forgive him.

Her mouth puckers into a perfect 'o.' "And?"

"I told him I'd think about it." He was so nervous when he asked. It was cute.

"And?" She rolls her wrist, telling me to get on with it.

"I haven't said yet. But I think I might do it."

"But you're scared."

"But I'm scared."

"Tara," she stops and sighs. "You got out once. You can do it again, and you won't let things get so bad this time."

"Yeah . . . But it'll hurt again." That risk worries me. I know I can get through it, but will I still be the same person? Or will I be bitter? And is it worth wasting more of my life on a doomed relationship?

"And it won't if you don't try?"

I open my mouth to argue and snap it shut. My mind never pursued the other path when he asked me that—the one where this is our new status quo. I only thought of what happens if I try and fail again. But not trying will hurt, too. *So what have I got to lose?* I fish my phone out of my purse and text Gabe.

My heart pounds as I type. I tap the send button before I can change my mind. **If the offer for dinner still stands, I accept.**

The message pops up in a little chat bubble, and the status quickly flashes from sending to delivered to read.

Gabe: Great! I'll make reservations. Can I pick you up at 5:30?

That works. What should I wear?

Gabe: Formal. The dress you were telling me about for next weekend should do.

Madi is smiling at me when I look up. She nods but doesn't get a chance to speak.

The waitress returns with food in hand, and I'm grateful for the natural end to the conversation. I'm not sure I'm ready to talk about my decision yet. Once the waitress is sure we don't need anything else, she hustles off to wait on a table of businessmen, judging by their suits, calling a promise to check on us soon.

I dive right in, scooping up half of what has become my second-favorite sandwich in the whole world, and stuff my face with gusto. I wasn't lying before. I'm *starving*. Madi doesn't, though. She watches me through her eyelashes while she toys with the condensation on her glass of tea.

I catch her eye and raise my eyebrows in query because my mouth is much too full for talking.

She cringes and blurts, "Would your boss still be a bitch if she offered to sell you half her business?"

"*What?*" I ask around a mouthful of sandwich because you can't *not* respond to something like that. I swallow hard, forcing the food down my throat and chasing it with a gulp of water.

Her nose crinkles, but she laughs and spreads her hands. "I dunno. I've been thinking about it for a few weeks now. I like working with you. Having someone to help shoulder the load would be nice. And we could expand, find a bigger storefront, buy new machines . . ."

I grab her hand and squeeze because I can't hug her right now. "I . . . I don't know what to say." Tears sting my eyes, and it takes everything I have not to break down and cry like a baby. This is more than I dared to hope for at this point in my life. *And I want it so much.* I want something to call mine. It might be *ours,* but my name would be on it.

Her eyes get a little watery, too. "Just think about it, alright? I've got some numbers for you at the shop."

Numbers. Reality crashes around my ears, taking my heart with it, and threatens to wipe the smile from my face. I fight to keep it in place for Madi's sake, though. I might not have that kind of money. Not even if I still cashed Gabe's alimony checks instead of shredding them.

"I'll think about it," I say, steeling myself for the potential of more heartbreak. I've sold a few more dresses, but what money I've put away after paying Madi back for the cost of the materials she purchased for me in good faith isn't going to touch something like this. *How much does half of a business cost anyway?*

Maybe if the house sells it could cover the difference. A bank loan is something to consider. And, as a last resort, I can ask Dad to lend me the money if it's not too much. I have options. I can figure this out. I *will* figure this out.

My, how far I've come. The journey was rough, but I'm proud of myself for making it to this point and finding the confidence I need to make my dreams a reality.

She picks up her sandwich. "Hey, you rub elbows with all those businessmen, right? We're a good investment!"

She might be onto something there, but I don't want to take advantage of my friendship with them. Ryan and Chris are an odd combination of computer and fitness gurus. I don't even pretend to understand what they do, but they did something big right out of high school and made a mint apiece. Austin isn't the top dog at CFI, but I know he's not hurting by any means. Mason *is* the top dog at CFI. He probably wouldn't bat an eye at the numbers. And there's always Gabe. *I can't ask Gabe. It would be wrong.*

I know he'd be happy to help, but I don't *want* him to. I want to do it myself. And I don't want to complicate this thing between us with something like that. That debt won't go away if things go badly between us.

"Right," I tell her, wondering if I could convince one, or all, of them to front me a low-interest, long-term loan. *I'll find a way.*

CHAPTER 16

Tara

A valet opens my door for me. He takes one look at the sky-high heels strapped to my feet when I carefully plant them on the concrete and offers me his hand to help me out. Gabe promised dinner was the only thing on the agenda for the evening. No dancing, no long walks through art exhibits, or anything like that. They're gorgeous, they do great things for my legs, and I love being eye level with Gabe, but they are *not* dancing shoes.

The beaded fringe lining the hem of my short skirt swishes around me as he pulls me up to stand. The man—though he's young enough it's generous to label him as such—swallows hard, his eyes lingering on the swaying fringe until Gabe clears his throat pointedly. The young man offers an apologetic smile and trades Gabe his keys for a ticket. It's a wonder his shoes don't lay rubber on the concrete as he hurries to get away from Gabe's angry glare.

Gabe looks me up and down for the third time I know of since I stepped out of my apartment and his eyes go glassy. Again. That look leaves me tingly all over as if my blood had been replaced with champagne.

I'm no better, though. The only thing better than Gabe in a suit is Gabe out of one, and he's wearing the hell out of the one he has on tonight. The last time I got a peek underneath it, his body was absolutely drool-worthy, but that was more than a year ago now. *A lot more.*

Of course, given the amount of time he devoted to sculpting those muscles, he damn well should be chiseled. I can see hints of all that work in the way the fabric clings in places. Memory probably doesn't do him justice now.

He only smirks at the disapproving look I'm aiming at him on behalf of that poor guy. "You're gorgeous," he murmurs, offering me his arm.

"Thank you, but that's no reason to be an ass to the poor valet. He's just a kid!" Calling him a kid is weird since he's probably not even ten years younger than me. Still, he's too young to catch my interest in any way other than a passing appreciation of his pretty eyes. At this point in life, I prefer a man who's had time to mature a little. I want to raise children, not my boyfriend.

Gabe shrugs. "Meh, s'good for him. Better than a jealous asshole who hits first, asks questions later."

A year ago, I would have argued that Gabe *was* that asshole. He's mellowed, though. *Mason must be rubbing off on him.*

The unassuming exterior of the building has me concerned we might be overdressed. The door opens from within, held by a waiting attendant in a sharp suit, driving that worry from my mind. The brightly lit, high-ceilinged dining room is dominated by a recreation of Michelangelo's *David* placed in the middle of a water feature that reminds me of a smaller version of the Bellagio fountains.

I used to beg him to take me places like this. Does he remember that, or is it a coincidence? Either way, I'm happy to be here.

The hostess greets Gabe by name and bids us to follow her. She leads the way to another wing of the restaurant that isn't as brightly lit. The dimness fosters a more intimate atmosphere and makes the illuminated reproduction of another sculpture the focal point of the room where the David relied on its size to draw the eye.

Once we're seated, I gawk around at other recreations of famous pieces and leave the wine selection and appetizers to Gabe. We have gone out together on a regular basis for the past two months but never anywhere this intimate. It's definitely a standout from the busy and brightly lit eateries we've frequented until now. *I wonder what else will be different.*

This is a date after all. Maybe that kiss we keep dancing around will happen tonight. Or maybe it won't. I can't decide which outcome is preferable. I hide my nerves about what might be with a smile and cast about for something to talk about.

"So, how'd the meeting go?" I ask, remembering that he mentioned having one on his schedule at lunch today.

Gabe beams at me. "Great! And I made a sale!" he says with all the excitement he had the first time he uttered those words to me.

My mind locks onto his good news. "Congratulations!" I say, genuinely happy for him.

"Thank you," he says, flashing me an easy smile that. "So, how was your day?"

"Ah." I'm at a loss for words. I *want* to tell Gabe about the fantastic opportunity Madi is giving me, but the news dies on my tongue. I don't want to tell him about it until I know it's going to happen. I don't want Gabe to see me fail when I'm finally getting what I've always wanted. *Some of it, anyway.*

But not being able to talk to him about it hurts. This is something else I wanted when we were married—open communication—and I'm the one withholding now. If I tell him everything, he'll have questions. He'll try to help. Turning him down might hurt his feelings. Accepting his help isn't an option because the knowledge that I couldn't do it without him will linger in the back of my mind. We don't need this complication between us.

I smile, but even I can tell it's not real. "It was good. Sketched a new design. Madi and I had lunch. Talked about the business and her plans for the future." *The devil's in the details.*

"That's great," Gabe says slowly, narrowed eyes examining every inch of my face. "Tara, what aren't you telling me?"

I force my smile wider, but it's pointless. If he's already suspicious, I don't have a prayer of pulling one over on him. We've known each other for too long. That doesn't stop me from trying to keep one of us from being hurt. "Nothing!"

"Tara . . ."

A lie of omission is still a lie. I can't win in this situation, but a lie will weigh heavier on my conscience. Besides, I need to know that he understands and supports my independence. "I didn't want to say anything because I don't know if I can make it work, but Madi wants me to be her business partner. She wants to relocate to a larger storefront, update equipment, all that good stuff."

Beaming again, Gabe stands and walks around to my side, pulling my chair back and guiding me to my feet for a hug. "T, that's wonderful! Why do you say you don't know if you can make it work?"

"Well, I don't know for sure yet," I say, reclaiming my seat. "I need to make some calls and see if I can get my hands on enough money for all that before I get my hopes up."

Gabe drops slowly into his seat and blinks across the table at me. "How much?"

And so, it begins . . . I stop pretending everything is fine and confess. "I honestly don't know. I've been too afraid to look. More than I have, for sure."

"T . . ." There's an edge of irritation to his voice that warns me it's time to change the subject. Before I can come up with a suitable topic, he's speaking again. "Text her, right now. Tell her you'll do it."

My head is shaking before he can finish issuing orders. "Gabe, I can't do that. Not until I have some guarantee that I'll be able to get the money. I'm going to call Dad tomorrow. If Dad can't swing it . . . Well . . . I thought I'd try Mason or Ryan. Or both. I'm afraid to go to a bank because what if—"

"Tara!" Hurt flashes through his eyes, but it's there and gone so fast I question what I actually saw.

"No, Gabe," I whisper before he can offer. "You don't owe me anything. I don't want to owe you anything. I don't want something else to come between us and ruin this . . ." I can't finish that thought because I don't know what this is. Whatever it is, it's good, and I don't want to lose it. I don't want to lose *him.* I just got him back, even if he isn't really mine.

He takes a deep breath. Silence hangs heavy between us for a long time, broken only by the appearance of our waiter to take our orders. We both grab onto our ignored menus like they're life preservers, and we've fallen overboard. Once the waiter is gone, I watch Gabe's face while he studies his hands where they're folded on the table.

"Text her," he says again, less demanding this time. "*Please*, let me do this for you like I should have done years ago. All I ever wanted was to do right by you, T. I know I fucked up then, but I'm here, and I'm trying now."

"*Let me do this for you . . .*" My pulse pounds in my ears, driven by irrational anger. There he goes again, thinking that I need him to buy all the things for me. He'll never learn, but my temper gets the better of me and I try again to make him understand. "I never needed you to *try* to do right by me. You did that without trying, at first. I needed you to *be* right by me, Gabe. To be the grown-up version of the kid I fell in love with."

My insides twist into pretzels when haunted gray eyes latch onto mine, obliterating the world around us. "Do you still love me?" The words are whispered but hit my eardrums louder than cannon fire.

"Gabe . . ." I sigh, hating that we're doing this here. There's no stopping it, though, sort of like the train wreck that our marriage became. I can't lie to him, but it would be so much easier. Admitting the truth feels like putting my heart out there for him to walk all over. Again. I may want what we used to have back, but making myself this vulnerable so soon is almost harder than signing the divorce papers. "I never stopped. I'll always love you, but I couldn't live my life on standby anymore."

He reaches across the table and latches onto my hand. "Let me try again, Tara. Please?"

"What?" My focus is locked on our clasped hands and his thumb caressing the fourth finger of my left hand. And the tingles traversing my spine because of that seemingly simple action. I can't focus on what he's doing and saying at the same time.

"Give me another chance."

"Another chance?" I murmur, struggling to break free of the spell his touch has me under.

"Please, Tara Bear. Let me come home."

"Home," I whisper, inwardly cringing at the hint of longing in my voice. I love my apartment, but it doesn't feel like home. Nothing has felt like home since the day we moved into the gaudy monstrosity he thought we had to have. I miss having a home.

My wits have gone a-begging. All I can seem to do is repeat after him like I'm some sort of parrot when he's asking me to put my heart on the line again. *Which is exactly what I wanted until he asked . . .*

So why is it a problem? *Because he just proved that some things never change.*

He ducks his head until his eyes are in my line of sight. "I love you, baby. I know I fucked up, but you're it for me. There's no one better. I'll be the first to admit that I didn't deserve you the first time. I damn sure don't deserve to have a second chance, but that's what I'm asking for. I can't promise I'll be perfect, but I promise I'm trying to be better."

His unexpected declaration shocks my brain into working order. Unfortunately, I don't have any words of my own to say. I *want* to believe him. I *want* to try again—no, not try again, I want to make it work. But I *need* to protect my heart and my newfound independence. I can't jump in headfirst just because we have history. I want this, but I want to be smart about it. "I don't know what to say."

"You don't have to say anything. Just think about it. Really, I'm not asking for anything different from what we're already doing. I only want to know that there isn't anyone else. And . . ."

"And?" I ask when he doesn't continue. Promising him that there's no one else is no big thing. There's never been anyone else, not since the day Austin's clumsy self knocked me over and Gabe caught me before I could hit the floor, hitting his head on a drinking fountain in the process. It maybe wasn't love at first sight, but I couldn't get him out of my head after that.

It's been nearly a year since I asked for the divorce, but my heart isn't ready to look elsewhere. Noel and Trista, and even Madi, have offered to set me up with guys they know, but the idea was repellant. I didn't want to be with Gabe, but I didn't—and don't—want anyone else, either. He said that I'm it for him. Well, he's it for me. He's my person.

Since that moment at the skating rink three weeks ago, all I can think about is *us*. I want to be with him. It's the possibility of losing everything I've worked so hard for that holds me back. I can't be with him if it means I have to go back to living my life on his terms. I need to know that he wants me for the person I am today, not the one I used to be, just as I've started to fall for this new Gabe.

He lets a deep breath whoosh out and scrubs his face with his hands before leaning back in his chair and crossing his arms over his chest. "And I'd like your permission to take our house off the market. We can always relist it later, but if things go well, maybe—"

"No." I've never been more certain of anything in my life. I don't care what happens next with us; I will never live under that roof again. I didn't want to move when he bought it. I hated it on sight. The only happy memory I have of that monstrosity is seeing it empty of my belongings as the door swung shut behind me for the last time.

His eyebrows shoot halfway up his forehead over eyes that betray his pain again. "No?"

I shake my head to drive the point home. "No. I've never liked that house, and I've never been quiet about it. It's a warehouse with windows! You bought it because it was a status thing, something you thought I wanted. I won't go back there."

His pale lashes flutter. "I'm sorry, T. I thought you'd learn to love it."

I mimic him, sitting back and crossing my arms. His eyes flit to my chest until I speak. "Gabe, that house felt like a prison to me. I hated it. I hated the neighborhood. I wanted something smaller, closer to family and friends."

"Alright," he says slowly. "I got an offer on it today."

I gasp and sit forward, both surprised and excited by the news. We'll both get a pretty penny from the sale, and it is precisely what I need to find a better place and become Madi's business partner. "Really?"

"Yeah," he frowns a little, "three-point-five mil."

I open my mouth, but it takes a bit before I manage to make it form words. "Th-three-and-a-half *million* dollars? Gabe, we paid half that!" *That's surely more than I need to take Madi up on her offer!*

He shrugs. "I listed it at five. Real estate in the neighborhood skyrocketed when they put the school in. Do you want to accept it? Or counter?"

His confession, more accurately his question, has me second-guessing myself. I don't want to be greedy, but this is his area of expertise. If he thinks that's not enough, maybe we should counter. Either way, that's enough money for me to buy a little house closer to my family *and* join forces with Madison. *Am I dreaming?* This is fantastic! More than I could've hoped for! "What do you think?"

His mouth twitches to one side. "It's a fair offer, if a little low compared to the asking price. I listed it high for two reasons. The first being I can always take less, but I can't ask for more. The second is that I really hoped the price would keep it on the market long enough for me to convince you to come back. I'll contact them in the morning," he says on a sad little sigh.

I'm so excited I'm bouncing in my seat. It's a careful, controlled bounce, though, to ensure my assets stay in my dress, much to his disappointment if the slight frown is anything to judge by. "Gabe, that's the answer! That's the money I need!"

"That's a lot more than the money you need, Tara Bear," he says. "I could write you a check for the money you need. Even without knowing how much, I'm confident it would clear."

Then why couldn't you do it for me years ago? Why did you change your mind and decide that I should wait until you were made a partner? *Stop.* It's our past. I need to leave it there. I can't move forward if I keep dragging myself back.

"No. Not unless you're writing me a check for my half of the house." I don't want him to do this for me now. This is *mine*. I'm making my dreams come true. Not him. He had his chance. "Hey, have you got any good listings close to Mom and Dad? I'm gonna be in the market for a house soon!"

He purses his lips. "I'll look tomorrow. Do you *want* me to write you a check for your half?"

"I don't know." Our original agreement was that we'd wait until the house sold. I didn't want to be greedy. I still don't, but I need that money now, and I didn't before. "I'll think on it."

Yeah, it's my money, but having him write me a check before the house has sold feels like asking him for help. I may be entertaining his request to give us another go, but I'm keeping my independence.

***

The high from Gabe's news about the sale and celebratory drinks have me walking on cloud nine. I should've stopped three margaritas ago, but they're so good, and I'm so happy!

The heat in his eyes when he thinks I won't notice him watching me only pushes me higher. Alcohol promptly dismissed any lingering concerns about the demise of our physical relationship. *It clearly wasn't anything to do with me.* Why would he look at me like he's imagining hanging my dress up on the floor later if he doesn't want me? The problem is, I want to let him. It's been too long, and my good buddy Al C. Hall tells me it's a fantastic idea.

A slow smile spreads across my face and Al cheers me on. "I miss you."

"I'm right here," he replies, answering my smile with one of his own.

Through my tequila shades—like beer goggles but classier—his smile is charged with *something* that sets my blood to boiling. It's just like old times, the good ones between college and him wedging his head so far up his ass he needed more power than a normal vehicle can manage to pull it out. Hearing him laugh is thrilling. My very skin is so sensitive I can feel his gaze like a touch.

It's not his gaze I want to feel. I want the frenzy we used to find ourselves in; the unzip-his-pants-move-my-panties-fuck-against-the-wall-because-the-bed's-too-far level of desire we used to know. That I'm-gonna-die-if-you-don't-get-inside-me-right-now feeling. And I want to know the feeling is mutual.

But I don't know that. I know what he said before, but the man sitting across from me is the next best thing to a stranger. I know everything about him. He likes his coffee black with just a teaspoon of sugar. He is deathly afraid of mice. He hates peanut butter and jelly sandwiches. He used to wear the same socks to every game, not the same brand, the same pair. His entire uniform went in the washer as soon as he got home to be sure they were ready for the next game.

I also know nothing at all. Sure he takes off for lunch, but does he still work until eight o'clock at night more often than not? Does he get up at five o'clock to hit the gym, run, shower, and eat before he has to be to work? Does he still sleep with one foot uncovered and snore just a little if he sleeps on his back?

Deep down, he's still the same Gabe. Nothing fundamental has changed except for his tendency to reassign blame, but he's different. Regardless, I know he can make me come so hard I scream myself hoarse.

My smile slips, and so does my happy. I gave up the right to know all there is to know about Gabriel Martin. He's offering me a chance to earn that right back, but is he really ready for that? Can he handle the new me? I take another drink, because I'm supposed to be happy tonight. It's hard to be happy when I'm worried I'm about to make a stupid mistake.

"What's wrong?" He frowns because he's being a good boy and staying sober. I admire his dedication, but it serves as a further reminder of how different he is. The old Gabe would've been drunk enough to dance on the bar by now.

"I miss you, but I don't miss you." The words come out in a wistful, sing-song way that makes absolutely no sense even to my alcohol sodden brain.

He tilts his head to the side, and his brow furrows. "I don't understand."

I get where he's coming from. Since he got out of rehab, we've spent more time together than we have in years. When we're not together, we're texting or talking on the phone. I see him all the time, so how can I miss him? It's not the same, though. "I like this new you, but I feel like I don't really know you anymore, and that makes me sad."

His smile rivals the one he had the day he found out he was going pro. "Do you *want* to?"

I can't remember what I said to figure out what he's asking. "Want to what?" *Want to invite you back to my place and find out if you still like it when I do that thing with my tongue? Yes, please.*

Gabe chuckles and takes his wallet from his pocket. Rising, he tosses a couple folded bills onto the table and comes around to my side. "Come on, T. Let's get you home."

"But . . ." He didn't answer my question.

"We can talk at your place."

***

I keep my eyes closed the entire ride back to my place. I've reached the elusive phase of drunkenness where the movement outside the car will make me dizzy. Puking is unlikely at this point, but it's not worth the risk.

Being closed up in a car with Gabe is not a good thing in my current state. He smells so *good*; sunshine and fresh air mixed with the subtle clean scent of his cologne. After all these years, I should be immune. I thought I *was* immune. *I'm never getting drunk again.* Drunk me sees through my own bullshit, even the bullshit intended to protect myself.

"Why did you let me drink so much?"

His chuckle grates on my . . . nerves. The ones between my legs that are currently begging for some real attention. "Because you were having fun, and you're entitled to cut loose on occasion."

"No occasion demands this kind of drunk."

A warm hand materializes on my thigh and squeezes it. "I like seeing you happy."

I swallow hard and try not to hope that hand moves higher to indulge the nerves his laughter keeps teasing. My skirt is short. It wouldn't be hard at all for him to slip a hand up it and a finger in my panties. I clamp my thighs together to keep them from spreading to offer easy access. "So buy me chocolate, not booze." *Chocolate wouldn't betray me this way.*

The car turns and slows. We're getting close. *Yay! Playtime!* "You never answered my question before," he says.

"Huh?" The promise of air that doesn't smell like Gabe and solid ground beneath my feet consumes my attention. I can't recall his question.

"Can we try again?"

"Try what again?"

He sighs. "Never mind. Let's do this when you're sober."

Blindly, I swat to my left and connect with what feels like his shoulder. I pull my hand away before I can forget that I have no right to feel him up. "Hey, I resent that! I'm perfectly capable of making sound decisions, even when inebriated." *Obviously, or I'd be in your lap already.* "It's your question that's confusing."

"Just because you're perfectly capable of using words that send the average idiot scrambling for a dictionary when you're sloshed does not mean you're capable of making sound decisions, Tara."

The car turns again and slows further. We've arrived. *Hallelujah!* He stops smoothly and my eyes fly open, only to be stabbed by the security lights in the parking lot. "Bah!" I hiss, shielding my eyes with my hand like an introverted shut-in confronted with the sun for the first time in months.

His chuckle becomes full-blown laughter when I turn to glare at him, and I can't help my groan as tingles shoot through me. He's *got* to stop doing that, or I'm going to spontaneously orgasm. The next time I get off, I want someone between my legs, damnit. Not a vibrator. Not a weird, spontaneous, laugh-induced O. I want the real deal.

"Sit tight," he says, opening the door and sliding out of his seat. I watch him walk to my side through slitted eyes because my pupillary response is on vacation, floating along in a lazy river of margaritas. He opens my door and offers me a hand. Gratefully, I accept and allow him to pull me to my feet.

"May I?" he asks. There's laughter in his voice, but I ignore it in favor of figuring out what he means.

In the end, I decide I've trusted him this far; what can it hurt? "Sure?" I make it a question that he doesn't deign to answer before scooping me into his arms.

"Oh!" I throw my arms around his neck like I need to hold on because he might drop me. *As if.*

Gabe winces, warning me that Al might be moonlighting as a megaphone in addition to occupying the position of devil on my shoulder. "Sorry," I stage-whisper though I'm close enough to his ear, the extra volume is unnecessary. *I wonder if he still likes it when I bi . . .*

Whoa! Down girl.

Before I can get myself into trouble, he sits me down in front of my door. He waits patiently while I fumble through my little clutch for my keys. There isn't enough room in the damn thing for me to lose them. Sober me would find them in half a second, but drunk me blinks at them stupidly for a few seconds before registering what I'm seeing.

Gabe saves me from my lack of coordination and takes the keys from me to unlock the door. He gets it on the first try, whereas I would still be deciding which doorknob is the real one out of the three I have to choose from. Somehow, I seem to be getting drunker instead of more sober.

"What the hell," I mumble to myself, shaking my head before I can remember doing so is a very, very bad idea. A strong arm wraps around me, keeping me upright and propelling me toward my bathroom.

Gabe closes the lid on the toilet, then helps me sit. "You should've left the last of that margarita in the glass instead of chugging it." Sage advice that's at least twenty minutes too late.

"Couldn't let good alcohol go to waste." I lean sideways and hold up the wall. It looks like it might fall soon if I don't. *I* don't need the support; it's totally the wall.

A squeak alerts me to the hot water being turned on. I know it's the hot because the cold tap doesn't squeak. "Let's get you cleaned up." A minute later, Gabe presses a warm cloth to my face and gently works at scrubbing off my makeup. "I'll stick around to make sure you don't fall and break your pretty neck getting into bed. I think I'll take a rain check on the good night kiss I was hoping for, though."

"Why?" A good night kiss sounds like a perfect idea. It might lead to good night orgasms.

"Two reasons. One, if you kiss me, I can't promise I'll stop unless you make me. Two, you're not sober enough to consent."

Option one sounds fantastic to me. *Damnit, Al!* I'm never drinking again. This is ridiculous. "Never stopped you before." Yeah, I never got *this* drunk when we were together, but I'd get drunk enough to make consent questionable.

He sighs and quietly continues washing my face. It's looking like I'm not going to get an answer when he says, "We were married then, Tara. I'm not going to say that consent is always implied in marriage, but most married couples don't wake up in the morning, see their spouse on the other side of the bed, and regret having sex."

He has a good point. All the same, sober me wanted the same thing. "I promise I won't regret it."

"I know you won't because it's not going to happen. There will be other dates."

"*. . . Other dates.*" I like the sound of that. It sounds like he might want the same things I do, which only makes me want him more. This new Gabe might be the Gabe he was meant to be, the one I needed him to be. "But I don't want you to go." I'm whining, and it's unattractive. Even worse, I'm slur whining. I need him to stay, though. If he leaves, he might change his mind about everything.

"I'll stay until you're asleep." He stands behind me, close enough I can feel his heat and the deliciously hard length of him pressed against my beaded backside while I brush my teeth. He says it's so I don't fall, but he doesn't need to be so close for that. He's teasing me. Torturing me. And I love it.

Two can play that game. "That for me?" I mumble, arching my back to press my butt firmly against him. I wanted proof he wants me as much as I want him, and I got it.

In the mirror, I watch him close his eyes. His groan is music to my ears. "Yes, it is. But not tonight."

Damnit. What's a girl gotta do to get dicked? A plan forms while I brush. I don't rush because it would only make him suspicious, but when I'm done, I'm armed and ready. "Would you unzip me? I can get it up, but down . . ."

"Yeah." He unzips my dress one-handed, taking care not to brush my skin with his fingers, which tells me he's holding onto his control by a thread.

"Thank you." I smile at him in the mirror. His answering smile is more of a grimace than anything. But he's distracted enough he doesn't see the trap he's walked right into. I slip my arms free and let the dress fall to a puddle at my feet, leaving me in naught but my pretty pink panties. My very *wet* pretty pink panties.

"Fuck!" He groans and turns away, shielding his eyes like my nudity might burn his retinas. "Damnit, Tara! That's not fair! I'm trying very hard to prove to you that I'm a better man now, and you're making it damn near impossible!"

What do I have to do to convince him? Do I have to spell it out? I will if that's what it takes because this hurts. "How does abstaining when I'm clearly willing make you a better man?"

He keeps his back to me. "Because you left me, Tara." There's no emotion in his voice to discern how he feels about that. The words are neutral, in your face, this is how it happened. "I'm not blaming you for that; I'm stating a fact. You asked me for a divorce because I turned into someone you didn't want to spend your life with."

He's right. That's a fact—two of them. But I won't apologize for it. My bathrobe is in easy reaching distance, so I grab it and shrug it on. Being rejected while mostly naked is worse than run-of-the-mill rejection. It doesn't matter that sober me would definitely agree with his reasoning. It's still rejection, and I'm still holding back drunk tears.

Gabe isn't done, though. "For all I know, the alcohol is the only reason you're offering right now. And the familiarity. I'm here, I'm not a risk, not like a one-night stand would be. Yes, I want to throw you down on your bed and fuck you until you can't walk. In the morning, if you still want that, I'm a phone call away. But I don't want this to be a drunken decision on your part. I want this to happen because it means something to both of us. And I'm not going to be a friend with benefits."

That only lessens the sting. I take a deep breath and swallow my tears down for good on the exhale. He's not rejecting me outright; he's protecting us both from more pain. *Cruel to be kind indeed.* I don't like him implying I'd use him for sex, but I'd probably feel the same way if our roles were reversed. Being logical when drunk off your ass is no fun. I can only come up with one answer that will ease the pain for both of us. "Why don't you stay then so I don't have to call you in the morning?"

He turns around. I catch the panic in his eyes before he notices my bathrobe and sighs his relief. "You mean it? You want me to stay?"

"There's a spare toothbrush in the drawer." It's not his fancy one, but it'll do. That should be answer enough.

I push by him and leave him alone to decide what he wants to do. While he thinks, I find my favorite sleep shirt. I only lose my balance and stumble into the wall once in the process of pulling it over my head. The bathroom drawer opens with a squeal during my free fall onto the dinky, full-sized mattress that is a concrete slab compared to the one we used to share. It was cheap, though. Really cheap for me since it was a housewarming gift from my brothers.

I'm on the edge of drifting off when the bathroom light shuts off, casting my little apartment into near cave darkness since I bought light-blocking drapes for the express purpose of ensuring no one outside could see anything inside. Soft footfalls slowly move my way, bringing tension with them.

"Tara?"

I grunt in response.

The footsteps stop in the area of my bedroom door. "You don't have a couch."

Thank you, Captain Obvious. My front room is too small for a couch, so I have a loveseat and a small chair. "Gabe, I slept beside you for years. Unless you snore for real now, get in here."

He hesitates in the door long enough, I'm sure he will leave. But he doesn't. After a short wait that seems like an eternity, he takes another step into the room. He doesn't hurry across the small space and tentatively crawls onto the bed.

"Damn, this is a small bed," he whispers when he bumps me in the process of settling in.

"Yeah," I tell him, yawning. "It does the job, though."

His arm hovers over me for just a moment before he jerks away. With a frustrated sigh, I roll over, grab his wrist, and take it with me when I roll again. When we're settled, I sigh again. But this time, it's contentment that brings it into being. I lost this when he stopped coming to bed at a reasonable time. At least, as far as I know I did. If he held me when he joined me, I was sleeping deeply enough not to know.

"G'night, Gabe," I mumble into my pillow.

"Tara?"

"Yeah?"

"I'm sorry I pushed you away."

"I'm sorry I let you." And there it is. The simple truth. It took both of us to ruin our marriage. He got lost, and I stopped trying to find him. I didn't want to admit it at the time, but I gave up on him.

CHAPTER 17

Gabe

It's too dark, even with my eyes closed. The bed is too warm. The room . . . isn't quiet enough. There's something warm under my arm. Something living. I don't have a dog and it's too big to be a cat. *Where the hell am I?*

Mom has a dog, but how did I get to Mom's after a night out with . . . Tara.

The room is pitch black when my eyelids fly open fast enough I'm surprised they don't roll up like window shades like an old Bugs Bunny cartoon. Tara tried, albeit clumsily, to seduce me last night! She was so cute drunk, but I'll take that to the grave. She'd kill me if I ever dared to voice it. I've never seen her cut loose to the point she made no sense unless she was using big words. I've never seen her drunk enough to stumble.

The steady, repetitive noise is her breathing, a once-familiar sound that was a distant memory before this. The warmth under my arm is the body she tried to give me last night. *Is she still so willing?*

No. After *that* much alcohol, she's going to feel like roadkill when she wakes up. Sex will be the last thing on her mind until the hangover wears off. I can help speed that process along, though. I hate to see her miserable. *That's rich.*

Apparently she was miserable for years, and I failed to notice. I didn't want to. I thought I was doing everything right.

"Mmmm," she hums, shifting in her sleep. Her movement presses her wonderfully round ass tighter to my morning wood, which is all too happy to be awake. If I were still sleeping, I'd probably be in the midst of a wet dream after that. Too bad there are too many layers of clothes between my skin and hers.

She shifts again, pushing her ass back even more and wiggling just a bit. "That for me?" she mumbles tiredly, repeating her words from last night.

"All for you." I push aside the fantasies about what I'd like to do now and focus on what's important: making sure she's okay. *Is it wrong to be proud of myself right now?* "How do you feel?"

Tara groans. "Like death chewed me up and spat me out."

Holding back a laugh is harder than holding back my lust. "Go back to sleep, Princess. I'll have something that'll make you feel all better when you wake up."

She wiggles some more. "Think you already have it," she says on a sigh.

God, she's going to kill me. I will not fuck my hungover ex-wife. I won't. I *won't*. At least not until she's not hungover anymore. "Go back to sleep. I'll be right back."

"Noooo!" She rolls to face me and throws a leg and over my hips and flings an arm around my neck. "You're warm. You can't leave."

"Do you want to be a functioning human being, or do you wanna feel like something the cat dragged in all day?"

"Hmph." I can picture the face she's making, her nose all scrunched and her bottom lip poking out. She'll try to behead me if I tell her she's cute when she pouts. A man's life depends on knowing when it's safe to tell his woman that she's cute. If there are negative emotions involved, it is *not* the right time; proceed with caution. Better yet, just don't. Tell her she's gorgeous and feed her chocolate.

"Let me do this, then I'm yours for the rest of the day." It's no real sacrifice, not with what I think she has planned. Staying in bed and worshipping her all day is not a high price to pay. She's my goddess and it's her due. I forgot to pray at her altar for far too long. Now I must atone for my sins. *Sucks to be me.*

Really, though, if I'd done this all along, we'd both be happier now. I made the wrong sorts of sacrifices.

She tilts her head back, but this place is a fucking cave, and I can't see anything. "Promise?"

"Swear it."

"You don't have a showing?"

"Nope. I rescheduled everything before I left to pick you up last night."

"Awww." She kisses my nose. Her morning mouth could gag a maggot, but she's so damn adorable, and I'm so damn happy, I don't care.

"I'll be back." Another promise I don't mind making.

Her hand deftly slips from my neck to my groin quicker than I can blink, and she's giving my wood a firm handshake. "Hurry back," she says, her voice husky with longing.

I am a fucking idiot. I passed up hot, drunken sex because I was afraid she didn't mean it. Tara means *everything,* even when she's drunk. I know I did the right thing, though. She might've been upset last night, but she'll respect me for it later.

"I will."

***

I check the clock on the dash and grumble a few choice words to myself. I don't have time to be stuck in this accident-induced traffic jam! I'm still ten minutes from Tara's. With any luck at all, she's sleeping and has no idea I'm not back yet. Fate hasn't been on my side lately unless you count Fern and my friends, so I fire off a text and hope it's enough. I promised I'd be right back, and I'm doing everything I can short of breaking the law to do that.

My fingers drum my impatience on the steering wheel, but I keep a leash on my anger—just like Dr. Dick taught me. Someone could be dead; I'm only minorly inconvenienced. Traffic inches its way along until I'm finally through. Luckily, the accident didn't look fatal. Just a fender-bender that caused a chain reaction because idiots follow too closely these days.

I skirt the speed limit the rest of the way to her apartment and pray every second of the way that she's still asleep. Or at least not angry that I took too long. I did my best, but I can't control the world.

The door closes behind me, plunging the room into complete darkness that breaks my heart. I might not know much about Tara anymore, but I know she loves light. Yet, here she is, living in the shadows because her neighbor gives her the creeps. *It's not permanent.*

Once I find her a house, I'll find a way to convince her to let me help until the money from our old house clears. Maybe I'll just tack a bit extra on her alimony checks to be sure she can make ends meet if she won't budge. I know she doesn't *need* my help. She's proven that. Hell, she probably never needed my help; she only needed me to get the fuck out of her way. She can make it on her own. But I can make it easier for her if she'll let me.

For the moment, I'll celebrate the darkness. It means I made it back in time.

Once my eyes adjust, I make my way to the matchbox-sized kitchen and flip on a light. I didn't count on her having a blender, so I bought one. Some snooping proves that I made the right call. She barely has the basics, but I find everything else I need and get to work.

I'm sure she has a reason for getting by with the bare minimum. Maybe she knew this place was only temporary and didn't want a lot of things to move later. I'm not required to understand her logic.

I know I'm sending her enough money every month to support herself, but I still blame myself for the situation she's in. Not only for pushing her away but for not insisting she come out of the divorce with more. She asked for next to nothing. *Why didn't I understand that sooner?*

The entire time, I expected her story to change, for her greed to make itself known. But no, anything she got beyond what she took when she left—which was nothing of any real value—her uncle insisted upon, and she fought him. She lost because I supported him, but she fought. I wanted her to ask me for things, to prove that she was lying when she said she didn't want anything from me. To prove that she needed me to support her.

I was a fool.

A click that calls to mind a nightlight and a loud groan emanates from the bedroom when I power off the blender. I knew I'd wake her, but it couldn't be helped. Footsteps pad down the hall and the bathroom door closes. I'm cleaning up my mess when it opens again, but she goes back to her room. I finish up, grab the two glasses of my best hangover cure, and follow her.

She's waiting for me, sitting cross-legged at the foot of the bed with her head in her hands, watching the door through her fingers. I have to bite my tongue to keep from smiling at the tangled mess of curls sticking up in odd places because she forgot to braid her hair before bed. Her eyes follow me while I make myself comfortable beside her, but the rest of her remains motionless until I hold out a cup.

"What is it?" she asks, cocking a suspicious eyebrow at the drink I'm offering her.

"Just a strawberry-banana-spinach smoothie with electrolytes added to help you rehydrate, and a little coconut oil because Ryan swears by greasy food for a hangover. Something about the grease coating your stomach, but coconut oil is healthier than deep fat fried anything." I can't cook, but any idiot can throw ingredients in a blender and turn it on. And I have a lot of practice with this particular recipe. It's what kept me functioning for years.

She takes her glass and sniffs it cautiously. Seemingly satisfied that I'm not trying to pull one over on her, she takes a sip and hums her approval. Her lips leave the straw long enough for her to say, "Yum," then she sucks it down with gusto.

"Slowly. You don't want to make yourself sick." A strong surge of pride takes me by surprise, with satisfaction following on its heels. I take a deep breath and try to determine the source of this feeling. Is it the smoothie? Could it be that she's enjoying it so much? I never knew *preparing* food for someone was more rewarding than providing the money for the groceries.

With a reluctant sigh, she lowers the cup. "Thank you. I'm already feeling better."

"Good." *I did that.* My chest swells with pride again.

A comfortable silence falls between us. It's nice—just the two of us, no distractions. No urgency to be doing something. No undercurrent of tension.

"You came back," she whispers after a while.

"What do you mean?" I ask, wondering if she's still a little drunk because she's not making sense.

She stares at her cup as if it is the most fascinating thing she's ever seen. "I thought if you left, you wouldn't come back. I was afraid you'd change your mind about . . . everything."

I take the cup from her hands and lean back to put it on the cheap, pressed wood nightstand so that I can hug her without worrying about a spill. "Is that why you wanted me to stay last night?" I ask once she's wrapped in my arms.

She nods. An empty space opens in my chest where my heart used to be. It shriveled up and died. *How did I not see that coming?* Years of damage can't be undone in a few months.

I took her invitation to stay at face value—she said she misses me. I'm in no position to be choosy when she gives me a chance to be close to her. The possibility of getting naked later was just a perk. I should've suspected she had other reasons because I knew then that she would be way too hungover to want to fool around first thing this morning.

"Oh, Tara Bear. I'm sorry." She doesn't respond, either content in the cradle of my arms or waiting for more. The fact that I don't know which leads me to believe it's the latter.

"I'm not going anywhere. I told you that I want another chance, and I meant it. One night that doesn't go according to plan isn't going to change that. I'm going to show you that I deserve . . . well, I don't *deserve* you. I never have. I'm going to do everything I can to make you happy, though, so you forget that part."

Her body heaves with her sigh. "I've missed you so much." The slight tremor in her voice betrays her. She's holding back tears that I don't want to see fall. I'm indifferent when others cry, but Tara's tears gut me every damn time. Even if I don't show it.

Acting on instinct, I lean away until I can see her face. She watches me with wide eyes—the whites stained a little pink from drinking too much and trying not to cry. I drop my eyes to her mouth and wait, giving her time to read my hint and act on it. *What if she's waiting for me?* What did I say last night? That if we were going to do this, I want it to mean something? She might think I'll tell her no again.

I slowly lean in, praying she doesn't pull away. We meet in the middle, and her soft little moan says it perfectly. *I could stay right here forever.* There's nothing sweeter than Tara's kisses. But we have too much left to say. I break away to whisper, "You don't have to miss me, baby. I'm right here."

"I can't do this again, Gabe," she says. "I can't let you hurt me."

The words sound like a goodbye, but I interpret them as a warning. *'Don't make me regret this.'* I hope that's what it is anyway. "You won't have to." I'll promise her the moon if that's what it takes, but Tara would never demand anything so unrealistic. *Apparently, time with me is unrealistic. Or it was.* No more.

"You come first. *We* come first," I amend, hoping she'll take the hint and agree that we're an *'us'* again. I don't want to rush her, but I want to know where I stand.

She rewards me by climbing into my lap and wrapping her long legs around me. "You damn well better mean that because if you break my heart again, I'm going to turn you over to Colt to be his new punching bag."

I shudder and my lip and jaw twinge. I've been her brother's punching bag once. I don't care for a repeat performance. I don't need threats to keep me in line, though. Memories of the time without her will do the trick.

I brush her hair back, tucking it behind her ear. "I never meant to break your heart to begin with, Tara. You have to know that."

Her mouth flattens. "No, I don't know that. But the road to hell is paved with good intentions. If what you say is true, you've paved your way more than halfway there. Don't get any closer, okay? The future will be what it will be. It's not worth sacrificing today's happiness just because it might result in a little bit more tomorrow."

Ouch. It hurts, but she's right. That's what I did. I poured my heart and soul into securing our future with no thought for the present. "I can do this, Tara. I did things right for a while, yeah?"

"Yeah," she says with a small smile full of nostalgia that gives me hope for the future. I lean in to steal another kiss but stop when that smile vanishes.

"Stef." That's all she says. But it's all she needs. I knew it was coming sooner or later, but it's a kick in the nuts after the progress we've made this morning.

Why now? There will never be a good time for this discussion. At least, not in my opinion. I prefer to pretend it never happened, but I knew it would crop up sooner or later.

Sighing, I fall backward onto the mattress, forcing her to either follow or let go. She chooses the latter option and scrambles onto the bed to sit facing me. It's never pleasant, but owning my mistakes has gotten more comfortable with time and practice. My Tara Bear has turned into quite the ball buster. It's best to confess my sins and atone for them in whatever way she deems necessary.

"I didn't cheat," I tell her. I need us to be on the same page here. If she thinks I cheated, she'll never take me back. "And I got tested at rehab. I'm clean."

"I know you didn't cheat." I smother a sigh of relief. She might know, but it doesn't change anything. She doesn't like what I did. I'm sure this will be the hardest for her to reconcile out of everything I've done. *It's not exactly easy for me to accept.*

I wasn't exactly celibate when I met Tara. Hell, I was a high school jock. And my parents were loaded. Girls were plentiful. But from the day I dove across the hall to catch her before she could crack her head on the concrete floor, she's the only one I've touched—until Stef.

I press the heels of my hands into my eyes because I don't want to look at her. *Coward.* I can't hide from this. I need to grow a set and own what I did. Tucking one hand under my head, I rest the other on Tara's leg to keep myself from using my hands as a shield again. She flinches at the contact but doesn't protest. She doesn't stop me from trailing my fingers back and forth over the soft skin of her inner thigh, either.

To give me more time to figure out how to explain myself, I take a deep breath and let it out slowly. "Stef was . . . Not supposed to happen. We bumped into each other at a bar one night. We were both a little under the influence. She came onto me, and I let her. For the next few weeks, we were a thing. I'm not sure what you'd call it, but we weren't happy, and I never touched her again."

Tara hugs herself and lifts her chin as if that small action can contain the tears welling up in her eyes. "Did you want to?"

Did I what? "No! God, no! You were all I could think of any time she tried. Back then, I blamed you for that," I add because it feels like I should. Like she needs to know that. I don't want to hide things from her. Doing so will only bite me in the ass later. "She'd change my schedule so that she could drag me off to some asinine *thing*, and the entire time, all I could think was *'Tara would love this.'* I didn't *want* the divorce, Princess. I wanted you. She quit and moved out of state because she said I wasn't giving her a fair chance, and if I wasn't going to make an effort, she couldn't work with me anymore."

And that was fine with me. I don't understand why I let her lead me around like she had a string tied around my balls to begin with. *Maybe I'll talk to Dr. Dick about it someday.* When Tara asked me to take time off, I'd refuse and get pissed. So why did I mostly take it in stride when Stef changed my schedule without consulting me? Yeah, I got mad, but I did the thing she wanted to do most of the time. It makes no sense. *Was I trying to prove to Tara that I could do those things?* If so, I was making the right effort with the wrong woman.

But it's over and done.

Tara exhales shakily and looks down at her lap, letting her hair fall forward to hide her face. "I just . . . I need to know that she's not going to pose a problem. That you don't . . . *miss* her."

Miss her? No. I regret what happened, but I don't want her back. I'm sure Tara's watching me though I can't see her eyes. But I didn't hide from her, and she's not gonna hide from me. Sitting up so that I can reach, I tuck her hair behind her ears before tilting her chin up until she looks me in the eye. "I haven't seen her since she quit her job a few months ago. I didn't want her then, and I don't want her now. I told you, Tara. You're it."

Her eyes squeeze shut. "What did I do wrong, Gabe?"

What? When? Oh! Understanding comes equipped with a knife in my chest. She's trying to take the blame. Yeah, we both made mistakes over the years, but this isn't her fault. It's mine. *And ain't that a bitch to admit?*

It must take me too long to formulate a reply because she fires a flurry of questions at me, each more ridiculous than the last. "Was I too naggy? Did I say something? Or did you get bored with me?" She takes another deep, shuddering breath in, and on the exhale, she whispers, "I just want to understand."

"No, Princess. None of that," I whisper, hating myself for causing her to question herself. I wipe away her tears and pull her into my lap again. "I got caught in an infinite loop. Everything was 'I'll do that tomorrow' or ' there will be time later' but tomorrow and later never came. I swear, baby. That's it."

Though she's crying, sitting here holding her feels like everything is right in the world. And I'm going to enjoy it as long as she'll let me.

CHAPTER 18

Tara

*G*abe's patience is astounding. He sits with me without complaint, combing my hair with his fingers and letting me cry myself out.

I've been dying to know about Stef, but this is the first time I've felt I had the right to demand answers. The question now becomes, can I let that go? If I can't, it will hang between us and fester until it drives us apart again. There's no point in trying if that's the case because we're doomed.

It's a huge relief to hear him say that nothing I did caused us to drift apart and for him to acknowledge his part in it instead of finding a way to spin it back on me. It's nice to know that he still wants me.

And I still want him, but is that enough to heal the damage that learning about him with another woman caused? It doesn't matter that he wasn't cheating. He had every right to sleep with someone else. But why could he find that time for her and not me?

There's only one way to know.

The voice in the back of my head needs to shut the hell up. My heart isn't sure that it's on board with taking risks.

No risk, no reward.

Fuck. Sometimes, I hate it when I'm right. But is the reward worth the risk?

Won't know unless I try.

Damn it all. Can't that voice take a vacation? I'm too hungover for this. Only I'm not. Whatever Gabe put in that drink helped tremendously. Drunk me and sober me seem to be on the same page.

The page that reads 'give Gabe another chance to destroy me.'

"Thank you." My voice breaks over the words from crying, but Gabe has seen me much worse than this. Like the time I broke down because I *still* wasn't pregnant after months of trying. That was around the time he started working more and coming home later. I wasn't fed up enough to let it go without a fight way back then. I confronted him about it, fearing that our lack of success was the reason. I believed him when he assured me that it had nothing to do with it, and I still do.

Gabe is indifferent to children. That's my dream, not his, but he was once delighted to help me make it a reality. He was content either way, as long as I was happy.

His hand stills for a moment before resuming the gargantuan task that is detangling my hair. "For what?"

A sigh escapes me. It's not a long list, but it's a big one. "For being a gentleman last night. This conversation would be a lot more awkward if you hadn't. And for answering my questions honestly. And for this," I gesture toward my face, indicating the tears.

I hate crying. Everyone hates crying. But, damnit, sometimes you just need to get it all out. Unshed tears and suppressed emotions weigh on your soul until it's drowning.

He chuckles. "How much of last night do you remember?"

My face immediately flushes. "Enough," I mutter, striving to hide my embarrassment. I practically threw myself at Gabe, and he refused. I know why, but sobriety only increases the mortification.

He didn't refuse Stef . . . What. The. Fuck! My brain needs to pick a side and stay there. But it's right. Stef threw herself at him, and he didn't turn her down.

But that was a different situation. This is also true. Things have changed since that happened, and he wasn't attempting to rekindle a relationship with her.

"You have no idea how hard it was to wait. Fuck, when you dropped your dress . . ." He sighs. "Damn, you are a sight for sore eyes."

"Yeah, well, I thought I was going to die of shame," I say, irritated with him for laughing at me.

"Try again and see what happens." His tone is still rich with amusement, but it's deeper now. Darker. Full of promises. Anticipation.

My heart slams against my ribs.

Do I dare?

If we were on the other side of the divorce, I'd be ecstatic right now. *At least on this side, leaving is easier.* The only things tying us together now are shared history and a few promises. Pie crust promises—easily made, easily broken. Nothing but my faith in Gabe says that things will be different this time, and he's given me no reason to doubt that faith since he left rehab.

Squeezing my eyes shut, I sit up straight and aim a kiss at him on muscle memory alone. His fingers sink into my hair at the base of my skull, grabbing a handful and correcting my trajectory. I used to hate that, but now, it sends a thrill down my spine.

Gabe's lips are searing hot against mine. There's no place for tentative, searching kisses between us. Those days are long gone, leaving us with desperation and need. He hauls me closer and holds me tightly enough inhaling is a struggle. His tongue pushes past my lips and tangles with mine.

I wiggle in his lap, turning to wrap my legs around him. Before I get where I want to be, he tries to lay me down. But that's not how this is going to work. I've waited a long time for this. I'm finally getting what I want, and it's going to be on my terms. I shove him flat on his back and straddle him.

It would take minimal effort on his part to resist, to take control, and do things his way. He would have in the past. But he watches me with wide eyes like he doesn't know what to do, or maybe he's waiting to see what I'll do next. He's only humoring me, but having him bend to my will is a heady experience—a different kind of drunk, a *better* kind. I want more.

The fire in my blood burns hotter, filling me with an all-consuming need to ride him hard as a reward for his good behavior. My pulse pounds between my legs, demanding relief from the pent-up frustration. *Soon.*

I pull my sleep shirt off and toss it away. Gabe reaches for me, and I allow his greedy hands to explore my body for the moment. I love the way his callouses scratch against my skin, but I'm not interested in foreplay. I don't need it. My panties are soaked through for him already.

I fumble my way through unbuttoning and unzipping his pants and slip a trembling hand through the opening of his boxer briefs to free his cock. My fingers close around him, and he groans. Or maybe I do. I want him inside me so bad, but I make myself slow down. I stroke him from base to tip and back again, enjoying the silky softness of his skin, the animalistic grunts he makes, and the throbbing of his pulse against my palm until I can't take it anymore.

I push my panties to the side. There's no way I'm moving to take them off, not when I finally have Gabe where I want him. I slowly sink onto him, finally taking what's mine. I suck a deep breath between my teeth while I take a moment to appreciate the sensation of fullness. Rightness.

"Fuck. Tara," He moans and rocks beneath me, testing my control.

I grab his wrists and pull his hands off me. As much as I'm enjoying the wicked things he's doing to my nipples, pinching and rolling them between his fingers, I have other plans. He resists at first but surrenders.

"Hands on the wall." I can't cuff him to the headboard or anything fancy like that, so I'll have to make do. Taking things that far might be a deal-breaker for him, anyway. It's not something we ever did.

"But—"

"Hands on the wall. Touch me, and I stop." And I mean it, too.

His eyes go wide again, but he puts his hands against the wall as directed. *This is fun.* He must like it, too, because he's not stopping me. I want him too much to tell him no if he takes over. He has the upper hand here, and I'm sure he knows it. That only makes this better. He's choosing to give up his control. That power is a heady sensation, and it makes me want him more.

I don't know what I'm doing. My entire plan was to get him to this point. Thinking has no place here, though. It's instinct. I close my eyes and tip my head back, enjoying the almost ticklish sensation of my hair against my bare back, and listen to my body. I lift my hips, sliding him out of me with excruciating slowness. Smiling, I open my eyes to watch him and slam back down, filling myself with him in a rush that makes me clench around him.

His upper body jackknifes off the bed. He reaches for me but stops himself. "Yes! Again!"

Grinning, I make him wait. We can do what he wants later. *He made me wait for years; it's my turn.* I tease him instead by touching myself in ways I know he wants to, but I won't allow. I trail my hands from my hips to my breasts and give them a squeeze. His eyes follow every movement while I play with my nipples. Wiggling my hips, I slide one hand down my belly to my slit to apply a little friction where I need it most.

"Please!" His voice breaks. He writhes beneath me, urging me to move again.

I smile down at him. His begging is better than any dirty talk I've ever read in a book. "You wanna touch?" I tweak my nipple tighter than he ever dared and gasp.

His hands jolt my way but stop when I shake my head. "I asked if you want to. I didn't say you can."

"You're killing me!" he groans, but he puts his hands back on the wall. "Please!"

"You wanna come?" I ask with a smile.

He bucks beneath me, but only once. "Fuck, yes. Make me come, baby."

Ladies, first. And I'm ready, too. Bracing my hands against his chest, I find a pace and an angle that works for me and ride him hard, taking what I want. He can get his when I'm through. I push myself over the edge, screaming his name and squeezing him tightly.

Gabe grabs me by the hips and moves me up and down, drawing out my pleasure and bringing himself to his own with a roar that will surely get the neighbors talking.

Gabe

What. The fuck. Was that?

More importantly, when can we do that again? It ended too quickly. Tara was never one to take charge before, which suited me perfectly because I like to be in control, but *fuck!* That was hot. So much hotter than when Stef . . . *Whoa, not going there.*

But Tara's *'I'm taking what I need, and you get the leftovers'* attitude was fire. It was different with *her. She* took control differently. It wasn't about what was good for her. She got off on making me serve her.

"Damn," I whisper, pressing a kiss to the top of Tara's sweaty head and thanking my lucky stars. Now that she's not calling the shots, my hands are refamiliarizing themselves with the dips and curves of her body, feeding my soul on her hums of pleasure.

Her heartbeat isn't pounding frantically against *my* chest anymore, and her breathing is smooth and even again. I'll flip her over in a few more minutes and show her who is really in charge here. For now, I'm content to bask in the little things: her slight weight pressing me into the hard mattress, her skin on mine, her warm breath on my neck.

Her body cradling my dick within her.

Simple pleasures. Tara hums her agreement with my eloquent assessment and sighs. A yawn takes me by surprise, and she echoes me.

"Why'd you stop?" she mumbles, her sleepy voice a warning that I don't have much time to put my plan into action before she nods off.

Her question catches me off guard. I stopped because I came. That's not what she means, though. I believe her mind is still in the past.

Sighing, I hug her closer and search for words to explain that won't spark a fight. I could lead with the truth—that I was a self-absorbed fuckwad—but she already knows that. No sense in beating a dead horse.

Why'd she have to go and kill my buzz? It's probably not a happy topic for her, either, and if it's so heavy on her mind she's bringing it up now, she needs an answer. So an answer she shall have. "At first, it was another one of those *'laters.'* Then, you were always asleep, and waking you up and foreplay seemed like too much of a chore. I convinced myself that if you really wanted me, you'd be awake and waiting for me."

She raises her head and props her chin on my chest so that she can see me. Cocking an eyebrow, she asks in a voice that could teach the Sahara a thing or two about dry, "And me sleeping in lingerie didn't clue you in that I wanted you?"

Well, that's embarrassing. I never noticed. A shrug is the only answer I really have. "I was an idiot?" We both know it was all a series of excuses I used to justify putting work first. If she needs me to say as much, I will.

She snorts and rolls her eyes. "Understatement of the century."

Holding her tight to my chest, I kick against the concrete slab she sleeps on and roll us both while she yelps and giggles. "Allow me to spend the rest of my life making it up to you." It's more of a solemn promise than a statement, but I refrain from pointing that out. It might spook her this early in our second stab at a relationship. *I'll show you, baby.*

Following her lead has gotten us this far. All I have to do is be patient and let her put us back together again, better than we were before.

I straddle her hips and contort myself until I *finally* manage to get my mouth one of her tits. The bud of her nipple stiffens under my tongue, resulting in a similar reaction in my dick, which never really backed down. My heart stops at her silence, but then the same high, needy whimper I've coaxed from her since the night I took her virginity rings in my ears, reassuring me that all is right in the world. *This is paradise.*

"You ready for more, Princess?"

She tosses her head back and forth violently enough I feel it in the mattress under my hands and knees. "I can't!"

It's an old argument—a futile argument. We both know she can. I just have to take my time. Build her up little by little. Eventually, I'll push her high enough she'll explode around me like an artillery shell firework, and it'll be worth every second of the wait.

"Yeah, you can. I'll prove it." I don't care if it takes me an hour. I strip her of her panties and undress myself to allow her a little more time to recover. I climb back over and nudge at her dripping entrance. Her pussy is so hungry for me, I slip inside with no resistance.

Her body responds, tightening around me to the point I could swear she's on the edge of coming again. "Gabe!" My name is a breathy whisper that sends chills down my spine. This is new. I like it. "Harder!"

I oblige, trusting her to know what she needs, and she rewards me with a moan. The muscles wrapped around my dick pulse and spasm their approval of a job well done. Surprise knocks my control out of play. I let loose, pounding her into the mattress, prolonging her orgasm until I join her in ecstasy with a shout of my own.

The neighbor beats on the wall, clearly unimpressed with how quickly I managed to get her off a second time, and shouts for us to shut the hell up. *Jealous prick.* He's just mad he's not getting laid.

We need a house. My apartment is better than hers, but neither has walls thick enough to keep the neighbors happy. The guy next door is in for one helluva long day. I'll give him a break, though.

I scramble off the bed and pull her to me by her ankles. "Shower time." I pick her up to carry her to her minuscule bathroom, ignoring her half-hearted protests until I silence her with a kiss.

I'll have her again in the shower. Eat her for lunch on the kitchen counter if there's room. Then it's back to her room for a nap before we pick up where we left off. *Always the man with the plan.*

CHAPTER 19

Tara

I shudder under Gabe's lips, which makes him chuckle. His relentless campaign to torture me to the brink of insanity continues. I thought he was joking when he asked me how many times I thought I could orgasm before the delivery driver arrives. I never imagined he'd take it as a challenge. A knock at the door stops the rain of lazy kisses on my shoulder and neck.

"Damn," he says on a sigh. He rolls off the bed and grabs his pants. I stretch and enjoy the show, though I usually appreciate it more when the clothes are coming *off*. Tonight, I'll make an exception, because I'm tired and sore. It's not a bad thing, but I need a break. "To be continued," he says, glancing over his shoulder in time to catch me admiring his ass. He grins and winks at me.

He opens his mouth, but another knock interrupts him before he can get a word out. His lips pull into an irritated snarl. "I'm coming, damnit," he mutters.

He turns, letting his eyes roam over my body before he leans over the bed for a kiss. "I won't mind at all if you eat dinner naked, but if you don't get out of bed, we'll be sleeping in crumbs tonight."

I smile on reflex, which hides my sudden panic. "*. . . we'll be sleeping in crumbs tonight.*" Does he think he's moving in here now? That we're going to pick up right where we left off like nothing bad ever happened?

Yeah, things were great today. They've been great since he got out of rehab. Will they stay that way, though? Or will we take each other for granted again and drift apart? It would be easy to get too comfortable, too fast. *He already is!*

What do I do?

I meant what I said this morning. I can't go through that again. I'd rather be alone forever than watch him gradually lose interest in me a second time.

I also meant what I told Madi. I want what Gabe and I used to have before we grew apart. Jumping back in headfirst isn't the right way to go about that, though. *Is it?* It's not too late to slow down and do this right. We only need to set some boundaries—treat this like a brand new relationship. But people in new relationships normally work toward spending more time together, not less. *What do I do?*

"Tara Bear? Are you coming?"

"Yeah." I crawl out of bed and rummage through my dresser for a shirt and some pants. Hopefully, getting dressed will act as a subtle hint that playtime is over and he'll go home. I've got to work tomorrow. I was supposed to go in today and pay my dues at the machine. *What was I thinking?*

I didn't plan to spend the *entire* day in bed with Gabe. Or in the shower. On the loveseat. The counter. The wall. I don't know what I thought, maybe that we'd part ways at lunch? But that didn't happen. Lunch was just a brief respite between rounds—an afterthought. We were both hungry, but not for food.

And I loved it.

I wouldn't change anything about today—except maybe the hangover. I loved waking up with Gabe here and every minute since, but I need some space. I need more time. I need him to prove that things won't change because I let him in my bed.

Gabe pouts when I shuffle into the front room. "That's how it's gonna be, huh?"

I fall into the recliner instead of the empty space next to him on the loveseat. "What do you mean?" I casually reach for the Styrofoam container he isn't holding.

"It's alright to tell me that you need some space, Tara," he says with just enough understanding to warn me he knows what I'm up to.

I freeze in the act of opening the container and try not to look guilty.

He smiles at me and saves me from deciding between a white lie to spare his feelings and the truth to spare my sanity. "I saw you freak out. I didn't mean anything by it, Princess. It was a Freudian slip, I guess. Obviously, I would rather stay with you, but that's up to you."

Well, shit. Heat spills across my cheeks. Now I feel like a bitch. I made a mountain out of a molehill. "I'm just—"

"Scared." He takes a bite of his dinner and watches me while he chews.

Greasy cheeseburgers—his suggestion, not mine—sounded heavenly at the time, but now my stomach is in knots. I'm not sure I can eat. "I'm sorry." I don't know what I'm apologizing for, but it seems like the right thing to say. I'm sorry I hurt him. I'm sorry I'm scared, and I can't trust him fully yet. That I had to go and mess up a good day with my insecurity.

"Don't be," he says, his attention seemingly fixed on selecting a fry. He swallows hard and looks at me through his lashes. "This isn't easy for me to say because I . . . well, you know. But I drove us to this point. I hate that I made you scared to include me in your life. I'm going to change that, you'll see. I don't care how long it takes."

I relax a little and berate myself for expecting him to turn it all on me. He hasn't done that in weeks, the occasional slip up over something silly aside. And in those cases, he acknowledged his fault once it was pointed out to him. Those were genuine mistakes, not willful ignorance. "I know you will."

He smiles, but it doesn't reach his eyes. "I have an appointment with Dr. Dick tomorrow."

My eyebrows fly up. "Really? I thought NA meetings were your only follow-ups?" Is he struggling again? Why didn't he say so? What if he's using again?

Gabe winces. "About that . . ."

I put my food aside. I can't eat right now anyway, and my concern for the turn this conversation has taken isn't doing my appetite any favors. ."What's going on?"

He sighs. "I'm sorry, I didn't tell you. I was afraid of what you might think . . . The meetings are great, but I asked to keep working with him. I saw him once a week for the first month. Now, it's every other week."

"Gabe! Why would you be afraid to tell me that?" There's no reason to hide something like that from me. Is that the only reason he's still seeing Dr. Johnson, or is there more to it? What else is he keeping from me?

He toys with a French fry, using it to scrape ketchup into a pile instead of looking at me. "Because I was afraid you'd think I was too big of a risk and wouldn't have anything to do with me."

That hurts, but I can see where he's coming from. My reaction proves his concerns were legitimate. *I have to do better, too.* I sigh his name and stand up. He blinks at me when I take the to-go box from his hands but doesn't resist. I climb into his lap and hug his head to my chest. "Gabe, no. I'm proud of you, you big goof!" That might be an understatement. I wanted proof that things would change for the better, and here it is.

He lets out a deep, shuddering sigh. "Thank you, Tara Bear. I'm trying, baby. I promise."

Gabe

By some miracle, I find a parking space close to my apartment. It's late enough on a Saturday night, I thought I'd have to walk. I don't reach to kill the engine after putting the car in park, though. Sitting out here, I can at least pretend that I'm on my way to see Tara instead of just getting home from her place. *If I'd kept my fat mouth shut, I could still be there.*

I didn't *mean* to make her think I was planning on sleeping over again. I wasn't planning on it. It was a hoped-for outcome, but I was following her lead. Too late now, though.

All those years, I took coming home to her every night for granted. I'd give anything to be able to do that again. And someday, I will. I'll find a way to prove myself to her, to show her that I'm not putting on a show to win her back. I know what I lost. I was telling her the truth when I said I don't deserve her. I only want her to be happy, and if that means I have to walk away . . . I might not be selfless enough to promise that, but I'll do everything in my power to ensure that I can make her happy. Everything.

I'll use this night to find her and Madi a new building for their business. I blew my chance to help her fund their venture, but this is something I can do. And I can find her a house she'll love. The perfect one is out there somewhere.

Now that I have a plan of action, I cut the engine and hurry to the door. From the corner of my eye, I notice someone on the sidewalk. Preoccupied with ideas for places to look, I give the individual a nod as I pass and continue on my way until they grab me by the shoulder and pull me off balance.

"Gabe Martin." His slimy voice sends chills down my spine. "Long time, no see. That speedball was a trip, huh?"

This isn't happening. Panic forces the air from my lungs. I shake off his hand and keep walking, calling back to him, "I told you, I'm clean, and I'm staying that way. Get lost."

"That blondie you went home with last night is a fine piece of ass, ain't she?" he asks, bringing me to a standstill.

I'm going to be sick. There's no way he's following me. He just happened to see us out. Hell, he might live near Tara. *Not helping.* He's only trying to get a rise out of me. If I attack him, which is probably what I would've done before, he'll have something to hold over my head. "Leave me alone."

He laughs, moving to stand in front of me. "I don't think you mean that, Gabe. Here." He holds up a little baggy like the one Chris found on me that morning. My stomach turns. The thrill of that high isn't such a distant memory that some part of me doesn't crave it, but it's not worth the risk of losing everything.

"A little reminder. You can catch up with me later." He tucks it into the breast pocket of my suit jacket and gives it a pat. "See you soon!"

Fear wraps its ice-cold fist around my spine, freezing me from the inside out. *What do I do?* If he really did follow me last night, I can't very well call the cops and report him. If he's crazy enough to follow me, he might be crazy enough to hurt Tara. Not only that, but I also have no proof that I didn't ask him to meet me here. Phone records would back me up, but he could claim I used a burner.

My best course of action is to flush that shit and pretend this never happened. Giving it back only prolongs my interaction with him. Flushing it gets at least a little bit off the streets. If I ignore him, maybe he'll get the hint. If he doesn't . . . Well, Tara will be moving soon. He won't be able to hold her safety over my head. I can call the cops then.

I can't tell anyone. If Tara finds out, she might not believe me. She'll freak.

CHAPTER 20

Gabe

irst thing the next morning, I drive to the office, knowing I'll find Dad there. I rap on his office door before I open it and poke my head in. "Got a minute?"

"Sure, son. What can I do for you?"

Tensing out of habit, I push the door all the way open and walk in while he stacks up the papers he was reading. I hate coming in here. More often than not, he lectures me about something when I do. But Dad handles most of the commercial properties that come through the firm, so of course, he's my first stop. I can handle him if it means finding the perfect building for Tara and Madi. "Tara's boss offered to sell her half of the business, and they're looking for a bigger space."

He holds up a finger and grabs his tablet. "This came in Thursday," he says absently as he thumbs through. "Ah, here we are."

He passes it across the desk and watches expectantly while I browse the pictures and relevant information. It's perfect. The girls will love it. "Can you sit on this for a while? I want to get a couple things in order before I show it to her."

His mouth presses into a hard line. "I can have that sold in a heartbeat. If she doesn't buy it—"

"I'm sure she will," I hurry to say, cutting his tirade short. *God forbid you might have to wait an extra day for money you don't need.* She'll buy it, though. I'm going to make it impossible for her to turn down. "I just need a week."

He stiffens and stares at me for a long moment for daring to interrupt him. "If she doesn't, I'm docking your pay for wasting my time."

"Fine," I snap at him. Anger drives my heart to pound in my ears, but I take a deep breath and practice some of the things Dr. Dick taught me. It's not going to cost him a damn thing to wait a week to list this. He's being an ass because . . . Well, I'm not sure why. Or that I want to know. I tap the appropriate button to print the information and hand his tablet back. "If you need me, I'll be in my office. She wants to buy a house, too," I tell him on my way to the door.

"Do you think you can win her back by finding her the perfect storefront and the perfect home? You had eleven years to make her happy, and you couldn't do it."

My hand tightens around the door handle. The edges cut into my palm, but the pain clears my head enough to keep me from lashing out at him. "Thanks, Dad. Good talking to you. Have a great day." He doesn't reply. I slam his door on my way out.

CHAPTER 21

Tara

One week later . . .

"**A**lright, ladies! Are you ready for this?"

Gabe's enthusiasm is catching. I'm breathless, like a kid at Christmas. It's the reason Madi and I switched off our machines and followed him to his car with nothing better to go on than his promise that he's found something we've gotta see. Sundays are our most productive days in the workroom because the boutique is closed. We don't like to be interrupted.

"This better be good," Madi says under her breath, giving voice to what we're both thinking before she sinks into the backseat.

Gabe closes the door before I can join her, then grabs my hand and drags me around to the other side to sit beside him. "It's good, I promise!" he fires over his shoulder on the way. *Maybe he's found a sale he thinks we'll be interested in or something.*

He double-checks to make sure we're both buckled before he backs out, ignoring our questions until he pulls up to the busiest open-air mall in town and parks in a conveniently empty spot in front of a storefront that appears to be vacant.

"Shut the fuck up!" Madi says, immediately pointing at the 'For Sale or Lease' sign in the window.

Gabe flashes us a smug smile. His eyes shine with pride. "They contacted Dad last week. I cashed in a favor and asked him to hold off on the listing until I could show you."

Her squeal is ear-shattering. "Are you serious right now?"

Her enthusiasm is bouncing the car, but mine is fading fast. I survey the storefront and the steady flow of foot traffic. Even on a Sunday morning, it's busy. This is prime real estate. We'd never have to move again. But it's gonna go fast . . .

We don't have time to drag our feet, and I can't come up with the money that soon without asking Gabe. I'm not counting on the money from the house until it's in my bank account. The buyers could back out. Stranger things have happened. And Madi and I agree that we don't want to take out a loan. Interest rates are too high. If we have a bad month or two and miss payments we could lose everything.

"Tara?" Gabe asks, clearly worried by my lack of reaction.

"We can't afford it yet," I say, hating to be the one to say it. This is Madi's dream, too. I'm holding her back. *What if she changes her mind?*

Where will I be if that happens? I wouldn't necessarily be out of a job, but to have this opportunity ripped away from me because the timing wasn't right would crush me. Would I even be able to work with her still, or would disappointment become bitterness and come between us?

"Lease, T. Lease!" Madi says, apparently forgetting the part about missing payments. "Hell, yes, we can afford it! Where do we sign?"

"She's right," Gabe tells me. "You don't have to have it all upfront with a lease. And it's a lease-to-own, so it'll be yours someday."

It is better than renting forever, but it's not a perfect solution. I know they want me to be excited, but I'm scared to get my hopes up. I'm too close to achieving my dream to have it snatched away from me. "Won't interest kill us? And what happens if we miss a payment? Could Madi make a large payment now to cut back on interest, then we'll make monthly payments until I have the rest of the money?"

Gabe turns his eyes toward the key to my dreams again before he answers. "I have a plan."

"Gabe?" Something is off. Why couldn't he look me in the eye and tell me that? I shift in my seat, turning sideways to face him. His plan better not be to cover my share until the check clears. I've already told him, if not in so many words, that's not happening.

Frowning, he drums his fingers on the bottom of the steering wheel. "I did some thinking after dinner the other night. You didn't come right out and say it, but you don't want my help, and that's fine. However, you mentioned asking the guys."

"Uh-huh . . ." *Impressive.* I didn't tell him that I don't want his help because I didn't want to hurt his feelings, even if I was upset with him for trying to take it over.

His head is still bent toward where his fingers are tapping out a rhythm on the wheel, but he's watching me from the corner of his eye. "What if all five of us buy it and sell it to you at no interest?"

"Yes!" Madi's enthusiastic bouncing sends the car rocking again.

"That way, I'm only a small part of it. One-fifth. You don't 'owe' me," he says over her backseat celebration.

That . . . sounds like it could work, but I'm leery. There's a flaw or a loophole that isn't obvious because I don't want it to be. "Can I think about it?" I ask.

"Girl! What is there to think about?" Madi asks, all but lunging over the seat to grab my shoulders and shake me.

"Sure," Gabe says. He probably expected that answer. "Would you like to take a look inside and see if it actually suits your needs?"

"Yes," Madi and I answer in tandem. I know better than to get my hopes up, but I want to go inside and daydream about my dresses on display in one of the windows. It'll hurt all the more later if this doesn't pan out, but for today . . .

We pile out of the car. Madi runs to press her face to the nearest window like a little kid while Gabe unlocks the door. A car slows down as it passes, reinforcing the marketability of this store.

I join Madi at the window for just a moment to imagine how things might look from a customer's point of view when planning our layout. Deep down, I'm just as excited as she is, but I'm erring on the side of caution. One of us needs to.

"There you are," a familiar voice says from the parking lot.

Automatically, I look to see Fern exiting her distinctive blue Camaro. The passenger door opens, and instead of Mason, a woman emerges. She's tall and model thin and my mind immediately takes over designing a dress that would show off her figure. Her short Afro compliments her delicate face and hints at African American descent, but it's a lighter shade of brown I'm not used to seeing, and her skin is on the fair side.

"Fern!" Madi says, delighted to see her again.

"Hi, Madi!" she calls back cheerfully. "Tara, Gabe," she adds, favoring each of us with a bright smile. "This is my study buddy, Jamaica Gunn. Jam, this is Tara, Madison, and Gabe."

"Gabriel Martin," Jamaica says, smirking at him. We both start because no one calls him '*Gabriel*' anymore. Her barely-there accent grabs my attention. It isn't one I'm familiar with. "Bloody shame about your knee, mate."

That was *years* ago. The only people who talk about his injury anymore are diehard soccer fans much older than this woman. Who the hell is she?

"Uhh, yeah . . . Thanks." His knee is a sore subject, but I suspect that he's not disgruntled with her for bringing it up, but he's trying to figure out her accent.

"Sorry." She winces. "Guess you don't like talking about that."

They come to a stop a few feet away. Fern tries to squash a smile and tells us, "Jam's family moved to Chicago when she was ten, but she always switches up her English when she's talking about soccer."

"Right, sorry . . ." Jamaica mumbles, her cheeks flushing. "Might as well get the rest of it out of the way. Mum is Jamaican, Dad is Scots-Irish. The accent is Jamaican, but I was raised in London."

"Thank you!" Madi says, smacking herself in the forehead with the heel of her hand. "I was going nuts trying to place the accent."

"Me, too," I say. That doesn't explain why she's here, but I like her forthrightness. Fern obviously likes her, so that's good enough for me for now.

Gabe grins. "Me, too." He sticks out a hand to the newcomer."Nice to meet you, Jamaica. What are you ladies doing here? I was expecting the guys."

Fern ducks her head and bites a corner of her bottom lip. "Weeelll," she says, stretching that one little word for all it's worth. "I, uh, heard you on the phone with Mason last night . . . And I decided to commandeer your plan."

"I don't follow." Gabe frowns and crosses his arms over his chest. I recognize the stance as one he uses when something or someone deviates from his carefully laid plans. He's not trying to come across as intimidating; he's bolstering himself to recalculate. The intimidation helps when he's determined to get his way, though. I've seen it in action.

Fern gives herself a little shake and lifts her chin, squaring her shoulders and standing tall. I never would have called her beat down before, but the difference between the Fern I used to know and the one standing in front of me is plain to see. She's much more confident now, even without Mason to shore her up.

"I'm your buyer," she informs him. To Madi and I, she says, "The guys are on standby if you're not alright with the change in plans, but I'm thinking bigger than they were."

I do a gut check. Her comment about thinking bigger seems like something someone interested in being a silent partner would say. While I like the idea of working with Fern on this, I can't help but wonder what's in it for her.

Madi and I exchange a glance. She shrugs, which I take to mean, 'let's see where this goes.' We don't have to agree to anything we're not comfortable with, after all.

My eyes bounce between Fern and Gabe like they're in the midst of a tennis match. He squints a bit, clearly displeased with this development. But he's a businessman. One who is smart enough to recognize a good deal when it's presented. And that's why I let him handle it instead of telling him to back off. He might think of something I don't. "How so?"

"Well, a bigger sales floor means you're going to need more racks, more displays, more of everything. And I heard you tell Mason that they plan to buy better sewing machines and Sergers, and more supplies, of course. You're going to need to make a lot of dresses to fill all that space."

"That's right," Madi says. We're operating with two second-hand machines right now and one Serger. She plans to add a Serger, an embroidery machine, and purchase three new machines, which don't come cheap if you want quality.

"What are you proposing?" Gabe asks, cutting to the chase.

She turns to look at Madi and me in turn instead of addressing Gabe. "I'll pay what you two can't comfortably afford, and you can pay me a percentage of your profit until we're even. I don't care how long it takes."

That sounds too good to be true. No one is just going to hand us money and tell us to pay them back whenever we can without getting something in exchange.

"What percentage?" Gabe and Madi ask together.

She shrugs her narrow shoulders. "Whatever you can swing, no interest."

"But why would you do that?" I ask her. It could take years to pay her back if the sale of the house falls through, and she won't make a dime. Sure, we're friendly, but we're not exactly besties. We could be, but I suspect that she's too shy to reach out, and I've been far too busy to try. Maybe this is an olive branch of sorts—a means to bridge that gap.

She shrugs again. "I'm a fan of helping people succeed."

My breath leaves my body as if someone punched me in the stomach. *Of course, she is . . .* Tears pool in the corners of my eyes. I quickly turn back to the window to hide them because I don't want her to mistake them for pity. I've only heard her story from Gabe, who only knows what Mason saw fit to share, and I'm sure it was nowhere near all of it.

"How's the scholarship going?" Gabe asks her.

I'd forgotten about that. It's another great thing she's doing with the money she never expected to inherit. *Oh, the irony.*

"Great!" she replies, her smile evident in her voice. "We've already started receiving applications!"

"Ready to make a decision?"

"No." She sighs and brushes her hair behind her ears. "I want to help them all."

"How will you choose?" Jamaica asks.

Fern shrugs. "The application includes an essay. I'm going to read them all and look for a few key things—shared values, so to speak."

With my eyes no longer in danger of springing leaks, I turn back around. "Let me know if you need help." I'll take time away from sewing for that. Not only is it a good cause, but it's also a good way to support Fern and get to know her better. It's a pittance compared to what she's offering to do for us.

She beams at me. "Thank you. I appreciate that."

I clear my throat. "You understand that I should have enough money to pay you back soon, right?"

She nods, beaming again, and I wonder how Mason ever stops staring at that smile long enough to get anything done when she's around. "But until then, there's no reason to miss out on this opportunity."

And that is a risk. We don't have time to drag our feet if we want to do this. The risks are minimal, and most of them are Fern's. If she's willing to do it, I am. This plan isn't perfect, but it's better. Better to work with one interested party than five who are only doing it as a favor. I nod my agreement. "Alright, let's go see it!"

There's a spring in my step to match Madi's when we walk through the door Gabe holds for all four of us.

"We're doing this," she states in an awed whisper as her eyes work to take in every inch of the sales floor. She's going to give herself whiplash if she doesn't stop trying to look at everything at once. "This is ours."

"I can't believe this is happening." I turn around to look out the windows to indulge in my daydream, but in my excitement, I bump into Gabe. "Sorry!"

He grabs my arms to steady me. I look up into smiling gray eyes, and butterflies take flight in my stomach. I *love* that look.

He ignores my apology and asks, "Do you like it?"

'Like' doesn't begin to cover it. I'm so happy that if I were a Disney princess, I'd probably burst into song. I can't contain my excitement any longer, but singing isn't my thing. He catches me when I throw myself forward and wrap my arms around his neck for a hug. "I love it! It's perfect! Thank you!"

He frowns at me. "I didn't really do anything."

I laugh and kiss the tip of his nose, then blush at the impromptu display of affection in front of friends. In Gabe's eyes, I'm sure that he didn't do anything. But he did. He cared. "Gabe, we never would've looked here. Even if we had, we would've missed out on it because we're afraid to take out a loan, and I wouldn't've asked the guys like you did. I know they'd do it, but I don't want to take advantage of their friendship."

"Where do we sign?" Madi yells from what will be the workroom.

"You're going to need a contract with Fern, first," Gabe says.

"Got it covered," Jamaica says.

Is that why she's here? Fern said they study together. I took that to mean she's a student. I look her way to see her pulling a manila envelope from the messenger bag hanging across her body. Maybe she's only holding it for Fern.

Fern rushes to explain, "Jam's dad is a financial lawyer, and Jam is pre-law. She wrote up the contract and had him approve it last night. And she's here as an impartial witness, not that we need one."

"I was bored," she says with a shrug and a grin. "And I love your car."

I shake my head, confused by their preparedness. "But we don't know how much we're going to need yet." We could always make another contract later, but I prefer not to have any surprises in the future. I don't want to have to call Fern and ask for more.

"Doesn't matter. The contract states any amount up to and including $500,000."

Fern smiles at me. "If that isn't enough—"

Madi cuts her off. "That's enough!" She comes jogging across the empty space, wide-eyed and deliriously happy. I'm glad she's still capable of speech because I'm not. "That's more than enough. I've been saving for this for a while. I have money to put with it, too."

Jamaica extends the envelope to me. "Take this and have your attorney look it over if you'd like, but I promise it's fair. Fern has already signed. Once the two of you have, make her a copy and keep the original with your records."

My jaw drops. "Fern, we haven't agreed on what percentage of the profits you'll get!"

Her attention seems fixed on a damaged spot on the wall and a crack in the ceiling, but she waves a hand dismissively. "Fill in the blank. Whatever you're comfortable with."

Gabe catches my eye and shrugs as if to say, *'what can you do?'* This is not a smart move on Fern's part at all. However, Mason surely knows what she's up to and either approves or gave up trying to talk her out of it. If the latter, he surely insisted on some sort of failsafe in the contract. And Jamaica would be remiss not to include a clause to protect Fern. Regardless, I have no intention of screwing her over.

The door opens, and Sam Martin, Gabe's father, comes strolling in like he owns the place. *What is* he *doing here?* I paste on a smile and pretend to be happy to see him when I'd love to tell him to take a hike. He's still Gabe's boss. It would only make things worse for Gabe at work.

Gabe isn't quite as tall as his father and got most of his mother's looks. Sam's face is round where Gabe's is angular, but they have the same eyes. Gabe also got his dedication to fitness from his mother, which is increasingly obvious each year because Sam's belly gets a little bigger.

Gabe got his work ethic from his father, though. And his temper and dramatic flair. Sam isn't a happy man. Maybe he was when he was younger, but I've only known him to be the kind of person who complains excessively. And when he can't find something to complain about, he says nothing.

He spares me a rare smile before turning his attention to the others. *Aren't I the lucky one?* "Ladies," he greets us, one nod encompassing the three of them. "Gabe." That one word holds so much disappointment; it's nearly unbearable.

"Hey, Sam," I greet him, striving for civility. He's always lovely to me—as lovely as he's capable of being, anyway. He used to be nicer to Gabe, too, before his knee injury. Since then, nothing Gabe does is right. He can say that he worked so hard to ensure we'd have a good life, but the reality is that he still needs his father's approval. And approval isn't something Sam does unless there are dollar signs in it for him. Gabe might not work so hard if Sam voices approval, so he never will.

Gabe's smile becomes strained. I feel for him. There's no reason for Sam to be here other than to make sure Gabe isn't fumbling the sale. Or to undermine him in some way.

"Hey, Dad. I'm not sure if you've met Fern," Fern smiles and shakes his hand, then Jamaica does the same when she's introduced.

"Dad helped me find this listing," Gabe explains when he introduces Madi.

Madi skips the handshake and hugs him. "We love it!" She backs away to smile at Gabe. "We'll take it!"

The look of shock and distaste on Sam's face has me hiding a laugh behind a cough. Fortunately, he doesn't seem to notice. "Excellent! I'll have the paperwork ready tomorrow, say one o'clock?"

You sonofabitch. He's going to screw Gabe out of at least half of this commission, probably for fear that Gabe would forgo payment to save us some money. And if I try to stop him, he'll find a way to punish Gabe.

"I'll pick you two up at 10:00," Fern tells us. "We'll go to the bank to get an account set up, then grab lunch."

"That all sounds perfect," I say, hiding my clenched teeth behind a smile. I can't do anything to help Gabe. He has to stand up to his father someday. The question is, will this be the transgression that spurs him into action?

***

"And Sean isn't too far from here," Madi says, chattering about how wonderful this location is while Gabe locks up. It's down to three of us now. "Hey, since we're not far, would you mind if we call it a day and I have Gabe drop me off there?"

"No, that's fine." We still have work to do, but I think this calls for a celebration. Just not one like I had last weekend. I'll skip the drinks and go straight to the dick.

"Actually, that's perfect," Gabe says. "I have more surprises for Tara. I was going to drop you off and—"

Madi slaps her hands over her ears and shouts, "I don't need details!"

I snort. Madi *loves* details. "Liar."

She whirls to face me fully and puts her fists on her hips. "Hey, I only want them after the fact. Sean and I both work too much. I need to live vicariously through someone."

"We're taking you to your boyfriend's house. You don't need to live vicariously."

She rolls her eyes. "Please. He probably fell asleep on the couch watching Netflix and won't even know I'm there."

"Then you're doing it wrong," Gabe jokes.

"Right?" I hold out my fist and he bumps it with his. However, it wasn't all that long ago that he was doing it wrong, too. He doesn't have much room to talk.

"Before we go, I wanna put a bug in your ear," Gabe says, shifting gears to more serious conversation.

"What's up?" I ask, choking on my curiosity.

"Mason's already got like seven groomsmen."

"Okay?" I knew Mason asked Gabe to be in the wedding party, and Gabe said the party was going to be huge. What does that have to do with Madi and me, though?

"That means Fern's going to have at least seven bridesmaids. Plus, her mother. And Mason's mother. And Ronni. You see where I'm going with this?"

"Yep!" Madi says. "If she comes to us for all of their dresses, and of course, she will because we're already doing hers, we can knock that off the tab!"

Gabe nods. "Exactly. And if you two branch into menswear . . ."

Wow. I can't believe he put that much thought into it. That could really boost our income.

"Oh, you're good!" Madi nods her approval. "I think we could do that. The girls already know how to take measurements."

Madi continues to babble on about expanding our line to include suits and tuxedos. I can't say I won't enjoy that, but my mind is elsewhere, puzzling out Gabe's surprise.

CHAPTER 22

Tara

*G*abe turns into the drive for an unfamiliar house in a ritzy neighborhood near the mall. It's a pretty Craftsman house on two or three lots. It has a huge front yard and a fenced-in back yard. I think I see a slide peeking over the top of the fence, which means there might be a pool. I definitely see a treehouse nestled in the boughs of a massive oak in the back.

"Who lives here?" I hope whoever we're here to visit doesn't mind if I explore a bit.

I like this community. Mason and Fern live a couple blocks up and a few blocks over if I'm right about where we are. It's a great place to raise kids. *Not that I'll ever know.*

A wave of bitter disappointment follows that stray thought. I guess I'm not as at peace with things as I thought. Or maybe I am, but that sense of loss will always live in the back of my mind, ready to pounce on a moment of weakness.

Gabe doesn't answer, so I glance his way to see what he's up to. He's watching me. The corners of his mouth twitch a few times, then stretch into a dazzling smile. "Well, Princess, you could."

"What?" I ask, much too loudly for the small space. We both wince, but Gabe laughs.

His excitement is palpable, charging the space between us and washing away my sadness. I can hardly breathe. "It's for sale. Not listed with us, but I've spoken to the competition," he says, brushing imaginary dirt off his shoulder.

"Are you serious right now?" My eyes pull my head back toward the house so they can roam over every inch of it, and it's not exactly small. *This could be* mine?

"Dead. Wanna check it out? I have a key."

"They just *gave* you a key?"

He chuckles at my skepticism. "I know the guy. He used to work for us. So, yeah. He's doing me a solid."

The excitement I lacked at the store sets every cell in my body to '*bounce*.' "Hell, yes, I wanna see it! I love it!" It's absolutely perfect. My dream house, at least on the outside. I grew up in a Craftsman, so I'm biased. This is the kind of house you make a home in—not that monstrosity we're selling.

Laughing again, he grabs my hand and kisses each knuckle before turning it over to press the key into my palm. "I thought you might."

My excitement lends me speed, and I run to the front door, pausing to admire the large porch before I fit the key in the lock and throw the door open wide. Behind me, Gabe laughs while I jump across the threshold and set about exploring every nook and cranny of the house. And the inside is just as perfect as the outside.

I make my way back to the front porch, my curiosity fully satisfied, and lean against the rail across from where he's sitting in a bent willow rocking chair. I'm surprised he didn't follow me around, talking up the finer points of the house like he would for a potential client. I'm kind of glad he didn't, though. Exploring was more fun than a guided tour would've been. "What gives? Why is it still on the market?"

His shoulders twitch just a bit like he's too relaxed to be bothered with a real shrug. "It's only been on the market a week. It hasn't even been shown yet. The company Kent works for likes to have homes inspected and appraised before showing and add that into their fees. It can save some steps for the buyer unless they choose to hire their own people to do it, but it takes a little longer to get listings up."

"You have got to be kidding me. First, the store, now this? How?" I push off the railing to check out the other rocking chair. They must be nice if Gabe is that comfy. It's a beautiful afternoon, and I don't get much time outside anymore, except for my morning run. I don't really have a yard to hang out in.

But I could . . . This one could be mine. My heartbeat quickens. I could sit here every day with a cup of coffee and my sketch pad, watching the world pass and the seasons change.

"Don't question it," he says with a warning look, stopping my daydream about decorating the porch for the season before it runs away with me. "Questioning it might jinx it! Sometimes, you just get lucky. I almost missed this one. I wasn't looking for things that weren't listed with us until the store came up. Then, I searched for houses in this neighborhood regardless of which realtor they were listed with. You said you wanted something close to family and friends. I listened this time. Your parents are only a few miles away. Colt is closer. Mason and Fern aren't far at all."

My smile is so big it hurts. I'm impressed that he listened. In fact, he's impressed me several times today. "Is it worth the asking price?"

"Personally, I'd offer cash but twenty grand less—maybe thirty. There are a few little things I'd want to have fixed myself."

"How much?" I ask, cringing. It's not going to come cheap. I probably don't have enough for a down payment right now. I should've asked more questions before I got so excited.

The silence stretches on, and the remaining kernel of hope in my heart withers away to nothing. It must be bad.

Finally, he says, "I want to talk to you about that. We never finished our conversation from dinner last weekend."

I search my memory, trying to put two and two together and figure out what he's talking about. Things get a little fuzzy after he told me about the offer on the house. "Alright . . ."

He reaches for my hand and squeezes it. "I said that I wanted to try again," he begins.

"Mmhmm . . ." I remember that. It's in the fuzzy area, but it's there.

"You never really answered. Unless the next morning was my answer."

"Gabe . . ." I hesitate, unsure of what I want to say. I didn't want to talk about it the next morning, either. *There were better things to do with my mouth.* I don't know what to tell him. I like the man he's become, but I'm not ready to put my heart on the line again. *Too late!*

"Hear me out, Tara Bear. I know you're sitting over there, freaking out about getting hurt again. I just want to point out that we're already doing it, Princess."

I don't so much as blink for fear that any reaction at all will give me away. I've done my best to call it everything but what it is out of sheer stubbornness. We've been dating for weeks, but it's easier if I don't think about it that way. But what does that have to do with the house? "So why are we having this talk?" I ask, hoping to distract him from labeling this . . . thing.

He squeezes my hand again. "Because I want to buy this together. I want to live here with you. I want to make this a home with you. Come home to you every evening. Eat dinner together while we tell each other about our day, share your bed, wake up in the morning, and do it all again. You said that I didn't need to *do* right by you; I needed to *be* right by you. I want to do both, Princess. Can we try again?"

My heartbeat quickens again. There's something stopping my lungs from working right. *Why do I want to say yes?* This is insane—the exact definition of madness; doing something again and expecting different results. *But it won't be the same . . .*

I've kept my guard up because I don't want to be hurt again. Yeah, we might already be trying again or working towards it, but there's nothing on the line here. As long as I keep my distance, I can walk away and never see him again and be okay. *Liar.*

Okay, so I'd be wrecked, but not like last time. Right now, Gabe is just my friend. My friend that I got stupid and slept with, but I wouldn't take that back. If

I agree to this, he's more. He'll mean more. It'll hurt more if he screws up. *But he won't because he's still working with Dr. Johnson.*

I can't lie to myself anymore; I want what he's offering right now. I regret that I ran him off that night because everything was perfect until I let my fear get in the way. I didn't ask for a divorce and set myself free to be caged in by fear. That's not taking control of my life.

"Gabe . . ." The words are on the tip of my tongue, but they're stuck there. I take a deep breath to try again, but Gabe cuts in.

"It'll be your house. In your name. If things go south, I leave, not you."

Breathing comes a little easier. He's thought of every angle. I appreciate that he's trying to make this easier for me, but it only helps a little. "And I'll live with your ghost," I whisper.

Gabe stands abruptly, causing the chair to rock wildly, and kneels in front of me, working his way between my knees. He grabs my hands and kisses them both, watching my face as he does so. It's impossible to look away, though the pain in his eyes cuts me deep. "Please, Tara. I know I'm asking a lot, but please! Give me a chance. I know where I messed up before, and it won't happen again. I swear it. I'll be home for dinner every night unless I have a late showing that you'll know about ahead of time. Those will be few and far between, though. I'll even go in late the next day to make it up to you."

My heart wants this even if my brain says it's a bad idea. My mind thought all those margaritas were a good idea last weekend, and it was clearly wrong. Gabe is working hard to fix the problems that drove us apart, but I have to give a little here, too. It took both of us to break it, after all. "Alright."

"Yes?" he asks, excitement bleeding into his tone. The pain in his eyes fades in favor of pure happiness. It's the same look he had on our wedding day.

"Yes."

Gabe

"Yes."

That one word reverberates through my body, lighting a fire in my blood. It sounds every bit as sweet as it did the night I asked her to be my wife. Maybe someday, I can call her that again. For now, I'll be content to call her mine in whatever way I can.

I don't remember standing, but I'm on my feet. "Really?"

She cocks her head to the side and grins. "Don't give me an opportunity to change my mind."

Heeding her advice, I pull her to her feet and kiss her as I've wanted to every time I've seen her since last Saturday. "You won't regret this," I promise. "Let me text Kent and tell him it's sold."

A shaky laugh is her reply. She turns her attention to examining the yard while I take care of business. He texts back immediately with an offer to meet us now. I'm so excited I nearly drop my phone. I hoped that would be his answer. I don't want us to have to wait one minute longer than necessary to move forward with life together as it should've been from the start.

"No!" Tara says. "I don't want to pull him away from his family! It can wait."

I relay her message and receive another quick response. "He's already in the car," I tell her. "He has his family with him. They just got out of a movie. He said they'll take the car, and he'll call an Uber when we're done."

That seems to mollify her. He's at least spent time with his family today. He knows as well as I do that the sooner we move on this, the sooner he gets his commission. Also, he probably wouldn't work on a Sunday for just anyone. And since I gave him my offer when I picked up the key, he might have an answer already.

Tara and I meet him at the driveway and are greeted by a carload of smiling faces.

"Thank you for letting us borrow him," Tara tells Kent's wife with a guilty grimace.

"It's no trouble at all," Kent answers for his wife. She nods, easing Tara's uncertain frown. "The kids weren't ready to go home yet, so Meg's taking them to the park until we're finished here."

"And you just *happened* to have the paperwork with you?" I ask, nodding to the file in his hand.

He waves goodbye as his wife reverses out of the drive. "Well, I had a feeling when you picked up the key. Especially since you told me what you'd be willing to pay based on my inspection and the appraiser's report."

Tara stiffens beside me. I wish he hadn't mentioned that. She's probably feeling set up now. "Gabe!"

"What?" I ask. "I couldn't help myself. I told him to sit on the offer until I texted him."

"And I did. I called the owners on the way over. They were thrilled to have an offer so soon, but I can't say that they were thrilled with the number." He pushes the envelope into Tara's hesitant hands.

"But you're handing her paperwork." He wouldn't be doing that unless . . . I hold my breath.

"Since it's you," Kent says, pausing for effect and shooting me a look, "I pitched them the low end. They countered with a number still in your range."

Fuck yeah! I bounce on the balls of my feet once and shake Kent's hand. Everything is coming together perfectly.

"Gabe!" Tara says again. "I don't have—"

I stop her with a kiss. "I'll cover it until the sell goes through on our place, then take the money out of your half."

I've already thought this through. She should know that I always have a plan. She might not always like them, but they're there. I'll jump through whatever hoops are necessary to make this happen and make her happy about it. The sooner she's out of her apartment, the better I'll sleep. I've been lying awake at night, worrying that my dealer is lurking outside her door.

"Thank you, Kent." I own him one. He has no idea how much he's helping me out.

***

"To us," I declare, carefully tapping my glass against Tara's. Her eyes shine brighter than the pendant light dangling over our table. She's still riding the happy high from signing on the house. Once she got over her stubbornness and accepted a short term loan from me, she was too excited to hold a pen long enough. We're both winning. She has her dream home, and I have her.

"To us." Her eyes go wide as she says the words, betraying her surprise. A hint of pink stains her cheeks, and she quickly turns away to look around the restaurant. When she looks at me again, she's smiling like nothing happened.

Surprise is good, though. That's three in one day. If I can keep them coming, life will be golden. Tara will always be happy. I've heard the phrase *'happy wife, happy life,'* but I've also heard *'happy spouse, happy house,'* and I think that one is more accurate. When one half of a relationship is unhappy, so, too, is the other. We both deserve some happiness because God only knows that neither of us has known much in the last few years.

It might've been my plan I was working to implement, but I wasn't happy. I was lying to myself and everyone else every time I said I was. I didn't see it before. It took hitting rock bottom to open my eyes. *Well, rock bottom, an angry Tara, and Dr. Dick.* The way she yelled at me that day in rehab brings a smile to my face.

She was so fierce—just what I needed. "I love you," I tell her without really thinking. It's a natural thing for me to say—as natural as breathing—because it's the truth. It has been my truth for years.

Her eyes widen again, and I realize it might not be an appropriate phrase to casually toss around outside of our soul-baring discussions about the past and the future. Not yet, anyway. *We'll get there.*

"I—"

"No," I cut her off before she can parrot the words back without really meaning them. I'd rather not hear it than hear it and wonder if she means it. "Forgive me; I wasn't thinking. That wasn't fair of me to say."

A small smile softens her face. "I *do* love you, Gabe, I'm just not . . . You just surprised me."

"You're just not *in* love with me. Yet," I finish for her, fighting back the tide of self-loathing. It sucks to hear, but I need it. It's a good reminder of what happened when I let life come between us. "It's okay to say it."

She ducks her head but not before I get a glimpse of her blush. "I'm learning to be."

"I'll take it." I have time to change that.

The waitress interrupts our conversation to slip me the check. Once she's gone, I polish off my water, wishing it were alcohol to bolster my courage. The next part of my plan is the riskiest. Well, maybe not. Putting in an offer without telling Tara was pretty fucking ballsy of me under the circumstances. This is the best place to spring it on her, though. She won't go off on me in public.

I clear my throat. Tara tips her head to the side and watches me expectantly, waiting for me to speak. The words are stuck in my throat, though. My hands are clammy, so I wipe them on my pants. *This is ridiculous.* I have no reason to be so scared of Tara. Even if she doesn't like my idea, the worst that can happen is her saying no.

"So, I thought that we should do a trial run before we give up our apartments." I watch her face closely, but she gives nothing away.

She rests her chin on her palm. "What do you mean?"

I resettle myself in my chair and lean back, resting one elbow on the back of the chair, hoping to look casual when I'm so anxious I'm beginning to sweat. "Well, once we have the house, there's no reason for us to keep our apartments. And if one of us needs some space after we move in, we don't really have anywhere to go. So, what if we spend some time playing house before we move? You can stay with me. That way, if you need some time to yourself, you don't have to ask me to leave."

Sweat rolls down the small of my back.

A little pucker appears between her brows and her head pivots to one side. "What about you, though?" she asks. "Where will you go if you need space?"

I smile on reflex but hold back my laugh. *She has no idea.* "Princess, I've had enough space to last me a lifetime. It's just a thought. Do with it what you will.

You're not going to hurt my feelings. I only wanted to give you the option to ease into this." *But I'll rest easier knowing you're not alone at night with my old dealer on the loose.*

I push my chair back and round the table to help Tara with hers. My palm finds its way to the small of her back like it belongs there on our way to the door. Outside, away from prying eyes, I pull her close and kiss her like I mean it, enjoying the taste of chocolate on her lips from her dessert.

"Mmmm. Is that an invitation?" She presses herself closer to me, grinding our hips together.

"Only if you want it to be, Princess."

She smirks at me. "Take me to bed or lose me forever."

I've never been so happy to hear a *Top Gun* reference in my life.

CHAPTER 23

Tara

Two weeks later . . .

I'm elbow deep in dishwater and dishes from two days ago, and my cell phone rings. My shoebox-sized apartment isn't equipped with a dishwasher, and I'm not here often enough to put this task off for another day. I might not be back until things are moldy. *I never would've considered letting them go before . . .*

Forget that noise. Before, I had nothing better to do in a day. Now, I go to work every day and do my thing to help make some bride's dream come true. Not only that, but I'm working my tail off to pack up a business without interrupting sales *and* pack up my home so I can move at the end of the month. Dishes can wait. Dreams can't. *I should know.*

I've misplaced my dishtowel, so I shake off one hand, swipe the screen without checking the caller ID, and cram it between my ear and my shoulder so I can multitask. "Hello?" I answer, curious to hear the voice on the other end.

"Hey, got dinner plans?" Gabe asks, his tone seemingly casual. I've known him long enough to know something is going on because his voice is a little higher pitched than usual.

"Nope." Excitement rushes from my head to my toes at the prospect of not having to cook, meaning I won't have more dishes to wash. *I really miss my dishwasher.* I like to cook, and I like to eat, but the clean-up . . .

"Are you at your place?" On his end, I hear a car door close at the same time I hear one close in the parking lot below. *What a coincidence.*

"Yep." I dry my hands on my jeans and round the bar that separates the kitchen from the living room.

He chuckles. "Good, come let me in."

I end the call without saying goodbye as I open the door. Gabe's blond head clears the top step right as I poke mine out to look for him. Seeing me, he smiles and waves. The rest of him follows, and I let myself drink in the sight of him in his suit. *It would look better on my floor.*

Disappointed with the lack of take-out bags in his hands, I ask, "Was asking about my plans for dinner a rhetorical question?" *Maybe I get dessert first?* I would be very okay with that. It's been . . . a week? We're both so busy right now.

He grins. "Nope."

With the promise of food between us, I step back and allow him inside. He pauses to kiss me in passing. "Happy Valentine's Day, Princess."

I gasp. "Oh, my gosh. I forgot!"

He chuckles again. "That's okay. I didn't. That's the important part."

I close the door behind him and lock it for good measure. The guy in the apartment next door is sketchy. I'm not lying awake at night worrying when I'm here, but I make sure to keep the door and windows locked. He has a lot of visitors in the evenings. I can't speak for the rest of the day since I'm at work.

"I'm so sorry! Everything is so crazy right now and—"

He cuts me off with a kiss. "Princess, I get it. We can have a real celebration when we move, okay? Our first night in our new home we'll do something special. I know you're busy."

"You're the best." I sigh, melting into him. His arms slide around me, and he rubs my lower back, somehow managing to find the spot that aches the most without being told. "Thank you for understanding. I feel like all I've done is run since we got the closing dates on both houses and the store."

"You have. That's why my gift to you is a quiet night in. You're going to park this cute little butt," he slips one hand down to squeeze my ass, "right there on that couch, and you're not going to lift a finger all night, got it?"

That would be so nice . . . I have so much to do, though. It's just not going to work.

There's no reason I can't pretend for a little bit, though. "What, are you gonna feed me?" I ask as a joke.

Grinning, he shrugs. "If that's what you want, then yes. And, I know how your mind works, so before you get ideas, I'm going to take over your to-do list tonight."

Oh, someone is definitely angling for a reward. I'd love to give him that, but I'm so tired. . . He might have to take an IOU. "You know I'm probably going to fall asleep as soon as my stomach is full, right?"

"We can make up for it later. All I want tonight is for you to take a break."

CHAPTER 24

Gabe

One week later . . .

No one answers the door at Mason's, so we let ourselves in. The smell of grill smoke wafting from the backyard beckons to my hungry stomach. I lead the way through the 'cozy little mansion,' as Tara calls it, to the kitchen and out onto the back patio to find our friends congregated around patio heaters. The crowd is bigger than usual this time because it's not our monthly 'meeting.'

"This is what passes for a bachelor party now?" I yell by way of a hello.

Everyone laughs, as I knew they would. Mason and Fern are eleven weeks away from tieing the knot, and they decided to forgo the traditional bachelor and bachelorette parties. Instead, they opted for a joint get together. I thought it was ridiculous at first, but now, I'm excited. Their bar is stocked with all of my friends' favorites. Fern's DJ friend has taken over the sound system and has music playing at a modest volume, loud enough to be heard but not so loud as to annoy the neighbors. There's a beer pong table and a few other games scattered throughout the yard, along with patio heaters to keep us warm.

Twenty-nine ain't old, but I must be mellowing with age. This looks like it'll be the most fun I've had with my clothes on in a long time. And Tara is here with me, so it's even better. It's only been a few weeks since we became official again, and this is the first time the guys have seen us together since then. I brace myself for their reactions, but they only smile and wave. I never told them that this was my endgame, but I don't think I had to.

Under my arm, Tara relaxes. She wraps an arm around my waist and gives me a hug. I know she was nervous, too. There was no reason for her to be; I wouldn't let anyone harass her. They can say whatever they want to me, but she's off-limits.

"Hey, you two!" Fern calls. She jerks her thumb over her shoulder, pointing to the bar. "Grab a drink and pull up a chair!"

Tara gets drinks while I drag a couple chairs to the circle. When we're seated, Fern introduces us to her sisters and their partners who flew in from Nebraska for the event. Tara is immediately pulled into a conversation about dresses. If it were anyone else, I'd be annoyed. It's hard to hold it against anyone in Fern's wedding party since the bride herself has done so much for Tara and Madi. She loved the idea of subtracting the cost of the dresses from what the girls owe. She even refused to take a discount on them when Tara felt guilty and offered.

The booze and the conversation flow freely. Mason's brother, Austin, and Jamaica bicker back and forth, purposely goading each other. Someone accuses them of flirting, and they both vehemently deny it. I'm not buying it. Somehow, the subject of flirting turns on Ryan. Chris loudly roasts him for being distracted at work and canceling plans, citing a secret girlfriend. Ryan doesn't do relationships, though, so he's probably wrapped up in some new project car he's not ready to show us yet. The bastard is secretive about the ones that are special to him. Even with all the shit-talking, no one mentions Tara and me. It's nice to kick back in my chair with my water in one hand and Tara's hand in the other and listen to my friends unwind, just like old times.

When I can, I sneak peeks at Tara and the couple we're here to celebrate. Their love for each other is evident in everything they do, and I hope that Tara and I can have that again someday soon. We *will* have that again. I will be the man she deserves.

After dinner, Fern's eldest sister, Ivy, and Austin—the matron of honor and best man—round us up for games. As tipsy as most of the others are, it's sure to be interesting. At least there's nothing that could hurt anyone, which was probably carefully thought out ahead of time. Being the sober one in the crowd is different, but I kind of like it. My head is clear, and I'll remember everything tomorrow.

And Tara is proud of me. I find her wedged between Fern's little sister, Aspen, and Noel on the other side of the huddle, and smile at her.

"Since they're a pair of sticks in the mud," Austin begins until Ivy elbows him in the side to stop him.

"Since our siblings decided to do things differently," she says, shooting him a *look*, "we decided to have a little fun." She grabs Mason by the arm and leads him to the beer pong setup, and Austin leads Fern to the opposite side with an arm around her waist.

"They're going to play against each other," Ivy says, sounding proud of herself. It must be her idea.

And it's a monumentally shitty one.

I bite my tongue so I don't yell that at them and shoot Tara a panicked look. This has the potential to go south really fast if either of them is a sore loser. It would be a disaster for Tara and me—we're both too competitive. Drunk and competitive is a horrible combination for us. There's a bar downtown we're still not allowed in because we were cheering for opposite teams that night. I don't want to see Mason and Fern at odds.

Tara smiles and shrugs. It's out of our hands.

"I don't like beer!" Fern complains loudly.

I release the breath I didn't realize I was holding. Fern's picky drinking tendencies will end this before it becomes a problem.

Ivy grins. "I know that. Which is why your cups all have whiskey and soda in them. And Mason gets bourbon and water."

Fuck.

"Oh, shit," they say together.

Austin runs through the rules in case anyone present lives under a rock and has never played beer pong while the rest of us jockey for better positions around the table. He wraps up the rules and says, "But forget the rules, we're doing things our way! Ladies first!"

Mason shouts a half-hearted protest but smiles and winks at his fiancée. More of their silent communication that probably says more than five minutes of non-stop talking. If I tried that with Tara, she'd probably think I was trying to get lucky. Fern blows him a kiss, then launches the ping-pong ball and sinks it like a pro amid hoots from the men in the crowd and cheers from the women.

He hangs his head and shakes it but then picks up his cup and tips it back. Fern cringes when he shoots, but he misses by just enough I question if he did it on purpose. I could never do that, not even for Tara. The drive to win is too strong. But I could see Mason giving Fern a slight edge. And I could see Fern being angry with him for it if she catches him. I edge closer to the table, ready to intervene. I don't know what the hell I think I'm going to do, but I can't stand by and watch them argue.

Watching any sort of game is usually boring for me. I'd rather be in on the action, riding the high of winning. Feeling the rush of victory when the game is finally over. This one, though . . . It's riveting, but not necessarily in a good way. I catch myself holding my breath with each shot, only breathing again when I'm sure there are no hard feelings on the other end of the table. Every time one of them releases a ball, my pulse pounds in my ears. The anxiety is killing me.

Fern holds her liquor like a champ. The only sign it's getting to her is her volume and the perma-blush on her cheeks. Of course, the drinks could be mixed weak. It's a close game; she has two cups left to his one. I should be rooting for Mason, but I want this hell to end. She closes her eyes, and her chest rises with a deep inhale. She holds it. Her eyes flutter open. She blinks a few times and in one smooth motion, brings the ball up, releasing it and her breath simultaneously. It sails across the table, bounces off the rim of the cup, and falls in.

Mason runs around the table and picks Fern up to congratulate her with a kiss. Relief leaves me dizzy. I know they're not Tara and me. They don't have the same problems we do. But they've both endured enough, and I don't want to see their relationship suffer like ours did.

"I can't believe you got your ass kicked by a *girl!*" Ryan shouts. His eyes shine with booze and mischief. We're contractually obligated to give Mason shit at times like this. It's in the best friend handbook. Somewhere. But I'll knock his ass out if Mason gets upset with Fern over it.

"I'll kick your ass, too!" Fern says through a giggle.

She's only joking—I think—but he holds his arms out wide. "Bring it, short shit!"

"Ryan," Mason says, a note warning in his voice. He should know that none of us would intentionally hurt her, my idiocy that night aside. And if he's busy worrying about her getting hurt, he can't be upset with her for winning.

Ryan scoffs, waving off Mason's concern. "I'm not gonna hurt her, man."

Mason shakes his head. "It's not *her* I'm worried about."

Intrigued, I watch Fern. She's sizing Ryan up like she's actually considering taking him up on his offer. I've met many women who act tough, but I don't think she's pretending. Alcohol might have something to do with that, though. No matter what she decides, I know in my bones Ryan would never hurt her. He might look like a mean motherfucker, but he's a damn marshmallow.

Ryan grins at her. "Gimme your best shot." Fern takes a step forward but hesitates. "C'mon, woman. I'm not scared of you. You couldn't hurt a fly. I do this every day."

That much is true, at least. He teaches self-defense classes at the gym he and Chris own. But watching Fern, I'm not so sure about his assessment. I think alcohol is clouding his judgment. She might actually know what the hell to do with him if she gets her hands on him.

He taunts her again, and she kicks off her shoes. "There we go! I won't touch you. Do your damnedest."

"Ryan . . ." Mason tries again to warn him. I open my mouth to back him up and snap it closed. Let Ryan learn the hard way. It's more entertaining that way. Tara sidles up beside me and ducks under my arm to hide her face in my chest. She's squeamish about violence for the sister of a semi-professional cage fighter, even the controlled variety.

Fighting was never my thing, so I have no idea what the two of them are up to, but in the span of three blinks, Ryan grunts in surprise, and his eyes go wide. In another two, he's flying through the air and lands on his back with an audible exhale. He slams his open hand on the ground three times.

"I've always wanted to try that," Fern says. She's so giddy with excitement she's bouncing on the balls of her feet. "We weren't allowed to do hip throws."

Ryan sits up and shakes his head like he's trying to rattle his brain back into place. "Muay Thai?"

She nods. "Ten years."

"Impressive." He stands and dusts off his hands and his backside. "You ever consider teaching? We have some ladies at the gym who are more comfortable learning from a woman."

She shrugs. "I'm not opposed. It's been a long time since I practiced." She grins and shoots Mason a sideways look. "Jabbing aside."

I don't want to know what kind of freaky foreplay they get up to. They don't offer any sort of explanation, either.

"Is it over?" Tara asks. She cants her head to peek up at me.

"Yeah, Princess," I say, grinning. *She's so damn cute.* "Fern showed him who's boss."

"Fern has boobs," Austin says, his voice carrying across the yard. "Anyone with boobs is the de facto boss."

"And don't you forget it!" Fern says, brushing her hands together as if dusting them off after a job well done.

While everyone is laughing at the two of them, I lean down to whisper in Tara's ear. "You wanna show me what makes you the boss later?" *Please?*

She's given me a taste of my own medicine lately, working almost non-stop at the boutique. Between prepping for the move and the tight deadline for the wedding, I'm lucky I got her to come tonight. She's always busy, coming in most nights after I've already gone to bed. If she comes in at all. Some nights, it's late enough when she leaves that she goes to her apartment instead so she doesn't wake me. The only 'us' time I'm getting is in my dreams.

I don't complain, though. It would make me a hypocrite. This is a temporary situation. I just have to ride it out a little longer. It's my turn to cheer her on while she works her ass off to grab her dream by the balls and make it her bitch.

Her smile grows by a fraction of an inch. If I hadn't watched it happen, I wouldn't notice the difference. But what a difference it makes.

It makes a difference in my heart rate. My ability to breathe. In my blood flow and in the way my pants fit.

I can't wait to get her home. I'm going to make her heart race. Make her pant. Make her so wet her honey drips down her legs. Make her crazy for me until she can't take one more second without me inside her.

She raises her eyebrows. "You wanna call it a night?"

My pants get even tighter. *Fuck yeah, I do!* "I thought you'd never ask."

I lace my fingers through hers and search the yard for Mason and Fern to tell them goodnight. There's another round of beer pong going on and three different games of cornhole. Everyone is happy, distracted. Instead of interrupting them, I tug Tara's hand and lead her through the house to the car.

Pulling out of their drive, I turn toward home and gun it as much as I dare. Getting pulled over will only delay my fun, and that's not acceptable. I have plans for my woman.

The seatbelt light in the dash comes on and the car dings, bitching about someone being unbuckled. "Hey, seatbe—" A hand on my thigh makes me swallow the rest of that word. *Nothing like a little foreplay to make the drive home seem endless.*

She shifts in her seat and reaches the other hand over to unbuckle my belt. "Tara!"

She ignores me and unbuttons my pants. The zipper follows. A warm hand slips into my underwear. I shudder at her touch. My hips surge upward, pushing my eager dick into her hand. "What are you doing, woman? Are you *trying* to cause an accident?"

"Home is too far away."

Fucking hell! That's sexy. I like knowing she wants me so much she can't control herself. But . . . traffic. We could get caught. And our lives are in my hands.

"You should've said something back there! They have guest rooms." Mason's got enough property; we could've slipped away into the darkness and found some privacy too. Or, we could've relived our high school days and climbed into the backseat before we left.

"You just drive."

I suck in a shuddering breath. "That's hard to do with your hands on my cock, Princess!" *Please, don't stop.* Her hand sliding slowly up and down my shaft makes it hard to remember why this is a bad idea. The danger adds to the thrill of it.

She leans over, and hot, wet heat wraps around me. My upper body tries to move away, but my hips thrust upward. "Shit! You're going to get us pulled over."

She giggles and kisses the tip of my dick. "You'd best keep both hands on the wheel and both eyes on the road. If we get pulled over or in an accident, you don't get to come."

Her threat makes my balls ache—a preliminary warning for the discomfort to come if I don't do as she says. *What's gotten into this woman?* But I want to come, so I play her game .

She takes me in again, not stopping until I feel the back of her throat. I fight to keep my eyes on the road when all I want to do is watch her. She retreats, tightening her lips around me and sucking hard. Pleasure radiates from that point of contact until it's all-consuming and I forget myself. "Oh, my God. Tara!"

"Shut up and drive, Gabe."

I hit the back of her throat again, and she moans like my dick is the best thing she's ever had in her mouth. It's indecent, and fuck, it's so hot. *When did she learn to do that?* She backs off and works my shaft with her hand while she sucks my head until I just want to scream, but I'm scared to. She might stop. Her tongue teases the tip, and I lose control. My hips jerk upward. She swallows me down again. I barely have time to grunt a warning before I give in to the best high in the world.

I look out the window, surprised to find that we're in the parking lot outside my apartment. The car is in park, and it's off. I don't remember doing that. I don't remember the drive. "Inside. Now. I'm gonna—"

"I'm gonna tie you to the bed and ride you until you can't come anymore."

I think that's supposed to be my line . . . I'm not dumb enough to turn down an offer like that, though.

CHAPTER 25

Gabe

Four days later . . .

nock, knock, knock.

"Come in," I call, looking up at my office door, hoping to see Tara's face when it opens.

"Hello, Gabriel," Dad says. The edge of disappointment in his voice is sharper than normal. *This isn't going to be good.*

"Hey, Dad. Grab a seat. What's up?"

He ignores my invitation to sit and crosses his arms over his chest. "Gabriel, your sales are down." *Right to the chase.*

I knew this was coming. Part of me hoped he'd cut me some slack, but deep down, I knew better. I'll always come second to his bottom line.

"Well, not all months are winners, Dad." In a perfect world, we'd sell a house the first time we show it, every time. That's not how it works, though, and he knows that.

"Your sales are consistently down since you got out of . . . that *place*," he says, wrinkling his nose in disgust. "And since you wormed your way back into Tara's life."

There was a time when I would've felt ashamed of myself for letting him down. My time with Dr. Dick has helped me move beyond that and recognize Dad's manipulation for what it is. It's not going to work for him anymore. I chew on my tongue to hold back the angry words that spring to mind. He's my father. And my boss. I can't lash out at him.

"You need to consider your life beyond your next breakup, son. If you continue this trend, you might not have a job next time she kicks you out. We're in the business of making money here. Not losing it because our employees aren't motivated enough to do their jobs."

And I wonder why I blame him for everything . . .

"Dad, I think I know how to do my job by now. I'm sorry I'm not selling houses fast enough for you, but my home life is every bit as important as my job. I can balance both."

His eyebrows climb to his receding hairline. "Can you?"

Yes, I can. And I'm happy to prove it. I'll enjoy feeding him crow.

My phone rings. I glance down at the screen. "Excuse me, this is my next appointment."

Dad nods and lets himself out.

"Hello, Mr. Griffin," I greet him.

"Hello, Gabe. I'm calling to let you know that our flight is delayed."

I stand up and start to pace. This could actually work out in my favor. They're my last meeting of the day. If they reschedule, I can go home early. "Hey, no worries, Nick. I have some free time tomorrow."

"I'm sorry, we can't reschedule. We fly out again tomorrow. If you can't make this work, we'll just have to go with one of the properties the other guy showed us. We're on a tight schedule."

Damnit! So am I! This isn't happening. I can't miss dinner, but Dad won't be able to complain about my numbers anymore after this sale. Not to mention the business this couple will send my way. They're moving to the area to establish a new branch of their company. Many of their current employees will be relocating.

Any other time, maybe I could be accommodating, but it's our first dinner and our first night in our new home. Tara will be crushed if I'm late. I pinch the bridge of my nose to ward off the oncoming headache.

"And how late will you be?" I ask, proud of myself for sounding perfectly reasonable instead of raging mad.

He makes a dismissive noise. "Thirty minutes. An hour, at most."

An hour. I relax a bit. That's not so bad. We can rush the tours. With any luck, they'll love the first property on sight and won't need to see the rest. "Alright, I'll be there. And you have the address?"

"Yes, I do. Thank you for being so flexible."

"Of course! Life happens sometimes. We can only roll with the punches!" I'd rather cuss up a blue streak, but it'll do me no good. *Dr. Dick would be proud.* I snatch up the stress ball the good doctor gave me and squeeze, imagining it's this guy's neck. *Maybe not so proud, after all.*

"Exactly. See you soon."

The rat bastard disconnects the call, leaving me to glare at my phone screen. I really want to throw my phone to vent my frustration, but I need it in working order. Instead, I fire off a text to Tara.

Might be a little late tonight. Six o'clock at the latest. Clients are running behind, and I need to stop by the apartment before I come home.

Why today of all days? My buyers can't help that their flight was delayed, though.

Tara

I pace back and forth in front of the stove, too anxious to stop myself. A glance at the timer says I have plenty of time to make another pass through the house to ensure everything is perfect. I've worked all day to have the house ready for tonight—our first night in our new home! I can't believe it's finally happening!

Gabe was right. I'd be freaking out right now if not for spending more nights than not at his place.

Who am I kidding? I *am* freaking out. We've practically lived together for a month now, but we're officially homeowners again. Only this time, everything is different. We're both happy. We've come full circle now. We're a week away from the first anniversary of the day I asked for a divorce, and look how far we've come.

Absence really does make the heart grow fonder, at least in our case. I needed time away from him to find myself. He needed time away from me to get his priorities in line. *They could use a bit more rearranging, though.*

Gabe still worries way too much about his father's opinion, but we'll get there. Together. He should be home any minute, and if things went well, we'll have two reasons to celebrate because he'll have another sale under his belt.

I compulsively adjust things that are already perfect, but I can smooth the little wrinkle out of the blanket draped over the corner of the couch and polish the little water spot off the faucet in the bathroom.

I check the table one last time to ensure I didn't forget anything and light the candles before I dash back to the kitchen to check the timer. While the last couple of minutes tick by, I clean imaginary messes in the kitchen and strain my ears for the sound of a car in the drive. I want to greet him at the door with a kiss and a glass of wine if he wants to try yet. It seems like a good thing to do to set the tone for this new chapter in our lives.

The timer beeps shrilly. I quickly turn it off and take the lasagna out of the oven, setting it aside to cool. I turn the oven off and slide a sheet pan of garlic knots in to warm in the residual heat. With nothing left to do, I wander to the front porch to watch for Gabe. He did mention stopping by his apartment to grab a few more things before coming home tonight. Maybe he couldn't find something? It's not quite six o'clock yet, though—nothing to worry about.

***

The lasagna is cool, so I put it and the garlic knots in the warming drawer and put the salad in the fridge. The wine waiting in the refrigerator is tempting, but I resist. If I start now, I might finish the bottle before Gabe gets home.

Maybe the buyers got chatty. That happens sometimes, and he can't really be rude and walk away from them. That has to be it. And he doesn't want to interrupt them to call me. I'm making a mountain out of a molehill. There's no reason to worry. I know he's doing everything he can to get home as soon as he can.

***

"Martin, Parker, and Warner Realty, this is Danielle. How can I help you?"

I breathe a sigh of relief. As late as it is, I didn't expect anyone at the office to answer. "Hi, this is Tara Martin. Could I speak with Gabe, please?"

"I'm sorry, Mrs. Martin." I don't correct her assumption. She must be new there—probably Sam's latest assistant. He has a high turnover rate. "Mr. Martin left hours ago."

My heart pounds. I thought she was going to say he is with a client. If he's not there, where could he be? "If you hear from him, will you tell him to call me, please?"

"Absolutely, Mrs. Martin. Is there anything I can do for you?"

"No, thank you, though. Have a good evening."

"You too."

I end the call and ignore the nagging doubt in the back of my mind long enough to dial another number. *Someone* knows where Gabe is. There's no reason to worry.

"Hey, T-Bird," Ryan answers on the first ring. "What's up?"

I skip the formalities and get straight to the point. Ryan will understand. "Is Gabe with you?"

"Nope. Haven't seen him today." He pauses before asking in a tone that promises misery, "Why?" Ryan is still pissed at Gabe for . . . everything. Most of the time, it's impossible to tell. They act like nothing ever happened. But if Ryan thinks Gabe is on the verge of putting even a toe over the line, he's ready to knock him back. With a sledgehammer.

"He said he'd be home an hour-and-a-half ago. He's still not here, he's not at the office, and he's not answering his cell."

His answer takes so long to come that I don't believe a word of his reassurance. "I'm sure there's a perfectly reasonable explanation, T. Do you know where the house is?"

"No." I should've asked Danielle. "I'll call the office again and ask for an address."

"Alright. Let me know."

"I will. Thanks." I end the call and dial the office number again. It rings and rings, but no one answers.

"Damnit!" She must've gone home. *Now what am I going to do?* I end the call and dial Ryan again. He answers on the first ring again, stopping me with my hand halfway to my mouth to chew on a nail.

"Got it?" he asks.

"No answer."

Ryan makes an unhappy noise. "I'll call Chris and see if he's heard from him. You call Mase or Austin."

"Thanks, Ryan," I say, barely holding back tears. *Keep it together.* Just because Ryan doesn't know anything doesn't mean there's a problem. There's no reason to panic.

I navigate to Mason's contact info and tap the call button with shaking fingers. What if he was in an accident? Would they call me? Maybe I should call Sam? But surely, he would've let me know. If not him, then Babs, Gabe's mother, would've. I'll call them next if the guys don't know anything.

"Mason's phone, Fern speaking!"

My breath rushes out in a sigh of relief. Gabe must be there if Mason isn't answering his own phone! "Hey, Fern. Sorry to bother you, but I'm looking for Gabe. He isn't answering his phone."

"Hmmm," she hums in my ear, making my heart drop to my toes. "We haven't seen him here."

I swallow my tears. I don't have time to cry. I can do that later when I know he's safe. "Damnit! He isn't at the office, and Ryan doesn't know where he is."

"Gimme a sec, and I'll ask Mason and Austin if they've heard from him."

"Thanks," I whisper. I hear the muffled sounds of deep voices shouting on the other end like she's covered the mic with her palm instead of muting the call.

"Time out!" she calls, and the shouts stop. "Either of you spoke with Gabe this evening?" Their answers are too soft for me to make out. "I'm sorry, Tara. Mason spoke with him over lunch but thought he'd be home by now. He says Gabe was excited about dinner."

"Thanks anyway, Fern," I reply automatically. At this point, I expected that answer. "Tell the guys for me?"

"Sure thing. If you need anything, you call, alright? And our door is always open." One of the guys says something, and she relays it to me. "Would you like one of us to go check his apartment?"

"No, but thank you. I'm going there now." I wasn't, but it's a good idea, and I need to be doing something. I should probably wait here in case he turns up, but I'm too anxious to sit still. I need to be out there looking for him.

"Keep us posted," she says.

"Will do. Thanks again." I hang up without waiting for her reply and dial Ryan to update him.

CHAPTER 26

Gabe

ritting my teeth, I direct the virtual assistant in my car to call Dad. I need to tell him the news. Best to get that over with on my way home instead of taking more time out of my evening with Tara. The dozens of missed calls are a sure sign that I'm in the doghouse, but she'll understand once I explain that I forgot my phone at the first property and had to backtrack to pick it up. I'll call her next.

"What's their offer?" he asks in lieu of a greeting.

"Nothing," I grit out. "They decided that they'd have to do too much work to both places because things weren't just so."

"You have got to be *kidding* me, Gabriel!" Dad shouts.

I cringe. "Sorry, Dad. I can't control everything."

"This was a slam dunk. All you had to do was talk up the good things about both places, spin it to make it look like doing all that work is worth it because then everything will be exactly to their standards!"

"I tried, Dad," I tell him, drumming my fingers on the steering wheel. I jumped through hoops to make them happy. I made myself ridiculously late trying to make this sale. He can't say I didn't give it my all.

Tara might forgive me but I can't forgive myself. I ruined our special night for nothing. I won't rest until I find a way to make it up to her.

"You didn't try hard enough!"

Fuck this shit. "Dad, nothing I do or say will be good enough for you, now or ever."

"I—"

"I'm speaking!" I growl, breathing heavily. I swallow the lump in my throat and grip the steering wheel harder. I've never stood up for myself to him, but I'm through with his abuse. "You have no right to talk to me—or anyone—the way you do. I'm tired of you acting like I'm an incompetent moron. I'm tired of letting you beat me down. You can shove this job up your ass. I quit."

"You're just like your mother," he snarls before I manage to end the call.

"Good," I tell no one in particular. "Better her than you."

Tara

Gabe's car isn't in the parking lot of his apartment complex, and neither of his parents knows where he is. Still, I get out of my car and make my way up the walk to check his apartment. Maybe something here will give me a hint. Between traffic and the darkness, we probably met each other in passing without realizing it, and I'm going to walk in to find that he's loaded his car as full as he can because he didn't want to make another trip. It probably took longer than he thought it would and he lost track of time. And his phone is dead because there's no way he'd ignore my calls.

A man steps out of the shadows, scaring the shit out of me and bringing me to an abrupt stop. I get the impression of high end, but unkempt clothing as my eyes sweep up to his. He's not tall, but I was focused on the ground in front of me.

He shakes his shaggy, greasy hair out of his eyes and gives me an equally greasy smile. "Ms. Martin. Fancy seeing you here."

Something clicks in my mind. I know this guy . . . "What are you doing here?" I ask, blurting out the first thing that comes to mind upon recognizing my old neighbor. The sketchy one that made me uneasy.

That same sensation creeps up my spine, causing goosebumps to spring up on my arms. I take a small step backward, putting more space between us. *Get away.* The little voice in the back of my mind wants me to run, but some sixth sense warns me not to. He'll only chase me.

I don't even know what I did to attract his attention.

"Same as you. I'm here to see your ex." He smirks at me. "Guess he's not your ex anymore, huh? Took me a while to figure out that the blonde bombshell who cost me a good customer was the same one who drove him to me in the first place."

"I don't know what you're talking about." I don't know him or any of his customers. I'm not sure I'd want to associate with anyone who does business with him. They're probably just as creepy.

His self-satisfied smirk stretches into a grin. "Sure, you do. Think about it. Gabe acting strange lately?"

I turn into a statue. Things fall into place, and the absurd number of visitors at odd hours suddenly makes sense. He's a drug dealer. *I can't believe I didn't see it before!*

But Gabe isn't using again. I'd know if he were. He hasn't missed any of his meetings, and he's been home for dinner every night. *Until tonight.*

The guy smirks again. "You tell him I'll forgive him for ghosting me this once, but if he does it again, there'll be hell to pay. I'm a busy man."

Ghosting him? Gabe arranged to meet him? That's ridiculous! But Gabe did say he had to come by here . . . Is this why? No. I have faith in Gabe.

I should walk away, but I can't make myself do it. Better to stand my ground. I stand up as straight as I can, doing my best to convey confidence because I'm not going to let him see my fear and shake my head at him. "I will not, and you will stay the hell away from us!"

The man surges forward and grabs me by the wrist, squeezing too hard and twisting. Pain shoots up my arm, and I cry out. My back collides with him, and his arms wrap around me, pinning mine in place.

"You gonna make me, *Princess?* Don't forget, I know where you live. And I'm betting I know whose bed to find you in when yours is empty. And I always know when yours is empty. You and your ol' man must be pretty serious. You're gone more often than not lately."

My heart takes off at a gallop, pounding sharply in my ears. *Oh, my God!* Is he *watching* us? Having us followed? Does he know about the new house? He's already hurt me. How far will he go? "Are you threatening me?"

He barks out a short, ugly laugh. "Yeah. I am. You tell your man that there's no such thing as a free high. I expect him to pay me back for what I gave him last month." He presses his nose to my neck and sucks in a deep breath. "One way or another."

My fight or flight instinct takes it up a notch, screaming for me to get away from him. I curl in on myself, hoping to find enough space to squirm out of his arms. He only holds me tighter.

He presses his face to my neck and sucks in a deep breath. "How 'bout we just settle this now, hmm? Me and your ol' man can call it even then. You wanna pay his debts, baby?"

I pull my knees in toward my chest to knock him off balance. Laughing in my ear, he leans forward until I can't hold my legs up anymore and my feet hit the ground again. There's no way I can get away on my own. He's too strong. One hand roughly gropes my breast—the other slips lower, toward the waist of my jeans.

No! I squirm, trying to free myself, but he holds tightly. *This can't be happening! I won't let this happen!* My lungs heave, but they still burn for more air. *Don't panic! Think!*

I work to suck in a breath and scream, "Let me go!" I read once that yelling 'fire' is more effective than yelling 'rape' in a situation like this. I never imagined I'd find myself needing that information, but I put it to the test. "Fire!"

With a wordless growl, he shoves me away, knocking me to my hands and knees. I land hard and pain spikes up my limbs. "Dumb little whore. You give him my message. One way or another. I hope we do this the hard way."

He slips into the shadows and disappears.

I scramble into the grass and vomit up what little food I sampled while cooking. Over the sound of my dry heaves, I hear feet pounding the pavement from the opposite direction. Someone heard me call for help. But are they here to help him, or me?

I climb to my feet and turn to meet the newcomers head-on. The odds aren't in my favor because there are two of them, but their uniforms label them as good guys. One of them stops to check on me, but the other blows right on by without a backward glance.

"Are you alright, ma'am? Should I call an ambulance? Did you know him?"

I shove my shaking hands into the pockets of my coat to hide them and rattle off the answers the nice security guard is waiting for. "I'm fine." I wince at the strained sound of my voice, but there's nothing to be done for it. *I'm safe now.* "Probably a little bruised, but I don't need an ambulance. I don't know him, but I know where he lives. Or where he used to live because he'll probably move now."

I'm so glad we moved. He can't find us anymore.

But where is Gabe? Is he dying of an overdose somewhere? Or did that guy give him something tainted? And where would he go? How could he do this to me?

My stomach heaves again. I stumble away from the security guard and retch some more. *Must be stress.* That guy's message to Gabe rings in my ears. *"... There's no such thing as a free high."* Did he really give Gabe something? Am I that naïve?

The other guard returns while I'm dry heaving, waiting for my brain to get the memo that there's nothing left to come up. Distantly, I hear them talking about cops and reports, but none of their chatter sinks in until they tell me I need to stay until the cops show up.

Part of my brain rebels because the guy is obviously dangerous and I'm making myself a target by going to the cops. The other part knows that I'm already a target, and I need to do my part to put that scum bag behind bars so he can never hurt anyone again. And I want to see him rot.

CHAPTER 27

Gabe

Oh no. The house is dark when I pull in. Even the porch light is off. Any hope I had of explaining myself, and her forgiving me easily fades away. Tara is definitely pissed, but I already knew that since she's not taking my calls.

The door slams behind me. The house smells wonderful—garlic and tomato sauce. My stomach rumbles, but it'll have to wait. I have to fix this first.

"Baby?" There's no way she's asleep this early. Mad, definitely. I can deal with that, though. I just need her to listen to me. "Tara?" I race up the stairs and throw open the bedroom door. "I'm so—" The bed is empty.

Déjà vu. Cursing, I run back down the stairs and try to call her once more. It rings and rings, and finally, voicemail picks up. "Baby, please call me. I'm sorry. They showed up later than they said they'd be, and then they went over every inch of both properties with a fine-tooth comb. I forgot my phone at the first house and had to go back for it. Call me back, please, Princess."

I end the call and pace the length of my car. Where the hell would she go? Trista? Noel? Madi? Maybe she went to the boutique to work her frustration out sewing?

I call them all in turn and get the same answer. They haven't heard from her in hours.

Waiting around is going to drive me nuts, so I yank open the car door and fall into the seat. I shouldn't take my anger out on the car, but I slam the door once I'm in and turn the key. Once I'm out of the drive, I hit the gas and burn rubber.

I don't know where I'm going, but I'll look all night if I have to. This isn't happening again.

Tara

Where could he be? I found nothing in his apartment to hint at where he might be—nothing save a baggy clouded with white residue. He isn't at the new house. His parents still haven't heard from him—at least his mother hasn't. His father wouldn't give me a straight answer. Chris, Ryan, and Austin haven't, either.

"Can you take me somewhere else, or do I need to get out?" I ask the Uber driver I hailed because I'm too emotional to drive right now.

"I can do it. I don't have another fare lined up," he says. So I rattle off an address from memory. Fern's reminder that their door is always open is a siren's song for me right now. I don't want to be alone. And if I'm right about Gabe, he'll come to Mason before he goes to Ryan. Ryan will kill him.

Not ten minutes later the driver turns into their drive and mutters a curse. "This the right place?" he asks.

"Yeah," I tell him, eyeing the gates. I've never seen them closed, but I've never turned up unexpectedly, either. "I'll get out here."

"You sure?" the guy asks, skeptically eyeing the gates again.

"Yeah, they'll let me in."

"I'll wait a minute, just to be sure," he says, glancing at me in the rearview.

"Thank you." I grab my wallet from my purse and hand him a twenty. "You have no idea how much I appreciate that."

He shifts around in his seat, muttering about how his mama would box his ears for leaving a woman in a situation like this, but he takes the money. I climb out and go to the security panel, immediately spotting the camera. I push a button and wait.

"Ms. Martin?" Len's voice asks through the speaker.

"Sorry to bother you, Len. Fern said—" The gate opens, cutting me off.

"You're not a bother," he says. "Have you found Gabe?"

"No," I say, stifling a sob that wasn't there before.

"I've made some calls."

"Thank you," I manage to get out through the fresh wave of tears.

"You're welcome. Let me know if you need anything."

Everyone is being so nice. "Thank you, I will."

I trudge up the drive, happy for the walk because it gives me time to get my tears under control. Len must've called because Mason and Fern are both waiting for me at the door. She opens her arms without a word, and I fall into them. "I think he's using again."

I didn't want to believe it. I didn't want to let that terrible man change my mind. But his insistence that Gabe was supposed to meet him, coupled with his offhanded comment about Gabe owing him for the drugs he got last month, slowly eroded their way into my certainty that Gabe wouldn't do that to me. And then I found the little baggy, empty save for some fine white residue, behind the toilet, like Gabe dropped it into the trashcan and it fluttered away.

"Why's that?" Fern asks, petting my hair as she would for Ronni. "Come sit down, Tara."

She takes my coat and leads me into the house, and I collapse onto the couch next to her. She carefully takes my arm—purple bruises already blooming where he held me—and probes with warm fingers. Gentle as she is, it still hurts. I grit my teeth and let her do her thing. Nodding her satisfaction, she releases me.

Mason sits on the other side of me, bracketing me between them and surrounding me with people who care. I walk them through my evening starting with Gabe not showing up for dinner. I gloss over the part about my encounter with the drug dealer, telling them he grabbed my arm when I tried to walk away from him. I don't want them worrying about me. I'm fine. It's Gabe we need to worry about.

"Do you want to stay here tonight?" Mason asks when I conclude with me turning up at their door.

"Could I please?" I should go home, I know. What if he turns up there? But I can't stand the thought of waiting in that empty house. Things were supposed to be perfect tonight. Not just tonight, from now on. The house feels like a symbol of what was going to be, and I don't want this to tarnish that.

"Absolutely," Fern says. "I'll get you something to change into." She gets up and makes it halfway to the stairs before turning around, wearing a funny little frown, and asking, "Have you talked to Noel and Tris?"

"No," I tell her. The thought crossed my mind, but Gabe wouldn't go to them if he's in trouble.

"Why don't you give them a call? And it's okay if they want to come over. We can go downstairs."

"Good idea," Mason murmurs. He and Fern lock eyes, and he nods a bit.

"I'll be right back," she says.

"I'm not sure I believe it, Tara," Mason says when she's gone.

I open my mouth to protest. I'd never lie about this! But he stops me.

"Not what happened," he says quickly. "That Gabe would use again. I feel like there's more to this story."

Tears pool in my eyes again. I try to speak, but sadness clogs my throat. I don't want to believe it, either. The evidence is hard to ignore. I've never in my life felt so betrayed. How could he do that to me? That question is stuck on repeat in my head, like an earworm I can't get rid of.

"I don't know what to believe anymore," I tell Mason. "But I can't bury my head in the sand and pretend this didn't happen. It won't help anyone."

He frowns. "No, but there could be another explanation for all of it."

"I hope you're right," I whisper.

Mason pats my shoulder. "We'll get it sorted. Call your friends. Tell them to come over. I'll go get you all a mountain of junk food, and you can camp out in the basement and do whatever it is you girls do when boys are stupid. Okay?"

Leaning sideways, I rest my head on his shoulder. "Thanks, Mase. That sounds good. But can I have a margarita, too?"

I shouldn't drink. I shouldn't turn to alcohol to deal with this. That's how it starts—or how it started for Gabe. One drink won't hurt anything, though. I think I've earned it.

"Oh, man . . . Now you're asking a lot," he grumbles. "We have that in the bar. Fern makes a pretty damn good margarita if I do say so myself. It's not bourbon, but it'll do."

"It's okay to admit they're yummy." I like this. Just a normal conversation. It's a nice distraction from . . . that thing I'm not going to think about right now.

"They shouldn't be so damn good. And you girls throw 'em back like they're Kool-Aid!"

"Shhhh! You've discovered our secret. We've worked hard for generations to buffalo you menfolk into believing those so-called fru-fru drinks are nothing but juice to protect your fragile egos. It's just easier if we let y'all believe you're better at something. If word gets out, we might have to kill you for ruining all our hard work."

He fails to smother a smile. "Your secret is safe with me."

Fern bounces down the stairs. "Did I just hear you reveling *The Secret?*" she asks, saying the words in such a way that they sound like a title.

I sit up because I'm basically cuddling with her fiance, never mind that we've been friends for years and I've got no reason to feel guilty, and hold up both hands. "He was on to us! I was trying to warn him!"

She sighs and pantomimes wiping sweat off her brow. "Whew. Thank you. I'd hate to lose him, even to the cause. Here," she holds out a bundle of clothes. "I grabbed you one of my shirts and a pair of Mason's flannel pants because there's no way any of mine will fit you."

"Sure they would," I tell her brightly as I accept her offering. "They'd just be capris!"

Mason stands up and shakes his head at us. Smirking, he rests his hands on his hips and looks at Fern. "Alright, get me my gun, woman! I'm off on a hunt for chocolate and ice cream."

I manage to hold a straight face for about a blink before I break into giggles. Fern does little better than I do. Laughing now is surreal, but it lightens the burden on my heart. It makes it easy to hope.

"Hey, you're the one over here talking about buffaloing the menfolk and our fragile egos. I've gotta go do something to reinforce mine," he says, winking at me.

"I'm just over here imagining you coming back with a pint of ice cream full of birdshot," Fern says, wiping at tears.

"A bar of chocolate with an arrow through it," I add.

"*Yes!*" Fern gasps, promptly succumbing to another giggle fit. She grabs a fistful of Mason's shirt and pulls him closer. "I love you. Safe hunting."

"Always," he says. He glances my way as if reminding himself they have an audience before he bends to kiss her.

I get my phone from my purse and wander to the kitchen to give them some privacy. The screen lights up, and the notification bar says I've missed a dozen calls from Gabe in the last five minutes. *Oh, thank God!*

No matter his reasons, I'm glad he's okay. I quickly navigate to my voicemail and tap to play the first.

His voice flows from the speaker, soothing the fear in my heart. "Baby, please call me. I'm sorry. They showed up later than they said they'd be, and then they went over every inch of both properties with a fine-tooth comb. I forgot my phone at the first house and had to go back for it. Call me back, please, Princess."

They were late? Could it be? That doesn't explain my run-in with his dealer and the baggy I found. *What really happened?* I move on to the next voicemail hoping for clarity.

"Tara Bear, where are you? You're scaring me. Please, call me back."

They're all about the same, only with increasing levels of panic and urgency. But they don't help me to feel much better. Yeah, I know he's safe, but I don't know who is lying—him or the drug dealer.

Guilt urges me to text him to let him know that I'm okay and to tell him to go home. I hate the idea of him out searching for me the way I was looking for him.

Thank you for letting me know you're home. I'm safe. Please give me some space.

I send a text to Trista, Noel, and Madi because it's faster than calling them all and explaining myself three different times, inviting them to a pajama party at Fern's. That way, there's no backing out if Gabe calls or texts and says something to sway me. I need time to think before I go home. *It would be rude to skip out on my own party, right? Right.*

***

Mason's basement is a thing of beauty. Most basements I've been in are glorified storage spaces. Not this one. It's fully finished and fully functional. Half of it is divided between a home gym, designed by Ryan and Chris years ago, and his 'man cave' where the guys usually disappear to once a month to drink themselves stupid, play darts, pool, and foosball, and watch ballgames on a projector screen that takes up one whole wall. The other half is split between a panic room in the event of a break-in or a tornado, storage space, and one empty room that used to be a play space for Ronni when she was younger.

Tonight, though, the man cave is ours. The five of us are crowded around the bar. The others are munching on the takeout Mexican food Mason was thoughtful enough to grab, but my stomach isn't happy with the idea of food. I pick up my margarita instead. The first sip of the wonderfully cold, bitter, sweet, burning elixir goes down easy, bringing with it a sense of bliss. Until it hits my stomach, which churns on contact.

Uh oh! I sit my glass down as carefully as I can manage and run for the bathroom. There's nothing in my stomach after the episode outside Gabe's apartment, so I'm stuck heaving up bile if anything comes up at all. It's the cherry on top of a monumentally shitty evening. Maybe I should just go home, lock myself in the bathroom, and wallow in self-pity by myself?

Someone taps on the open door. Sure hands gather my hair, and a cold cloth is draped around my neck. I don't need to look. It's Fern. Trista is a sympathy puker, and Noel can't handle vomit.

"You okay?" she asks softly.

I shake my head. I'm not okay. "You don't have to stay," I tell her, trying to hold back frustrated tears.

"Don't you worry 'bout me, Tara. Get it out of your system."

My reply is cut off by another wave of dry heaves. "Thanks," I tell her when they subside.

"Don't mention it."

"I think I'm good." I *hope* I'm good. This is ridiculous. I haven't even done anything to deserve it. Yet.

She takes the cloth off my neck and helps me stand, then hands me the rag to wipe my face with. "Maybe you shouldn't be drinking?"

I wrinkle my nose at her suggestion. "Well, I disagree, but my stomach doesn't. Hopefully, it'll change its mind after some food." Since rinsing my mouth out with margaritas is off the table, I opt for some tap water. Satisfied that it's as good as it's going to get, I lead the way out of the bathroom, ignoring the curiosity written all over Fern's face.

"You okay?" Noel asks, leaning away like she might be next if she gets too close to me. "You're white as a sheet."

Before I sit, I push my glass away. I don't even want to look at it right now. Or smell it. "Yeah. It's been a night."

Fern claims my drink instead of pouring one of her own, clearly unafraid of cooties. There's enough alcohol in it to kill anything I might have if stress isn't making me sick, I suppose. "Let's hear it," she says.

My lack of emotion surprises me while I fill them in. I've hit the point of numbness, where nothing can hurt me anymore. At least for the time being. That'll wear off much too fast. I've learned that the hard way. Tomorrow, it'll hurt again. I'll relive every last second as soon as I wake up.

While I'm regaling them with the tale of my evening, I eye the margaritas longingly. It's too soon to try again, though. I conclude my tale with the five of us in Fern's basement.

Fern frowns and exchanges a look with Madi. "I'll agree that it doesn't look good, but are you absolutely certain Gabe is using again? Being high wouldn't keep him from coming home or calling you."

I fold my arms on the table in front of me, shoving to-go containers out of the way to do so, and drop my head on them. "No. I'm not sure. But it's hard to ignore that baggy." I can't get that image out of my head. "He did call, finally. He says he was working late."

Hopefully, she and Mason are right and that perfectly rational explanation for this evening is the truth. I want to forget everything his dealer said, but it doesn't change much. I cannot forget what I saw.

I'm mad at him for being late or not answering my calls or texts. For not telling me that he was stressed to the point of relapse if that's the case. Did he *know* my neighbor and his dealer are the same person? Even if he wasn't using the whole time, he set up a meeting with his dealer. *Maybe I should call Dr. Johnson?*

I'll do that in the morning. He needs to know, but I'm hoping Gabe will call him first.

"Maybe I'm jumping the gun?" I ask the girls.

"Not like you don't have reason to," Noel says. She'll be the first one to shout 'I told you so' if it turns out Gabe is off getting high—and not even to rub it in my face. To her, it's a teaching moment, like when your parents tell you not to do something and you do it anyway. Only, she never really did say not to get back with Gabe. . .

A flash of something catches my eye. Fern is drumming her fingers on the bar. Her bright purple, glittery polish—no doubt Ronni's doing—gleams in the light. "Under the circumstances, it does look pretty sketchy. However, it could all be a . . . well, maybe not a misunderstanding, but there really might be more to this than meets the eye."

I get where she's coming from. A series of misunderstandings almost proved disastrous for her relationship not too long ago. This is different, though. There's not much to misunderstand. Someone is lying to me. The dealer doesn't have anything to gain by lying to me, but Gabe does.

"Definitely give him a chance to tell his side of things. But be pissed at him in the meantime," Madi says.

"But how will I know if he's lying?" I ask, sinking further into the misery pit. "I believed he was better all this time. What if he lied from the beginning?"

Trista lays her head down to look me square in the eye. "Maybe that guy was lying?" she asks, paralleling my thoughts.

"Why would he do that?" I ask.

"Why *wouldn't* he do that?" Fern says so softly I barely catch it over the music. I lift my head to look at her, so she elaborates. "He's in the business of making money. If he splits you two up and Gabe goes back to his old ways, that guy benefits."

She has a good point. . . "I didn't think about that. But why would he be there if Gabe didn't ask him to come?"

She bites her bottom lip. "That I can't answer."

CHAPTER 28

Gabe

I pound on Mason's front door hard enough to hurt my hand. Ryan wasn't home, he was out looking for me, and Chris and Austin haven't heard from her in a while. Her family hasn't heard from her tonight. She says she's safe, but that's not good enough. I need to know where she's at. And we need to talk about this. She can't run out on me the first time something doesn't go right.

The door opens just far enough for Mason to stick his head out. "Ronni is *asleep!*" he growls at me, his lip curled into a snarl. I know better than to do *anything* to disturb his girls, but I'm desperate.

"That's why I didn't ring the bell! I can't find Tara!"

His stern glare vanishes. Bright blue eyes slide away from mine, and the door opens wider in a silent invitation. "She called earlier freaking out because *she* couldn't find *you.*"

I rush inside and follow him into the family room, but I'm too anxious to sit. He watches from the comfort of his couch while I pace around and catch him up on the situation with my late buyers and my forgotten phone. "Her car is at my old apartment, but she's gone. Security says she was there and some guy accosted her. Said she refused medical treatment. I've called every fucking hospital and urgent care facility in the damn city, and she's not at any of them."

"Would they tell you if she was?" he asks dryly, no doubt drawing a parallel to his stint in the hospital not so long ago.

"I lied and said we're married." It's not too much of a lie. We were once. And I'm probably still her emergency contact on her records because she hasn't thought to change it and we share a last name.

Mason sits forward and rests his forehead on the heels of his hands. "Damnit, Gabe . . ."

"What?" I'm not going to listen to a lecture about honesty from the man who lied about his relationship for weeks. I didn't do anything he didn't do.

He doesn't answer for a long moment. "She's fine," he finally grits out. "As fine as can be expected anyway. She showed up here in an Uber. She doesn't want to see you, though."

Relief nearly knocks me on my ass. "Oh, thank God. Which room is she in? I just want to talk to her, to explain!"

He moves his hands to look at me. There's a war going on behind his eyes, deepening the lines on his face. "Gabe, she doesn't want to talk to you right now."

"I don't care!" I nearly shout. This is so unfair! I don't deserve this for being *late*. "Where is she?"

He glares at me and jerks his chin toward the ceiling to remind me about his daughter sleeping upstairs. "I promised her I'd honor her wishes. But she didn't tell me everything about the incident outside your apartment. That changes things . . . If she had, I would've called you already."

If he were anyone else, I'd be in his face, screaming and demanding answers. But if he were anyone else, Tara wouldn't have come to him in her hour of need. She knew she could count on him and that he'd keep his word. That's who he is.

He looks at me, and I watch the war rage on. He doesn't want to break her trust by telling me, but he probably understands the position I've found myself in. "Let me make a call," he says.

He stands, and I follow him upstairs to his room. I'm too worried to be polite and wait downstairs. I want to hear the answers as he gets them. He looks over his shoulder at me and his eyes narrow, but he doesn't say a word. I take the hint and stop just inside the door, though. I don't want to bother Fern anymore than I already have by showing up in the middle of the night and beating down their door.

The giant television on the wall across from their bed is the only light in the room until the backlight on his phone comes on. He raises it to his ear. "Hey, sweetheart."

My eyes dart to their bed for the first time. It's empty. It's relatively easy to connect the dots. Their bed is empty; he's calling her about Tara. Is Tara even here? Where would she go? But at least she isn't alone. If Fern is with her, she's safe. Fern can hold her own. There's a good chance Len is with them as well because Mason is overprotective. No one will touch my princess. But I should be with her, not them.

I try not to fidget while I listen to his side of the conversation. "Yeah, he's here. What's this about her being attacked? No shit? No, I don't think so. Sober, but scared. Yeah, I'll tell him."

"Tell me what?" I ask as soon as he disconnects the call. "Where are they?"

He sighs and runs his hands through his hair. "She says that Tara is pretty upset and she doesn't want to see you right now. And that she advises you to disregard that. As mad as she's going to be when you turn up, it's better than the alternative."

Every muscle in my body tightens. "What's the alternative?"

"I have no idea. I don't even know if it's good advice. Fern sounds a little . . . *happy*." He grins to himself, probably thinking ahead to what happens when she gets home. I know I would be. He gestures toward the door.

I follow him down the stairs, wondering where he's taking me. Now that I know Tara is safe, I feel bad for being such an ass when I got here. I'd be pissed if I were in his shoes. There's a time when I probably wouldn't have answered the door. "Hey . . . thanks, man. I'm sorry I came busting in here like this. She wasn't anywhere else I checked, and I couldn't think of anywhere else she would go. I was so worried."

He huffs out a laugh. "Gabe, I tried to break out of the hospital when I thought Fern was going to leave me. I told Austin to come sit on her until I got home if he had to. I get it. I don't know what's going on. I don't need to know either. Just fix it. You owe her that much."

I owe her so much more.

He stops outside the door to access the basement stairs. "They're in the game room," he tells me. "Good luck. I'm going back to bed. Don't do anything to make me have to come down there," he warns.

She's here? Oh, thank God. I breathe freely for the first time since I pulled into our driveway. "As if Fern needs your help," I mutter to his retreating back.

I make my way down the stairs and pause outside the closed door of the game room. I take a deep breath, say a little prayer, and knock on the door.

It opens a crack, and blue eyes peek out. "Oh snap," Madi says. "Tara?" she calls, her face disappearing from view.

"What's up?" Tara asks.

"You have a visitor."

The door opens a little more, and Tara is there. She looks at me, and her eyes well up. Mine do too.

It's such a relief to see that she's okay, but I want to hear from her what happened. "Tara, I'm sorry! Are you okay?"

She shakes her head. I reach for her, and she backs away. "No. I'm not. I'm confused, and I'm tired, and I'm heartsick, and I really just want to be left alone."

"Princess, please—" I reach for her again, but she holds up a hand and stops me.

"Give me tonight, Gabe. Please. We can talk tomorrow, but I need some space."

"What did I do wrong?" I ask, taking a step back to give her the space she wants.

"Please, just go."

She said please, but it's not a request. She backs away from the door and turns around, hugging her middle and collapsing in on herself as she goes. Fern and Noel immediately fill the frame.

"I'm sorry," Fern says. She grabs me by the cheeks and pulls my face down to her level. The haze of alcohol is absent from her eyes, which are darting around like they're searching for something on my face. After Mason's assessment that she was *happy,* I expected her to be drunk.

"What are you doing, woman?" I grab her wrists, taking care not to hurt her so Mason won't kill me, and pull her hands away.

She looks at Noel and nods. "He's sober."

"Of course I'm sober!" Some cold slides through my guts. "Is that why she won't see me? She thinks I'm drunk?" Bile climbs the back of my throat as another possibility occurs to me. "Or high?"

They both nod.

That cold feeling spreads to the roots of my hair, the tips of my fingers, and the soles of my feet. It feels like dying dreams.

"I thought we had her talked into hearing you out," Noel says.

Coming from Fern, that statement wouldn't be a shock. But from Noel . . . I look closely, but she appears sober, too. It's enough to pull me out of my shock. "I'm sorry, what did you say?"

She rolls her eyes at me. "Look, you're an asshole, and I'd love to knee you in the junk for all the times you've hurt her, but no one else will ever love Tara like you do when you're head isn't buried up your own ass."

I guess I'll take that as a compliment. "Uh . . . Thank you?"

"Just give her a little space, alright?"

I can't do that! I didn't do anything wrong! What if she doesn't give me the chance to prove it? I need to talk to her now.

Noel grabs my shoulders and tries to shake me, but she moves herself because I don't budge. "We're trying, alright? Call her five million times so she knows you're thinking about her but give her some physical space."

I sigh and concede to their superior knowledge of how to handle an angry woman. If Tara really believes I'm using, I might not be able to fix this. I have to find a way. I'll hate every minute of it, but giving her some space will allow me time to do that. "Alright. Until tomorrow. And only if you promise you won't let her go back to her apartment." I will do anything to keep her away from there— from *him.*

Fern pats my arm. "I'll drive her home tomorrow."

"And tell her I'm still clean!"

"We will."

CHAPTER 29

Tara

"Thanks for the ride," I tell Fern before I get out. I might not have a hangover, but my stomach is churning, and I could go for a nap. "I'll bring the clothes back tomorrow."

"No rush," she says, waving away my worry. "I have something for you, though." She reaches into her purse and hands me a familiar pink box.

I frown at it. "A pregnancy test?"

"Tara, you ran to the bathroom to throw up the second you woke up this morning. Humor me?"

"Alright. I'll humor you." One more can't hurt anything as miserable as I am. "It's only stress, though."

She smiles. "Sure."

I take the box and climb out. "Thanks again," I say before I close the door.

"Let me know either way!" she says, nodding at the test.

"Will do. Have a good day!"

"You too."

I close the car door and head for the porch. I would rather be at my apartment, but Fern insisted I needed to be here. I still don't understand, but she wouldn't budge. Gabe isn't here at any rate. He texted to say he was staying at his place. That's the part that matters. I'm not ready to face him yet.

Once my door is unlocked, she taps the horn lightly and backs out of the drive. Inside, I look at the stupid box and curl my lip. *I hate these things.* They used to represent hope. Now, they only mock me. Fern was nice enough to care, though, so I'll do it for her.

I run upstairs to change clothes and get it over with. If I put it off, I might actually get my hopes up. No matter how much I want a baby, being pregnant right now would be disastrous since my relationship with the supposed baby's father is questionable. I don't want to bring a child into a toxic situation.

My timer chimes at me. I roll my eyes and pick up the stupid stick. She bought the fancy ones with a digital readout, so I don't have to consult the paperwork five times wondering if I'm reading it right. *Not that I've ever done* that *before.*

Come on, one glance, and it's done. You can do this.

Holding my breath, I glance down at the dumb thing like it might sear my retinas. One word fills the screen.

Oh, my God.

Oh, my God!

Oh, my God . . . This changes everything. I have to protect us both.

***

Pounding on the door pulls me out of my stupor. I glance at the phone dock on my nightstand to check the time. *How has it only been an hour?* I wanted to sink into the blissful relief of sleep and forget my troubles for a while after reading the results of the test, but those troubles wouldn't let me rest. The future is too heavy to escape that easily.

He knocks again. It has to be Gabe. He must've forgotten his key. Or maybe he's respecting my request for distance and waiting for me to give the okay. *I'm still not ready.* I'm not sure I'll ever be ready now. This situation is more complicated than I thought. But I roll out of bed and hurry down the stairs. *Best get this over with.*

"Come on, Tara Bear. You can't ignore me forever! Fern let me know when she dropped you off. You know I can just come in, right? I have a key too."

The door muffles his words, but it can't stop the pain. Nothing can. Letting him in again was a mistake. And now, I have to cut him out again. *It's for the best.*

I unlock the door. He turns the handle and hurries inside. "Tara! I'm so—" He tries to hug me, but I step back. I might lose my resolve if I let him hug me, and I can't afford to do that. Not anymore.

"Gabe, I'm sorry, but I can't do this." I'm proud of myself for how steady my voice sounds. I need to do this quickly and cleanly. He might swear he's clean this time, and Fern might believe him, but what about next time? What if he hadn't missed the meeting with his dealer? I can't afford to take chances with my baby's future.

"Tara, I—"

I cut him off before he can find some sort of foothold in my heart. "Stop calling."

"But—"

"Stop harassing my friends." *Deep breath. You've got this.* I just have to stick to the script.

"You're not even going to give me a chance?" he shouts, throwing his arms out wide. His overreaction isn't a surprise. It's his default setting when he's upset. It hurts, though, because it means he's hurting.

How can he ignore the obvious? I could forgive him for being late and for ignoring my calls. At least this once. But I can't look the other way if he's using again. "I found a little baggy with white residue in it behind your toilet last night. And you asked your *fucking dealer to meet you again!*" I scream so hard it hurts the back of my throat. My ragged breathing is the only sound for a long time.

Gabe opens his mouth and closes it several times before he finally says, "I swear, I have no idea what you're talking about with my old dealer, and I haven't used since the night before I went to rehab."

That he can look me in the eye and spout that bullshit almost hurts worse than what he did. "Don't lie to me, Gabe! He was there!"

He shakes his head. "He was where?"

"At your apartment!"

"When?"

Why is he playing stupid? Does he think he can confuse me? "Last night!"

The blood drains from his face. "The man who grabbed you," he whispers. "I need to sit." He drops to his ass in front of the door and puts his head between his knees. "That's why you thought I was using again."

"How'd you know?" I ask him. Fern . . . Mason called her last night before Gabe came downstairs.

His eyes drop to my bruised arm. It doesn't hurt much, but it's spectacularly ugly. "Security at the apartment told me you were there and someone assaulted you."

So he was there later . . . Anger makes the words easy. How I'll feel later is a problem for another time. "He said to tell you that you still owe him. And he threatened to . . ." I choke on a sob but try to force the rest of it out. "He said . . ." I can't say it. I'm shaking too hard. I hug my middle and join Gabe on the floor. *Just breathe.*

I thought I was alright after it happened. I told myself that I was lucky and there was no reason for me to freak out. And when I did freak out, I told myself it was due to stress over Gabe. That what happened to me wasn't bad enough to justify panic attacks. There are so many people out there who have suffered so much worse. I have no right to feel violated because he didn't *do* anything.

But it wasn't nightmares about Gabe that woke me up last night, drenched in sweat and screaming. It was the *what-ifs.*

What if he'd followed me to the apartment and forced his way in? What if he'd knocked me out and shoved me in his car? *I could've lost the baby.* I know I was lucky, but that doesn't stop my brain from conjuring up all the bad shit that could've happened when I let my guard down.

He's still out there somewhere. He could come after me. And that haunts me.

I press the heels of my palms into my eyes to try to obliterate the memory of his face burned into my eyelids. It doesn't help because I can still feel his breath on my neck and his hands on my body. "He said he'd get what you owe him one way or another and asked me if I wanted to pay your debt."

"I'm so sorry, Princess," Gabe whispers. "Did he—"

I shoot to my feet. I don't want to talk about what he did. "Don't *princess* me!" I yell. "You ruined your second chance when you decided to invite that man and his poison back into your life!"

"I didn't invite him! I swear it! I'm clean, Tara! I can prove it." He stands up and pulls a folded piece of paper from his back pocket. "I got tested last night after Fern said you thought I was high. I've been tested monthly since I got out of rehab. We can go right now, and I'll get tested again if that'll make you happy."

I take the papers out of habit, but I don't read them. I need a chance to go over them and think it all through. I want to believe him, but I'm not sure I can. That doesn't explain the baggy I found. It has to be new. Ryan told me they searched his place top to bottom before they took him to rehab and would've found it then. I have to protect myself—protect us.

Gabe rubs the back of his neck and looks at the floor instead of looking me in the eye. "There's something I should've told you weeks ago . . . He was waiting for me when I got home from that first night we spent together. He must have followed us. I didn't mention it because I didn't want to worry you." He tells me the rest of the story and things the man said that night begin to make sense, like how he knew I was Gabe's ex-wife.

I hate that bastard even more now if it's possible. I'm not too pleased with myself, either. I should've trusted Gabe from the start. But I let that scumbag manipulate me and come between us because I was scared—scared that this new start for us was a lie.

"He didn't follow us," I say when he's through.

"What?"

I clear my throat to rid myself of the lump of guilt wedged in so tightly I can barely breathe. "He didn't follow us. He was my new neighbor—the sketchy one. I recognized him last night."

All that time, he was one wall away. One door down. My stomach turns. I clamp my hand over my mouth and run for the bathroom.

"Tara?" Gabe shouts, thundering down the hall behind me.

I fall to my knees and skid the last few inches to the toilet, barely making it in time. Gabe holds my hair and rubs my back. When my stomach abandons its attempt to turn itself inside out, he scoops me up and carries me to the stairs.

My head slumps onto his shoulder. The scent of his cologne and something that is unique to him soothes me with my next breath. The world is right when I'm in his arms. *I don't deserve this.* Why is he helping me after last night? I lost faith at the first real test, and here he is, taking care of me. *I'm a horrible person.*

"Put me down," I say, but I'm too tired to mean it—physically and emotionally. I feel like hell.

"You need a clean shirt," he murmurs.

I look down and gag. *Not so independent now, am I?* But I allow it because I'm still scared, and I need him. That isn't as terrifying as it was a few weeks ago. He's proven more than once that I can rely on him. A fact that makes my reaction last night that much worse. *But will we survive this?*

In our room, he helps me get my shirt off without getting vomit on me. He takes it to the bathroom, and I hear water running. I shuffle to my closet to find a new shirt.

"What's this?" he asks.

I turn around but have to finish pulling my shirt on before I can see what he's talking about. My eyes zero in on the little stick in his hands, and my stomach churns again. *Shit.* I swallow hard and try to look him in the eye, but guilt makes it impossible. "What does it look like?"

I risk a quick peek, but his eyes are glued to the object in his hands. "It looks like a fucking pregnancy test, Tara."

I swallow my tears. "You're right, it does."

"A *positive* pregnancy test." There's the barest hint of excitement in his voice. I hope I'm not imagining it. I don't want our child to grow up without his father in his life—as long as he's clean. I'll understand if Gabe can't reconcile my lack of faith in him, but this baby is innocent.

"Huh . . . Hadn't noticed." I'm too tired to do this right now. *I'm too tired to do this ever.* Nothing is going according to plan.

He finally looks up and locks eyes with me, and I could swear he's about to cry. "Is . . . Is it mine?"

"Nope. Milkman's." I'm almost offended that he feels it necessary to ask. Of course, it's his! Who else's would it be? We were stupid, and we never used condoms. After years of trying and failing, it didn't seem like much of a risk.

He makes an unhappy sound. "I didn't want to assume . . . I know we were . . . apart for a while." He scrubs his face with the back of his hand. "When were you going to tell me?"

Looking at him is too hard again, so I drop my eyes to the test. It's finally happened, the one thing I wanted and could never get, and the timing couldn't be worse. "Well, until a few minutes ago, the plan was to tell you when I asked you to give up your rights."

I used to daydream about breaking the good news to him when we were still married. I had lists of ideas saved on my computer, searching for the perfect one. A photoshoot? The first ultrasound? Instead of planning the best way to tell him, I've spent the brief time between taking the test and him beating down the door to figure out how to ask him to sign that paperwork.

Gabe sniffs. "And now?"

"Moot point now. You know." Maybe it's better this way. I don't have to put myself through the stress of worrying if he'll be happy. I look into those gray eyes I love so much. "I'm sorry."

I believe he's sober, but I also know that my accusation had to hurt him. I'll apologize for it, but I won't beg his forgiveness. I was doing what I thought needed to be done to protect our child. If he can't understand that, maybe it's best if he exits gracefully now. We can still be friends. We can co-parents. We'll work it out.

He finally looks up at me and cocks his head to one side. "For what?"

"For not believing you. I was just so scared that it would be an endless cycle and I couldn't put myself through that. And then Fern gave me the pregnancy test, and once I saw the results, I *knew* I had to do everything in my power to take care of the baby and—"

He crosses the room and pulls me into a hug. Horrible person that I am, I sink into his arms and accept the comfort he's offering when I've done nothing to earn it. "Princess, I'm not mad at you."

My throat is so tight I almost can't get words out. "You mean it?" He nods, and I bury my face in the crook of his neck. And I cry, because pregnancy hormones are evil little bitches with no regard for my dignity. "I was so scared!"

"Me too." He holds me tight, and it feels like home. "I'm sorry I didn't tell you about that asshole turning up the first time. If I had, we could've avoided all of this. Will you tell me about it?"

There's nothing I want more than to get it all off my chest now that everything has come to light. But it can wait. I don't want him getting into trouble. "Aren't you supposed to be at work?"

He tenses. "About that." He pauses to clear his throat. "I quit."

"What?" I ask, wincing at my volume. The neighbors probably heard me.

I'm so happy for him, but I don't understand. That job was his *life* for so long. He put his blood, sweat, and tears into that place, and he's going to walk away? "What the hell happened?"

He shrugs like it's no big thing. But it's a huge thing. He's finally free. "After all the bullshit the clients put me through last night, they didn't buy either property. Dad was pulling his normal shit, and I realized I've had enough. I've never been happy working there, and I'll never *be* happy working there because he won't let me. So I told him to shove it up his ass."

Tears run down my cheeks again, but I don't care. I grab his face and kiss him. "I'm so proud of you!"

"Thanks, Princess. I'm pretty damn proud of me, too."

EPILOGUE

Tara

"Last chance to change your mind," Ryan calls through the bathroom door.

I know he's joking, but I give what I'm about to do some serious consideration. I've done the research on 'boomerang' couples, the ones who reconcile after divorce. I know the statistics. Our chances are good. All the same, there's no guarantee it'll work this time around. But the only certainties in life are death and taxes. The rest of the time, we have to cross our fingers and let it ride.

"I'll be right out." I flush the toilet and go to the sink to rinse my mouth.

"Did you puke again?" he asks.

You ask that like I ever stop . . . "Yeah."

"So much for waiting until the morning sickness passes."

It's never going to pass. I'll be puking my guts up the day I deliver. I dig through my purse to find the little tin of crystallized ginger from my mother. "The 'morning' part of morning sickness is a myth."

"Well, tell the future soccer star to give you a break so you can come out here and marry his daddy. Again."

I chuckle and hug my middle. "The future designer will do whatever she wants, and we will deal!" *Mama would appreciate a break, though, little one.* "Is he freaking out?"

"Oh, yeah. He thinks you changed your mind and ran."

I open the door. Ryan frowns at me and fusses me with my hair a bit. "Thanks."

"You bet," he says with a grin. "Ready for this?"

"Let's do this. Before I need to puke again." I take his arm so I don't fall if I have another dizzy spell. The doctor assures me it's perfectly normal, but they freak out everyone around me. Everyone loses their shit when the pregnant lady falls. If they keep up, Gabe will make good on his promise to buy me a walker.

"And before you're late to your own 'surprise' baby shower," he adds.

I grin. Little do the guests know, the surprise is on them. "How do you think it'll go over?"

Ryan snorts. "Oh, your mom is going to be out for blood. You left her out."

Tears sting my eyes. "I know." Maybe we're doing the wrong thing, but neither of us wanted to fuss that would come with a 'real' wedding. We've done that once. We want to keep it simple this time. "She'll get over it, though."

Just like she got over us getting back together.

Ryan grunts. "As soon as she has a new grandbaby to distract her."

"That, too." Once the baby is here, nothing else will matter. I hope. . .

We walk into the office of the justice of the peace. All eyes turn our way, and Gabe visibly sighs. "Finally."

"Hey, you know you can't rush her," I tell him, rubbing my barely swollen belly. If she ever lets me keep food down, I might have a baby bump.

"It's a boy," Trista argues, going over to the team boy dark side. "A girl wouldn't be this hard to get along with."

Ryan taps his smartwatch. "Places to be, people!"

"Right." I nod and reach for Gabe's hand, hoping he doesn't notice mine is shaking. "Let's do this."

"Sign here," the justice of the peace says, sliding a piece of paper and a pen across the desk.

Well, I did want simple. I scrawl my signature on the line, forcing aside memories of the day we signed our divorce papers, then pass the pen to Gabe, who gives it to Ryan, and Trista signs last.

"Congratulations!" the man says, sounding bored. "I now pronounce you man and wife."

"That's it?" I ask. I expected . . . I don't know what I expected really, but something more than that!

He smiles at me. "That's it."

"Should've done that the first time," I whisper to Gabe on our way out. It would've spared me months of listening to my mom cry about her only daughter—her baby—getting married.

He wrinkles his nose. "Nah. You looked beautiful in all that white lace. Definitely worth the hassle."

Outside, he pulls me to a stop. "I got you something." He pulls a little velvet-covered box from his pocket. I smile, happy that he thought of bringing our wedding rings today. I left mine on my nightstand when I moved out. I didn't know he kept them.

I open it, and my heart sinks. "Gabe! It's beautiful, but that's not my ring."

He swallows hard. "It is, but it isn't," he says. "I took your ring and had it remade. You keep calling this our new beginning, so I wanted your ring to reflect that while still being a part of our history."

I try to speak, but my words get lost in happy, hormonal tears.

"You're spending too damn much time with Mason," Ryan grumbles. "Ow!"

He makes a valiant attempt to glare down at Trista for the smack on the arm, but it's like glaring at a kitten, so he fails miserably.

"I think it's sweet!" she says, glaring right back at him, which is astounding to me. It's very un-Trista-like behavior.

"I love it," I say, sniffling as Gabe slips it on my finger. And I love that he's been spending more time with Mason. That man is more of a father-figure to him than his own father ever was, as weird as that might seem.

***

I smile to myself as we turn from the empty street into our drive, anticipating the surprise when we crash our own surprise party. Everything is going off without a hitch, other than the impossible-to-plan breaks for me to be sick if I so much as think about food. I think about food a *lot*. As planned, Ryan and Trista go to the door. They'll wait two minutes and go in to distract everyone.

Mason's sister, Nicole, is waiting for Gabe and me in the back yard, out of sight of the windows. She holds up her camera to let us know it's ready to go. This is going to be the most epic surprise in the history of surprises.

"Do I finally get to know what's going on?" she whispers.

I almost feel sorry for her, but we didn't trust anyone to keep our secret. Ryan and Trista only found out today, and Trista helped plan the shower. "Everyone inside thinks I had a doctor's appointment today. They think they've been invited to a surprise baby shower."

"But?"

"The joke is on them." I'm too excited to contain it anymore and do a silly little dance while I explain. "We know about the shower. Trista let it slip a month ago. The surprise is that we just got back from the courthouse." I hold my hand up to show her my ring, a princess cut diamond flanked by two sapphires and a band of channel-set diamonds.

"Congrats!" she whisper-squeals, diving at me for a hug. "This is going to be so much fun!"

We hear our cue and rush to the back door. "Ready?" Gabe asks.

"Let's do this!"

He throws open the door. Nicole goes in first, her camera already clicking and whirring, then we run inside, yelling, "Surprise!"

A note from Cara

Thank you for reading Right By You! If you enjoyed reading it as much as I enjoyed writing it, I hope you'll consider taking a moment to leave a review and share your thoughts. Reviews are magic fairy dust readers use to help good books fly. Your review could help other readers decide to read this and the other stories in the Tarnished Hearts series.

My newsletter is a great way to stay up-to-date with the newest releases. If you haven't already signed up, you can do so on my website, caradsmith.com. You'll get a free short story about the day Ronni, Fern, and Mason met when you sign up, and there are sure to be more short stories made available to subscribers along the way!

I never intended to write Right By You. To be honest, I never intended to write I Kinda Do. The story came to me one day and it wouldn't leave me alone. I already knew I wanted to publish a book, so I decided that I Kinda Do would be my test run so to speak. I've written a series that's very near and dear to my heart. I will someday release it but I wasn't ready to give it to the world yet. I wasn't ready for it to be picked over by editors and criticized by readers. I needed something I wasn't so attached to, and I Kinda Do served that purpose.

Then, I wrote Austin. He's a handful, but he's so fun. I knew I'd write his story. It was supposed to come next, but I felt bad for Gabe after the Easy Speak scene and my conscious demanded I tell his tale. And so, the series was born.

Acknowledgments

As always, thank you to my little family. This one was crazy, but we made it!

Thanks to Shannon for helping me find Tara's why, Kelsey and Katie for helping me through it again, and Teresa for answering the hard questions.

Thanks again to Nancy, Dawn, and May for helping me make this story the best it can be.

Many thanks to you, dear readers, for each page you turned.

And thanks to my parents for their unquestioning support.

Follow Cara

My website:
www.caradsmith.com

Facebook:
www.facebook.com/CaraSmithAuthor

Instagram:
www.instagram.com/caradsmith

Also by Cara D. Smith

Tarnished Hearts:
*Hired—Newsletter bonus short story
I Kinda Do—Mason and Fern
*Surprise!—Deleted Epilogue
Right By You—Gabe and Tara
Dare To Love—Austin and Jamaica
(TBD)Tarnished Hearts 3.5—Noel and Colton
It's Not You—Ryan and Trista
A Second Glance—Chris and Heidi
(TBD)—Logan and Madi

Each book in the Tarnished Hearts series is a stand-alone, meaning each story is self-contained and they can be read in any order. Some jokes, conversations, and references might make a little more sense if you read them in the order in which they were written, but it is not necessary. Each story has a guaranteed HEA.

*Find these on my website, caradsmith.com

Dare To Love is available now! Can Austin and Jam stop fighting long enough to realize they may actually like each other?

www.ingramcontent.com/pod-product-compliance
Lightning Source LLC
Chambersburg PA
CBHW050140110726
47898CB00008B/2605